breaking

Also by Danielle Rollins

Burning

breaking

Danielle Rollins

BLOOMSBURY
NEW YORK LONDON OXFORD NEW DELHI SYDNEY

First published in the United States of America in June 2017
by Bloomsbury Children's Books
www.bloomsbury.com

Bloomsbury is a registered trademark of Bloomsbury Publishing Plc

For information about permission to reproduce selections from this book, write to
Permissions, Bloomsbury Children's Books, 1385 Broadway, New York, New York 10018
Bloomsbury books may be purchased for business or promotional use. For information on
bulk purchases please contact Macmillan Corporate and Premium Sales Department at
specialmarkets@macmillan.com

Library of Congress Cataloging-in-Publication Data
Names: Rollins, Danielle, author.
Title: Breaking / by Danielle Rollins.
Description: New York: Bloomsbury, 2017.
Summary: Charlotte, an outsider at prestigious Underhill Preparatory Institute,
must decide if she is willing to risk her own safety and sanity to discover
the truth about her two best friends' suicides.
Identifiers: LCCN 2016037740 (print) • LCCN 2016058839 (e-book)
ISBN 978-1-61963-740-5 (hardcover) • ISBN 978-1-61963-741-2 (e-book)
Subjects: | CYAC: Suicide—Fiction. | Secrets—Fiction. | Best friends—Fiction. |
Friendship—Fiction. | Boarding schools—Fiction. | Schools—Fiction. |
Self-esteem—Fiction. | BISAC: JUVENILE FICTION / Social Issues / Friendship. |
JUVENILE FICTION / Law & Crime.
Classification: LCC PZ7.1.R666 Bre 2017 (print) | LCC PZ7.1.R666 (e-book) |
DDC [Fic]—dc23
LC record available at https://lccn.loc.gov/2016037740

Book design by Jessie Gang
Typeset by Westchester Publishing Services
Printed and bound in the U.S.A. by Berryville Graphics Inc., Berryville, Virginia
2 4 6 8 10 9 7 5 3 1

All papers used by Bloomsbury Publishing, Inc., are natural, recyclable products
made from wood grown in well-managed forests. The manufacturing processes
conform to the environmental regulations of the country of origin.

For nice girls and monsters

Prologue

I still think about the blocks.

Their smell seeps into my head—the smell of sawdust and chemicals and paint. They used to give me headaches, until, finally, Mother scrubbed them down with bleach and dish soap and left them to dry in the sun. I can feel their weight in my hands. I hear the clicks of wood hitting wood as Mother stacked them into their precise, angular tower.

I wasn't allowed to watch. I'd turn my back and cover my eyes with my hands until she said, voice clipped:

"All right, Charlotte. Begin."

She started the stopwatch the second I lowered my hands. Two minutes. I'd reach for the blocks while my eyes were still adjusting to the light, before I got a chance to study the shape of the tower she'd built. Always different. Always impossible.

The concept was deceptively simple. I had two minutes to

take the tower apart, revealing the tiny, wooden princess at its center. Every block had to be removed in the correct order or else the entire tower would fall and the princess would be trapped. It was a genius test, designed to separate the exceptional children from the mediocre. The mundane. The hopelessly normal.

I never completed it.

"Again." Mother's voice would cut through the sound of clicking wood. I'd lower my hands, blinking, and reach my chubby, eight-year-old fingers toward the blocks. Sometimes I'd get two out. Or three. They were balanced so carefully. One wrong move could send the whole tower toppling. Sometimes the clock would run down before I even made my first choice. Mother would sigh when that happened and take the entire tower down in a few, swift moves. The princess waited at its center, her pink dress creased and frayed, her painted eyes pleading.

"You're not concentrating," Mother would snap, holding the wooden doll in front of my nose. "Pay attention this time."

We spent hours working on the block tower. There were other tests, too. Impossible puzzles, math problems I could never get my brain to work through, riddles that left me with headaches long after I stopped trying to solve them. But we always came back to the wooden blocks, the tiny princess.

"Again," Mother said.

She took me with her to a conference the summer I turned nine. I stayed behind in the hotel room while she attended lectures and lunched with old friends and passed out business cards. I entertained myself with books and my computer. I tried one of her cigarettes and I threw up, but she thought it was food poisoning and sent me to bed with a cold can of ginger ale. I went through her purse. I put on her lipstick and shuffled through her credit cards and counted the pills in the plastic orange container with her name printed on the front.

Then I found it. A small blue bag nestled at the bottom of her Prada tote. I knew what was inside, but I dumped the bag out on my bed anyway. I watched the blocks bounce across my bedspread and settle near my knees.

All the anger I'd ever felt for my mother hit me in a sudden punch to the gut. I actually doubled over, clutching my stomach, struggling to breathe.

My mother had dragged me along to her stupid conference like a pet she didn't want to leave home alone. My mother didn't realize I'd been smoking even though my hair and breath reeked of it, even though the crumpled pack of cigarettes was still sitting on my bedside table. And she'd brought these horrible blocks knowing how much I hated them. Knowing that I'd never be smart enough to solve any of her puzzles.

You have to understand. I hadn't found the others yet. I didn't have Ariel to tell me Mother was miserable and middle-aged and living vicariously through me. I didn't have Devon to urge me to try one of her pills, just to see how it felt. I was alone then. I was alone for a long time.

I waited until I caught my breath, and then I gathered the blocks in my shirt and hurried across the room to the window. I wrestled it open with one hand, and I went up on my tiptoes and dropped the blocks, one by one. I watched them bounce across the sidewalk and disappear into some bushes. I hid whenever someone walked past.

I saved the princess, though. I tucked her into the pocket of my shorts before I pushed the window closed and crept back into bed.

Just that one time, I saved her.

Chapter One

"Charlotte, wake up." Zoe leans over me. She's so close that her dark eyes look like a single Cyclops eye in the center of her head. Her jet-black hair sticks up at odd angles.

I blink. It's still dark. Moonlight streams through the windows behind us, doing little to illuminate our messy, crowded dorm. Zoe didn't unpack so much as explode into the room when she moved in. Boxes of rolled-up vintage movie posters and makeup and fencing equipment are everywhere.

I hear whispering on the other side of our door. Footsteps.

"Charlotte?" Zoe says again.

"What's going on?" My words blur together—*wasgonnon*? I groan and raise a hand to brush the hair off my forehead, but there is no hair on my forehead. It takes one slow moment before I remember that I cut it all off two weeks ago. I swear I can still feel it, like a phantom limb. Phantom hair.

Someone giggles in the hall outside our dorm. More

footsteps. It isn't unusual for the girls of the Weston Preparatory Institute to sneak out at night. It's easy to trip the lock on the door leading to the courtyard. But they don't usually sneak out all at once.

Zoe leans back onto her heels, the floorboards creaking beneath the weight of her knees, and I'm finally able to focus on her face. She looks like she's not sure she should've woken me. We're just roommates, after all, not friends, and we haven't been roommates for long.

She's standing, but, since she's not quite five feet tall, her head is just a few feet above me. Zoe Hoang is French Vietnamese, tiny with giant eyes and big lips that never seem to smile. I sit up in bed and we're practically eye to eye.

"Is everything okay?" I ask.

"No," Zoe says, her speech taking a trace of French accent. "Something happened."

Anyone else would make her say more, but I learned long ago to be comfortable with mystery. My old roommate, Ariel, never bothered with *where* or *why* when she woke me in the middle of the night. She'd just crook her finger and smile, and I'd come, like a puppy. Like a shadow.

I pull a robe on over my T-shirt and follow Zoe out of our room, down the hall, and outside. It's almost like old times, almost like Ariel's the one hurrying through the darkness ahead of me. Only Ariel never hurried. She walked like she had all night to sneak through the school. She dragged her fingers over the doors lining either side of the hallway, daring someone to open one. To find her. I let myself smile and, for a minute, I actually see her. Her red hair falls in tangles down her back, and she's wearing that vintage slip she loves—the lime-green one with the broken strap, no matter if it's freezing outside or if there could be boys wandering around. Especially if there could be boys.

Dry leaves crunch beneath my toes, and wind claws at my ankles. I shiver, my teeth chattering. My robe is too thin and there's a hole at the elbow. I've always hated the cold. It hits me harder than it does other people. It seeps into my skin and curls around my bones. Girls in pajamas flit past us through the trees, their voices trailing behind them like scarves. Moonlight paints their bare arms and legs silver.

I wrap my arms around my chest, holding the warmth close. Ariel would love this. The trees, the dark. The mystery. I start to turn, a joke for her on my lips. But then I don't. It's been a month. I've almost stopped talking to her.

Zoe glances over her shoulder to make sure I'm still following. We're deep in the trees now, and I can't really hear the other girls' voices, but I feel them moving around us. I yawn, still half asleep. Red light flashes through the branches and, for a second, I think of sunlight. Then it flashes blue.

"No." I stop walking. My hands go to my chest and I press them there, flat. My fingers find the skin at the edge of my T-shirt.

Zoe turns. "Are you okay?"

I nod, but my voice cracks, betraying me. "Is it Devon?"

Devon, my second-best friend since we were sophomores, which feels like forever and ever ago instead of eighteen months. Or first-best friend now, I guess, with Ariel gone. Devon disappeared two days ago, but everyone, even her teachers, thought she hitchhiked into the city to go dancing or see a concert. It wouldn't be the first time, or even the fifth time. We were never worried—just pissed she didn't invite us.

Zoe hesitates. "I don't know," she says carefully. "I just heard that the cops were here. They found . . . something."

She darts through the trees. I walk slower, aware of the wet on the leaves beneath my feet, the wind on the back of my neck. I hear Ariel's voice in my ear, but it's a memory of a voice, not a real one.

Why are you so surprised?

The trees open onto a clearing. Police tape weaves between the branches, a shocking spot of fluorescent in the middle of all the black and gray and brown. I see faces, but most of the girls don't creep close enough to be recognized. Dean Rosenthal kneels in the dirt, and her assistant, Mr. Coolidge, stands behind her. He has one hand pressed to his mouth. The emotion on his face is raw in a way that makes me blush and avert my eyes. I feel like I've just seen him in his underwear.

Their bodies form a barricade, blocking my view of what they're staring at. I hesitate behind Zoe, but just for a moment.

"*Charlotte,*" Zoe says, but I'm already moving closer, ducking below the police tape. She grabs my wrist, her tiny hand surprisingly strong. I shake her off. An arm lies across the leaves. Brown skin and long, tapered fingers with bright red nails. The last time I saw those hands, they were wrapped around a tumbler of whiskey in her daddy's office.

Now Devon holds a syringe. Her knees are bent, like she'd crumpled to the ground after it happened.

Doesn't she look perfect? I imagine Ariel saying. I nod, because wouldn't it be just like Ariel to say something so horrible? But she's right. There are no marks on Devon's body. No blood.

"Like she's sleeping," I whisper. I close my eyes and wrap my arms around my chest. Devon isn't lying here in the dirt. Devon is dancing at a party in the city. Devon is drinking martinis and flirting with a thirty-year-old businessman who hasn't guessed yet that she's only eighteen. Devon is wearing a ridiculous dress that shows off too much skin and that she bought with the credit card she stole from her mother. She's not here.

When I open my eyes again, they settle on a shape in the trees across from me. I recognize Jack by his height, which is nearly two feet taller than everyone around him. His hair bleeds into the shadows, his pale skin a spot of brightness in the night.

If he's out, the rest of the boys' dorm is out, too. I pull my robe tighter around my body, suddenly self-conscious.

Jack takes a few steps forward, and red and blue lights flash across his face. His shaggy black hair is messy with sleep, and his faded T-shirt strains against his broad chest. He finds me in the dark, his gaze lingering for a second too long. Heat creeps up my neck and spreads over my cheeks.

There's a part of me that doesn't want to look at him, in case Ariel sees.

But Ariel's dead. So that's impossible.

Chapter Two

Much later that night, when I'm back in my dorm and Zoe's breathing has deepened, and even the moon has fallen asleep, I roll onto my side and curl my knees toward my chest. And I cry.

Devon is dead. Devon, who told me that red lipstick made me look fierce, and who once brought a kitten to the animal shelter, a kitten so tiny and weak we'd had to feed her with an eyedropper. Devon, who always sat with me at lunch when Ariel was being a bitch and giving me the silent treatment, even though we both knew she liked Ariel better.

Devon followed Ariel to that dark place knowing I would never be brave or strong enough to meet them there.

I cry silent sobs. The ones that claw at your throat and dig their way up from your chest no matter how you try to choke them back down. The ones that hurt, deep.

If Ariel were still here, she'd slip into my bed and knot

her fingers through my fingers and lean her forehead against my forehead, like she did that night last year when I found the baby bird someone had run over with a bicycle. I replay that night in my head. How I squeezed my eyes shut because I was crying, and I don't cry in front of anyone.

"Charlotte," Ariel said. She traced a finger down my cheek, catching a tear beneath her fingernail. "I know your secret."

"Shut up," I said, hiccuping.

"You act all tough, but you're soft inside. You're a kitten."

The words tiptoe through my head on feet made of needles. They dig their points into the soft tissue of my brain. It was a conversation we had a lot, when Ariel was alive. She was the only one who saw the real me. She told me that "nice" wasn't something to be ashamed of, but I think she never really listened to herself say that word.

"Nice." It doesn't even leave an imprint on the air after it's been spoken. It doesn't slash at you, like "daring," or enchant you, like "magnetic." It's empty. A bubble that glitters and gleams, then disappears when you apply too much pressure.

Nice girls don't kill themselves. Nice girls get left behind. Nice girls cry in their beds alone.

I turn my head, letting my tears soak into my pillow. I want to sleep, but Devon and Ariel wander through my brain all night, refusing to let me. They laugh and dance and, for a moment, it's like old times, when we'd sneak out to the cave in the woods and drink and tell secrets. It's like it's supposed to be.

But then they disappear into the trees, and no matter how hard I look, I never find them.

"They're saying it was an overdose." Dean Rosenthal grabs a tissue from her desk, then leans back in her chair, dabbing at the corners of her eyes. She cried at the emergency assembly this morning, too. Her tears don't seem real. They're like props, like the tasteful strand of pearls around her neck and the sensible black heels she wears with her Chanel suits.

I am appropriately sad, the tears say. *I am having a healthy emotional reaction.*

"Who's saying it was an overdose?" I ask.

"The police."

"But Devon doesn't do drugs," I say.

Rosenthal raises an eyebrow, calling my bluff, but I don't correct myself. Like hell am I going to admit the truth to the dean of our school.

Rosenthal balls her tissue in one hand, shifting in her seat so she can look at me. *Really* look at me. The way adults look at teenagers who concern them.

Let's take inventory of what she sees: Eyes, dry. Hair, freshly (and badly) cut, probably done with a plastic razor in the girls' bathrooms. Too tall. Too thin (anorexia!?). Skin, ashy and pale. Deep circles under eyes. Not smiling.

In other words, I am *not* having a healthy emotional reaction.

Rosenthal clears her throat. "A few of your teachers mentioned that you haven't been turning in assignments. Since . . ."

"Yeah." I take a pristine crystal ashtray off Rosenthal's desk and turn it over in my hands. What's the point of an ashtray you don't use? Is it art? "I know. I'm trying to catch up."

"You were barely keeping up with your classwork before."

Before. Since. Rosenthal's become quite the pro at dancing around difficult subjects.

"I've always passed my classes," I say.

"Mr. Carver says you won't pass physics unless you hand in your take-home test today by three. Ms. Antoine says you've missed her last three classes, and you still haven't completed a ten-page essay on *Brave New World* that was worth seventy-five percent of your grade."

"But I'm getting a B in drama."

Dean Rosenthal pushes her glasses up with two fingers and pinches the bridge of her nose. "In light of . . . recent events, we think it might be best for you to take a break from Weston for the remainder of the year."

The air in Dean Rosenthal's office grows several degrees cooler. Weston isn't the kind of place you "take a break from." Not without sacrificing a pound of flesh. People donate entire buildings to get their children considered for admission. The entrance forms and tests and interviews take months to complete. There's a 3 percent acceptance rate.

Unless your mother is very important, of course. Like mine.

I place the ashtray back on Rosenthal's desk and fold my hands in my lap. "We?"

"Your mother and I."

A knife pierces my back and twists. I bite the inside of my lip to keep from doing something stupid, like forming an expression. My mother, who forced me to come to this idiotic school, has decided that I'm not good enough. My mother, who's always been hopelessly embarrassed by how very ordinary I am. How unlike the cutthroat, genius sociopaths who attend this place.

The logical part of my brain knew something like this would happen eventually. Growing up, Mother was always switching me from school to school. I attended three very different prestigious day cares, not to mention a rotating door of private grade schools and junior highs and summer camps. Weston is my second high school, and the place I've been the longest. I was kind of hoping it would stick. Silly, silly Charlotte.

"Did she say why?" I ask, and my voice doesn't crack. Thank God for small victories.

"Why?" Rosenthal frowns. A tiny wrinkle creases the skin between her eyes. "Charlotte, your two best friends committed suicide within a month of each other."

I stare at the wrinkle. It takes me longer than it should to recognize the look of sympathy on her face. I'm not slow or anything; it's just not the kind of thing you see at Weston. Pity, yes. But not sympathy.

"You were in a . . . a kind of a club with Devon Savage and Ariel Frank. Is that correct?"

I cringe. I hate the way she says Ariel's last name. Frank, with a hard *k*. It sounds like a cough.

"We were friends," I say.

"Friends who were in a club?"

"God, it wasn't a *club*. We're not seven years old."

Rosenthal leans back in her chair and folds her arms over her chest. "How would you describe it, then?"

I stare at the heavy velvet curtains covering the window behind her head. What is it with fancy private schools and *velvet*? Velvet and oak and marble and leather. Have there been studies done detailing how these materials are more conducive to an academic environment? Has someone made up charts and spreadsheets and highlighted things with yellow markers?

"Charlotte?"

"Ariel liked fairy tales," I say, pulling my eyes away from the curtains. "She used to joke that we were all like characters from the stories."

It wasn't really a joke. Ariel thought this was brilliant. "Weston looks like a creepy-ass castle," she used to say. "And we're the princesses they're keeping locked in the attic."

I don't know what story she got that from, but it was hard to argue with her. She was charismatic. She made things like pretending to be a fairy-tale princess when you were seventeen sound dangerous and exciting. She'd wake us after it got dark, persuade us to sneak out into the woods with her, and drink stolen wine straight from the bottle. She said our lives were going to be like fairy tales.

Across from me, Rosenthal nods. She's waiting for me to speak first. I could outlast her patience, if I tried. Years of wordless dinners with Mother have taught me to be very comfortable with silence.

"Devon was Snow White," I say, because I want to get this over with. "It was kind of an irony thing, because she's—she was black. Ariel thought it was funny."

"Who are you?"

I close my eyes, letting breath escape from my lips in a rush that's almost a sigh. "Cinderella. Because she had all those animal buddies."

Rosenthal stares for a moment, and then understanding passes through her eyes. "Ah, right. Your shelter."

I press my lips together, nodding. Weston is in the middle of the woods, and there are stray cats and lost dogs and injured bunnies that find their way onto the grounds. I used to hide them in our dorm until Ariel complained that it made our stuff smell like woodland creatures. Then I went to Dean Rosenthal to see about opening the shelter.

I don't tell her the rest of it. That I was Cinderella because Cinderella was loyal and kind and easy to manipulate. That Ariel teased me about it.

"See how nice she is to those awful stepsisters?" she'd say. "That's just like you with Dev and me. You never call us on our shit."

I clear my throat. "And Ariel was, well, duh, she was Ariel. You know, the Little Mermaid? Because of her hair."

Maybe that was why Ariel loved fairy tales. Because of

her hair. Her hair was like something of legend, like something old tribes would sit around the fire and tell stories about. It hung past her waist, this cascading wave of red that I swear to God I never saw her brush.

She called it mermaid hair. She said you don't need brushes when you live under the sea. We used to hitch a ride to the river after lunch hour, blowing off our afternoon classes. I'd stand on the grass, watching Ariel walk in fully clothed, laughing when the water licked the edges of her skirt. She'd make me dunk my head into the water, and then she'd spend hours weaving my hair into perfect, tiny braids. We'd take them out after it dried and, for a little while, I'd have mermaid hair, too.

"You can see why we're concerned," Rosenthal says. "Three girls in a club, and now two of them are dead."

I'm still at the river, with Ariel, and her words take a long time to reach me. I blink and sit up in my chair. "Do you think it was, like, a *suicide* club?"

"You can see why—"

"Do you—wait, do you think *I'm* going to kill myself next? Is that why you're booting me?"

"Charlotte, your teachers are telling me you don't participate in class. You don't talk to the other students or come down for meals." She casts another pointed glance at my too-thin frame. "Or eat at all, for that matter. The Med Center's volunteer coordinator tells me you stopped showing up for shifts, and you seem to have given up on reopening the animal shelter. Your new roommate says you rarely leave your dorm."

I place my hand on my lap and curl my fingers into a fist. *Screw you, too, Zoe.*

"Since Ariel's accident last month, we've been advised to look for warning signs. Even you must admit that your behavior has been . . . alarming."

I open my mouth to argue with her. There's no way my mother buys this theory. Mother doesn't believe in cries for help.

But my argument dissolves on my tongue like soda fizz. What am I fighting for? This school isn't right for me. Devon and Ariel could blow off classes and homework, then show up on the day of a pop quiz and answer every question correctly, all while reapplying their lipstick as soon as the teacher's back was turned. They'd start an essay at midnight the day before it was due and, somehow, hand in something so beautifully written their teachers would feel compelled to read it out loud in class.

No matter how much I studied, or how hard I worked, I could rarely manage to pull my grades above Cs and Ds. If I'd been any other student, Rosenthal would have expelled me years ago. But she didn't. Because of who Mother is.

The only things I ever liked about this place were my friends. Ariel and Devon. Devon and Ariel. And now they're gone.

I roll my lower lip between my teeth. Ariel would fight to stay, just because they told her she couldn't. If I were stronger, I'd fight, too. But I've never been strong.

"I'll pack my things." I stand and walk across the room,

feeling a little like I've left some part of myself behind in that chair. An arm, maybe. Or some fingers. I reach for the door.

"You know, I did my thesis on fairy tales," Dean Rosenthal says, just as I'm about to turn the knob. I hesitate, and glance back over my shoulder.

"I had to research all the original stories that inspired Hans Christian Andersen and the Brothers Grimm. Fascinating stuff," she says, pushing her glasses back up her nose. "Very dark."

I try to look interested. "Were they?"

"Oh yes. The original Little Mermaid didn't actually marry her prince. The story ended with her walking into the ocean and dissolving into seafoam." Rosenthal frowns, and that wrinkle appears between her eyes again. "You know, I believe Snow White died in the original story, too. She chokes on the apple and it kills her. Did you girls know that? That they both died?"

"I didn't," I say. And before she can say another word, I open the heavy wooden door and step into the hall, pulling it shut behind me.

Of course we knew they died.

Chapter Three

Ariel always said her mother should have been a nun. She went to church more often than she slept. She talked about Christ like he was a lover.

Devon's mother was a dancer until an unplanned pregnancy made her feet swell two sizes. She always complained that she could never get her body to move the way it did before she had a child. She married rich and blamed her daughter for all those lost years onstage.

And my mother . . . well, you've already met my mother.

They never wanted us, so we were each other's mothers and sisters and family. Ariel taught us all the domestic things her mother thought a lady should know: how to sew buttons back onto our blouses and bake cookies and iron the pleats in our skirts. Devon explained how to tell when you were ovulating and faked my mother's signature on every less-than-stellar report card. I stole Mother's booze and showed them both how to take a shot without cringing.

After a while, we forgot we had mothers. We forgot we had anyone but each other.

We liked it that way.

Back at the dorm, I pop my laptop open, scroll through a column of playlists, and find one called "for when you're pissed."

I click and music thunders through my speakers. Screaming voices. Hammering drums. There's no melody or pretty singing or soothing chorus. This is sound for the sake of sound. It's an assault. I close my eyes and let it course through my veins and rub against my nerves until I'm twitchy and hot.

Ariel's voice, whispering in my ear: *This is your brain on anger.*

I slide the top drawer of my dresser open and stare down at pile after pile of neatly folded plaid skirts.

Pack your bags, I think. *Take a break.*

I want to yank the drawer out of the dresser and smack it against the wall. I want to watch the wood splinter and crack. I want to fill my ears with the sound of something being destroyed.

I should have tried harder to stay. Ariel would have come up with just the right argument to change the dean's mind. I sat there and let it happen. The way I do with everything.

I remove a stack of skirts from my drawer and place it on

my bedspread. A plaid brick of cloth that I will never need outside this building.

I smooth the skirt on top of the stack with one hand. I have no reason to take them with me. But I pull the suitcase out of my closet and place it on my bed. I fill it with useless plaid, stiff oxford shirts, and scratchy wool vests. I hum to myself as I work, a different song from the one blaring on my computer. The sounds crash together like fighting dogs.

I finish packing up my dresser and move to my closet. Heavy winter coat, heavier winter coat, heaviest winter coat. Three pairs of clunky black loafers that Devon and Ariel made fun of me for wearing. Three pairs of Repetto flats in cute colors that I bought once I realized the teachers don't care what's on our feet as long as our shirts are tucked in. A pink bag filled with lacy black underwear that Ariel made me get for someday. My desk is empty except for dried-up pens and textbooks I haven't opened in months. I toss them into the trash can.

Zoe walks in, hears my music, walks back out again.

Almost done now. Everything I own fits into one suitcase and one weekend bag. Everything except for the little pink bag of underwear. I think about leaving it behind for Zoe. Like a going-away present—French girls like lingerie, right? But then I think of how she told Dean Rosenthal that I never leave my room, and I decide I don't want to give her a present. I dump the bag onto my bedspread and a tangle of black lace falls out, followed by a tiny glass bottle. The bottle rolls across my bed and drops onto the floor.

"The hell . . . ," I say, kneeling. I pick up the bottle and hold it between two fingers. It's impossibly small, barely as wide as my pinkie, and filled with a clear liquid the consistency of cough syrup. A tiny label dangles from the lid on a thread. I recognize Ariel's spidery handwriting.

Drink me.

The angry music goes silent, replaced by a kind of static. Like bees. The whole room seems to dim and fade at the edges. I press my finger over the label, marveling. Ariel dotted her *i* with a tiny smiley face. She smeared the *e*, leaving a trail of ink across the label.

When someone dies, the strangest things become time machines. You'll be going about your day, and a sound or a smell or a word will tear you away from real life and send you tumbling back through memories you didn't even know you had. I stare at Ariel's handwriting, and suddenly I'm slumped at my desk in math class, doodling a picture of a ladybug in the margin of my notes. She pokes me in the back with her pen and drops a folded piece of paper onto my desk.

Mr. Dooley is kind of hot, it reads.

I scribble beneath it. *Gross. He's old. He has nose hair.*

I pass it to her. A second later, it bounces back onto my desk.

I bet he has a big dick, she wrote, dotting both of the *i*'s with tiny smiley faces.

When I come back to the present, I'm sitting on the floor next to my bed, the tiny bottle still clutched in one hand. My cheeks are wet, and my head aches. Music pounds around me, and I swear to God it's louder than it was before. Like it's trying to tell me it won't be ignored. I flick the "drink me" label with one finger.

I don't know when Ariel left this for me. It could have been ages ago, back when we first bought the underwear. I was dating Kevin Norbuck then, and the whole point was that I needed cute underwear for my first time. I can picture Ariel sneaking something into the bag, something she thought might make the night more memorable. Sisters do that for each other. She would have wanted me to enjoy my first time.

Or she could have left it for me during that last month.

I lean beneath my bed, fumbling around for the booze I hid there. My fingers brush glass and I pull out a half-full bottle of fifteen-year-old Glenfiddich. Ariel and Devon could never handle hard liquor, but Mother doesn't stock much else, so I've been trying to develop a taste for it. I unscrew the cap and take a deep swig. It burns down my throat. I cough. Angry music blares around me. My ears feel like they're bleeding.

Ariel was a different person during her last month on earth. She was mean. Not catty or sarcastic like she always was. Just *mean*. She stopped laughing at my jokes and listening to my stories. She'd say something cruel to see if she could make my face crumple. She never could, but that just made her try harder. Devon was the same. Worse, sometimes.

They were into something, but I don't know what. They'd whisper, then stop as soon as I stepped into the room. I'd wake up in the middle of the night and Ariel's bed would be empty, sheets tangled and kicked to the floor. I'd know without going to Devon's dorm that hers would be empty, too. The next day, I'd ask them where they went, and they'd lie, right to my face.

You must've dreamed it, they'd say, smiling these strange smiles that didn't meet their eyes.

I turn the itty-bitty bottle in my fingers, watching the liquid coat the sides of the glass. I take another drink of scotch, and this time I don't cough. The liquor feels like velvet heat as it slides down my throat. I haven't really eaten anything today, and I'm already feeling a little drunk.

I always wanted to know what had happened to them. What they were doing that they didn't think I could handle. And now they're gone. And I'll never know.

Drink me.

Music screams from the computer behind me. I imagine it filling the air with zigzagging lines, like in a cartoon. I pinch the tiny cork between two fingers and then—*pop!*— the bottle's open. My head feels soupy and warm from the scotch, so I take another drink.

It's probably nothing, I tell myself. Maybe a little GHB— Ariel knows how stiff and nervous I get. She probably wanted me to keep calm for all the sex I never did get around to having.

Still, there's something about the bottle that makes me think it's more than that. The mystery of it. The little "drink me" label, like in *Alice's Adventures in Wonderland.* Ariel didn't just love fairy tales; she loved all children's stories. *Alice's Adventures in Wonderland,* and *The Wizard of Oz,* and

The Lion, the Witch and the Wardrobe. Anything where the hero finds a secret entrance to another world. Anything about running away.

I picture her grinning at me from across the room, a wicked glint in her eyes.

Come on, Char, she'd say. *I dare you.*

I dare you. She got me with that every time. It persuaded me to follow her out of our room after curfew, to sneak into secret parties in the boys' dorms, to explore the woods late at night.

My head hums. Scotch burns the back of my throat. I roll the delicate bottle between two fingers, watching the syrupy liquid coat the glass. I lift it to my nose and sniff, but it smells like nothing. I should dump it out. I should throw it away.

"Here goes," I whisper. I lower the bottle to my lips, and I tip it back, hoping it leads me down the rabbit hole.

Chapter Four

Sometimes I say the word "family" over and over. Until it loses all meaning.

Family. Fam-ily. Fa-mil-y.

Family used to have a purpose. Parents taught their children to walk and talk and behave. Fathers hunted bison and made fire and fought off predators. Mothers tended to the babies and cooked the bison meat and, I don't know, gathered berries and shit.

But now we have Seamless and nannies, so what's the point? Why do we need family anymore?

Ariel said we were family. Her and Devon and me. She said we had to look out for one another. At first, I thought that just meant that she wanted someone to lie for her when she didn't show up for homeroom. But then, during lunch last year, Jennie Lawful said I had a butter face, and Ariel slapped her so hard that her hand left a mark on Jennie's cheek.

After that, Jennie was dead to us. We'd pretend we didn't hear her when she spoke. We didn't see her in line at the water fountain or save a seat for her during lunch. She simply vanished.

Poof.

Chapter Five

"Are you drunk, or are you dead?"

A finger jabs my shoulder. I groan. Light burns my eyelids, and my skull throbs. Someone is pounding a nail straight through my forehead. Someone has fitted a vise around my temples and started to squeeze.

"Charlotte? Seriously, are you okay?"

I have to wake up before Zoe runs off to get the school nurse. Here I go.

I open my eyes. There's something thick and sticky crusted into the corners, holding them closed. I blink. The room blurs. It's like looking through foggy glass.

"What time is it?" The words scrape at the sides of my throat. I imagine them leaving thick red slashes on my vocal cords. I lift a hand to my neck, almost expecting to feel blood.

Water. I need water.

"It's eight fifteen," Zoe says. "Jesus. What happened to you last night?"

Last night I tried to find my dead best friends at the bottom of a bottle. I remember lifting the mysterious liquid to my lips, but everything after that is blank. I must've passed out. So much for wild experimentation.

I blink again, and the room slams into focus. Everything is in Technicolor, too rich, too vibrant to be real. I try to swallow, but there's no moisture in my mouth. My gums and tongue feel tacky. Swollen.

Zoe stares. I'm supposed to say something. She asked me a question.

"Water," I croak. Zoe's lips curl—half sneer, half smile. I can't tell whether she's grossed out or amused. She pulls a water bottle out of her backpack and tosses it to me.

"You look like that furry apple in our fridge that we should have thrown out last week," she says. "I'm not even kidding. You look like moldy, rotten fruit. Except greener."

"Thank you." I unscrew the lid from her water bottle and drink deep. The water is warm, but it tastes like heaven. I suck down the whole thing, the plastic bottle collapsing beneath my fingers.

"Did you really get booted?" Zoe asks. *She* doesn't look like a fuzzy apple. She looks like a sixties movie star mixed with a ninja. She's dressed in workout gear—black leggings, black sports bra, slouchy black T-shirt. Liquid liner flicks away from the corners of her eyes.

Last year she was more meek, less chic. Puberty: it works wonders.

"I was asked to take a break," I say. I screw the cap back onto the now empty water bottle and set it on the floor next to my feet. Zoe frowns. Actually, it's more of a pout. I wonder if she practices in the mirror.

"How is that different?"

"It probably isn't." I push myself up to my knees and glance around the room. My luggage sits next to my bed, neatly packed and ready to go. I groan and press a hand to my forehead. At least I wasn't a complete failure last night. "Have you seen my phone?"

Zoe plucks the cell off my bedside table and hands it to me. My fingers feel like they've doubled in size, like they're too big and clumsy for the tiny device. I click over to my home screen, and one unread text message glares up at me. It's from Mother.

Car. 8:30. Main entrance.

I check the time at the top of the phone's screen—*8:22.* "Shit," I mutter, standing. "I have to go."

"Like *that*?" Zoe wrinkles her nose. "You aren't even going to shower?"

I glance down at myself. I fell asleep in my uniform. The heavy skirt hangs low on my hips, limp and creased. A yellow stain dribbles down the front of my top. I can picture Mother's expression when she sees me like this: her eyes narrowing, her upper lip curling in distaste. I jerk a hand through my spiky hair—dammit, my *hair*. Mother hasn't seen it since I played drunken stylist.

I dig my nicest coat out of the suitcase—black wool, double breasted with gold buttons—and tug it on over my disheveled uniform. Then I spit into my hands and finger-comb them through my hair. Gross, I know. But at least I get it to lie flat. I peek at my reflection in the mirror on the back of our closet door. Zoe was right. I do look like rotten fruit. My complexion has taken on a greenish hue, and deep circles color the skin below my eyes. And I look so thin. My cheekbones cut hard angles away from my face, and my chin comes to a near-perfect point.

At any other school, I'd pass for strangely beautiful. I'm skinny and my hair is messed up, but my face isn't so bad when I, like, wash it and throw on some blush. I have a sharp chin and good eyebrows. Ariel used to say I looked like a hot alien.

"She's more like an Alexander Wang model," Devon would counter. "Wang likes thin, odd-looking girls."

I wipe the crusts from the corners of my eyes and smooth down my eyebrows. Strangely beautiful doesn't cut it at Weston. The girls here are insane-looking. I could never do better than average. I pinch my cheeks, hoping for a burst of pink. But the color fades as soon as it appears.

"Better," Zoe says. She pushes herself to her feet and grabs her practice saber from the floor. She had one specially made. The handle is hot pink. "Look, I gotta go. Practice."

I glance at my phone: *8:26.* "Yeah, me, too. I'm going to be late."

We stand awkwardly at the door. Zoe's only been my roommate for a month. I don't really know her. Rosenthal decided I shouldn't live alone after Ariel's suicide, and, for reasons I never quite understood, Zoe agreed to give up her private suite to sleep in Ariel's bed. For a while she even tried to be my friend. Everyone else acted like suicide was contagious, but she ate lunch at my table. She asked me questions.

Zoe parts her lips like she might say something. I feel the moment hovering in the air between us. This is when she'll explain why she moved in. What she wanted from me.

Zoe closes her mouth and the moment's gone, a balloon popping. She shrugs. "See you, I guess."

She pulls the door open and steps into the hall. I count to five before following, giving her enough time to get to the gym so we don't run into each other. Then I pull my duffel over one shoulder and wheel my suitcase out of the room.

The last of my hangover burns off as I drag my suitcase through the school. Maybe there was something in that bottle Ariel had left for me, because I feel great. Like a fog has lifted. I glance around with clear eyes, taking in the glittering trophies in their cases, the blue ribbons lining the walls behind them. Wax shines up from the floor, and the smell of freshly cut flowers hangs in the air.

I've never seen a broom or mop inside the walls of Weston, but the floors are always polished, the bookshelves dusted, the wastebaskets empty. Ariel used to say that a team of elves cleaned the school while we were sleeping, like in Harry Potter. Devon rolled her eyes and said it was normal cleaners, but she'd heard a rumor that Rosenthal threatened to fire anyone who was seen by the students or faculty.

I have a theory of my own, though I was too embarrassed to admit it to Devon and Ariel. I think the school doesn't need to be cleaned. It's exceptional, like the students who go here.

I pause next to the gym's double doors and peer through the glass. Zoe's already inside, dancing across the far end of the room with her whip-thin saber clenched in one hand. She darts forward, the capped tip jabbing into her competitor's side. I used to take fencing with her, back when I actually attended classes. She's deadly.

Jack was on the fencing team for a hot second earlier this year. He and Ariel hadn't been dating long, so we went to a match to cheer him on. Ariel thought it would be sexy, but it was just a bunch of dudes dressed up like marshmallows poking each other with sticks. Ariel covered her eyes with her hands and asked me to tell her when it was over.

Then the girls' team came out, and Zoe stepped up to compete.

I'd seen her in class before, but watching her during competition was something else. She had this way of moving, this slow, easy elegance. Almost like a snake. She'd ease up on her opponent, ducking out of the way of their sword so casually you'd think it was luck.

Then, out of nowhere, she'd strike. She'd come at her opponent again and again, giving them no time to retreat or catch their breath. It was merciless. I hear she's headed to the Olympics.

"Can we keep her?" Ariel whispered to me. She was leaning forward, elbows on her knees, practically salivating as she watched Zoe dance around the gym. "Please? She could be our Sleeping Beauty."

Ariel was always saying shit like that. She loved talent, had a thing for anyone who was the best. She'd constantly threaten to recruit someone else to our little group. I remember how my cheeks flared. How I tightened my hands into fists and tucked them beneath the folds of my skirt, where Ariel wouldn't see them.

But Ariel could always tell. She took my hand and squeezed.

"You know I love you best, right?"

It was her promise to us. No matter who came into our lives—boys or family or other friends—Dev and I were always her favorites. Devon made the promise, too, and so did I, and I really meant it. Until I didn't anymore.

"Charlotte?"

I turn. Jack stands behind me, his hair slicked with sweat. He wears gym shorts and a white T-shirt that sticks to his skin in patches.

You know when you're on an elevator and it kind of . . . *lurches*? And your stomach clenches before you even know what's happening—like your body has started preparing for the elevator's inevitable plunge while your brain is still stuck on what you had for breakfast or that pop song you can't remember all the lyrics to?

That's what happens to me right now. I stare at Jack's face, and every muscle in my body tightens, like I'm on lockdown. Jack and I haven't spoken since before Ariel died. Thirty-one days—wait, no, thirty-two now. The last thing he said to me was "After a while, alligator." It was a joke, because he was always mixing up words.

Jack's eyes move from my face to my suitcase. "You're leaving?"

I blink. *Leaving.*

"Dammit!" I dig my cell out of my pocket and check the time. *8:42.* "I'm sorry, Jack. I'm so late. I should—"

"Wait. Stop for a second." Jack shakes his head, like he's trying to get the information in his brain to fall into the right places. "Are you quitting school? You never quit anything."

I tilt my head in the special, asexual way I reserve for Jack. Half kid sister, half one of the boys. "This from the expert on quitting?"

Jack has the decency to look embarrassed. "Hey, that's not—"

"Lacrosse your junior year? And chess club? And remember when you wanted to be an actor for, like, five minutes?"

"You know that was just to piss off my dad."

Impressed with our banter? We've perfected it over the last year, all the better to fill awkward silences that seem to stretch for days and months and years. I'm not even paying attention to what we're saying. I'm too busy staring at his hands.

Jack has big hands. Strong. Ariel used to talk about them in hushed, reverent tones. She said he could wrap them all the way around her waist, his thumbs touching. She used to paint his fingernails pink. And he let her.

He lifts one hand to scratch his chin, and I have to remind myself not to stare. He used to cuff me on the shoulder and ruffle my hair and hug me with one arm. Like I was his little sister. Then one day he stopped. All of a sudden there was this two-foot barrier of space between us, like I gave off some sort of toxic gas that only affected Jack. I try to remember what his hands felt like. Were his fingers soft? Callused? Were they warm, or always cold like mine?

"Are you really leaving?" Jack asks, cutting into my thoughts.

I clear my throat, grateful that I don't blush. "I'm taking a page out of your book."

Jack stares at me, too. Don't think I don't notice. His eyes always wander to this spot on my neck, just above my collarbone.

"Take a different page," he says, and his voice sounds deeper than it's supposed to. Husky. Less protective older brother and more illicit lover. We're verging on dangerous behavior here.

I tug my coat closed. "I'm going to be late."

"I don't quit everything," Jack says. "Not always."

His voice reminds me of rain. Does that make sense? Is it

possible for someone's voice to remind you of rain? I want to kiss him. No, I want to slap him. And then kiss him. I want to grab him by the collar of his shirt and scream in his face, and bang my fists against his chest. And then kiss him.

Unfortunately, none of those things are appropriate. Not when the guy in question is your dead best friend's ex-boyfriend.

"That's right," I say, clearing my throat. "You never gave up on Ariel, and she gave you a million and a half reasons to."

For a second, Jack looks like I really did slap him. He shuffles backward, his tennis shoes squeaking against the floor. "That's not fair."

"Who said I was playing fair?" I start to move past him, wheeling my suitcase behind me.

"Wait," he calls before I make it to the door. "I'm sorry about Devon."

I stop, but I don't turn back around. "Me, too."

"I hate how weird things are between us," he says. "I get why you didn't want to see me after what happened with Ariel. But now Devon—"

"Things aren't weird between us."

Jack is quiet for a second. "Aren't they?"

"I really have to meet my mother," I say. For a long moment, the only sound in the hallway is my suitcase's wheels grinding over the wooden floor. I stop at the main entrance and reach for the door.

"I don't know why you're so mad at me," Jack calls.

I lower my hand to the doorknob. Tighten my fingers around the cool brass. I close my eyes, and I pray that he won't keep talking.

Please. Please don't say it.

"About what happened," Jack continues. "It's not the reason she . . . that she killed herself. She was messed up, Charlotte. Devon, too. It wasn't about you."

"You have no idea what it was about," I say.

Chapter Six

Ariel and I met Jack on the same day. In the same class period. At the same moment. He walked into our homeroom, and we looked up and—*boom*—Jack was in our lives.

He was a transfer student from the city. Started at Weston our junior year. I had the new-student thing down to a science by then, and I knew the drill. No sudden movements or loud noises. No unnecessary eye contact. You don't want to spook the animals.

Jack . . . did not follow those guidelines. His first week at Weston, he signed up to do a comedy set at the under-eighteen club in town. Every single student at our school showed up to see him. We figured he was a theater kid, that he must be some sort of comic genius to take such a big risk.

He was not a comic genius. In fact, he stank. It was like watching an oddly charming train wreck. He grinned like an idiot when we all finally booed him off the stage. He bowed and doffed an invisible hat. Everyone at Weston fell in love with him at the same second.

If Jack were a dog, he'd be a golden retriever. If he were an inanimate object, he'd be something bouncy and determined, like a tennis ball. He tries too hard and does too much and doesn't care about what anyone thinks, except that of course he cares about what everyone thinks.

"Dibs," Ariel whispered to me that night, while we were watching him bomb onstage. It took me too long to realize what she'd meant. Jack wasn't her type. She liked dark, brooding boys with leather jackets and bad attitudes. She liked tattoos and no futures and older, bordering on inappropriate. She didn't date goofy high school guys. She didn't appreciate determination and charm.

But Jack was different. Jack was worth it.

I felt something shift then that I couldn't quite name. The sudden emptiness that comes with losing something you hadn't realized you wanted.

The floor was wet. I'd noticed that first. I was coming home from the library that night, late because I didn't want to talk to Ariel about what had happened the day before.

Ariel liked fights that lasted for days. She liked to scream. She thought drama was healthy. That getting our blood boiling was the best thing that could happen to our relationship. I'd never been a yeller before I met her. I came from a house of silent dinners and single kisses good-night. But Ariel didn't live like that. She'd push and push until I was standing across the room from her, screaming myself hoarse. And just when I got worked up, just when I decided exactly what I wanted to say to her—the thing that would make her understand why I was so hurt or angry—just when I'd perfected the phrasing in my head, she'd shut me out. Her face would go blank and I'd get the silent treatment for an hour. A day. A week.

I hated the silence even more than I hated the fights, so I'd been hoping she was in the mood to yell when I pushed the door to our dorm room open that night. I was wearing my loafers with the thick soles, and I almost didn't notice the water. But then I took a step into the room, and it sloshed around my heels. It made empty, sucking noises when I lifted my foot.

I'd muttered something then—a curse, maybe. I don't remember. I set my book bag on top of the narrow dresser by the door, and I tried to switch on the light, but the bulb had burned out.

A sliver of light cut across the room. It leaked out beneath the bathroom door, glimmered over the inch of water sitting on top of the floorboards.

I think that was when I knew something bad had happened. Right that second, staring at the light from the bathroom.

I called out Ariel's name. I crossed the dorm room in two long steps.

The bathtub faucet was still running. That was where

the water was coming from. There were candles lining the windowsills, sending flickering light onto the peeling paint of the bathroom walls.

Water flowed over the sides of the tub. I took a step forward.

Ariel floated just below the surface. Her hair fanned out around her, drifting in the water like tentacles. Her pale skin was luminous. Her eyes open.

I didn't scream. I didn't even cry. I bit back the vomit rising in my throat and stumbled. Then I turned and ran. I grabbed my bag on the way out the door.

I ran all the way back to the library. I huddled in the stacks at the back of the room, and every time I closed my eyes, I saw flickering light and flowing water and Ariel's red hair.

Hours and hours later, some freshman I didn't recognize came and found me.

"Are you Charlotte?" she asked. I'd nodded, and I remember thinking how easy it was to nod, to pretend that I hadn't seen what I'd seen in our dorm room. To pretend everything was fine.

"You need to come with me," she said. "There's been an accident."

"What kind of accident?" I asked. It hadn't even sounded like my voice. I don't know why I asked that.

"Your roommate," she said. "Just . . . please come."

Chapter Seven

You're wondering if I slept with Ariel's boyfriend.

If that was why we fought. Why she killed herself.

You think the guilt is driving me crazy. You think that's why I'm so messed up.

Well. I didn't.

What I did was so much worse.

Chapter Eight

I'm out the door, and cold like the sharp end of a knife slices through my skin. Mother's black car waits at the curb. I hurry down the front steps, suitcase smacking against the concrete behind me, worn-out ballet flats slipping off the backs of my feet. A crow caws, then leaps from a half-naked tree branch, sending a shower of dead leaves to the sidewalk. Even this is like something from a story. Like Weston wants to send me off on an ominous note.

I glance back at the school one last time. Ariel was right—it does look like a castle. The building itself is made up of a half dozen spiky towers, with intricately carved gargoyles peering over the windows and around columns. Its stone walls gleam unnaturally against the dull backdrop of the woods. Arched passageways twist around the school, and wild gardens grow over the courtyard. It's like something alive. Wind blows through its walls, making it sound like the building is weeping.

I shiver and tug my coat closer. The car engine purrs, exhaust leaking into the early morning.

Darren, the driver we've had since I was four, steps out of the car and takes my bags.

"Miss Gruen," he says, opening the door for me. "A pleasure to see you, as always."

"Hey, D, how's the new puppy?" I like to pretend Darren and I are friends, but he probably complains to his wife about the obnoxious rich girl he drives around as soon as he's off work. Now he just nods, a slight smile curving his lips.

"Finally house-trained," he says as I slide into the car. "It's a miracle."

I want to say something else, but he closes my door before the words can escape my lips. The car closes in around me, all butter-soft leather and shiny wood paneling. It feels like a very expensive jail cell.

"Charlotte," Mother says without looking up from her phone. Her short blond hair sweeps over her forehead, hiding her eyes. Her signature accessory—a gold rose pin—flashes from the lapel of her stiff black coat. She taps a manicured nail against her phone's slick screen.

My mother, Dr. Rose Gruen, is the president of the Underhill Medical Center, a sort of famous hospital and research clinic in Underhill, New York, which is just fifteen minutes away from my school by bus. She's used the clinic's deep

pockets to stock Weston's library, finance renovation proj-
ects, and set up a prestigious internship program specifically
for Weston students. The school considers her a kind of folk
hero, the brave woman who takes from the rich to give to the
rich. And makes everyone—including herself—much richer.

I clear my throat and shift on the leather seat. Mother
doesn't say she's upset with me, but the words hang in the air
around us like perfume. If her disappointment had a scent, it
would be something expensive. Chanel No. 5 or Shalimar.

The car pulls away from the curb and rolls smoothly down
the driveway. I lean against the window, my breath fogging the
glass. I play a game of tic-tac-toe against myself. And then I play
three. And then five. I win every time.

Finally, "What did you do to your hair?"

Her voice is deceptively sweet. Honey and maple syrup. I
look up and see that she's tucked her phone back into her
purse and folded her hands on her knees. She fixes her icy
blue eyes on me, head cocked like a bird.

I touch the edges of my hair, then drop my hand into my
lap again. "I got tired of having it long."

Mother studies me, eyes narrowing. "It looks hideous.
I'll make an appointment with Anita when we get back to
the city."

Anita, Mother's stylist, who hates me for my "wasted
potential."

"Thanks," I mutter.

Mother's eyes shift from my head, over my torso, and
stop at my knees. My coat has come unbuttoned, displaying

the limp, dirty hem of my uniform skirt. I tug it closed, cheeks flaring.

Mother lifts an eyebrow. "I've spoken with Dean Rosenthal, and she's recommended several of the better tutors back in Manhattan. I thought you could meet with them over the next week and let me know your preferences. And it'd be wise to get you started with a new therapist. Dr. Gillespie is still taking clients, but I seem to recall that you didn't like him."

Dr. Gillespie smelled like mothballs and stared at my ass unapologetically. "I'll find a new therapist," I say.

"Good." Mother is still staring. She's back on my face, and something about it must upset her, because the skin around her eyes crinkles. She'll get wrinkles if she isn't careful.

"What?" I ask. She rests a long finger against her lower lip.

"You look different."

I wrap my arms around my chest, making sure that no other part of my offensive uniform is poking out from under my coat. "You mentioned. I know you hate my hair. I'll see Anita—"

"No, not your hair. Your skin." She leans forward, the leather seat groaning beneath her. She takes my chin in her hand and moves my face first to the left and then to the right. "Are you using that vitamin C serum I sent you?"

I swat her hand away. "No."

"Something else, then. A new foundation? Did one of your friends lend you something?"

"I'm not wearing any makeup." I grab my shoulder bag off the floor and drop it onto my lap, digging through crumpled-up homework assignments and old tampons for my compact. "I happen to know for a fact that my skin looks like the outside of a fuzzy, rotten—"

The rest of the words fizzle and die on my tongue. My compact reflects a face back at me, and I guess it's my face. It has to be my face. But it looks nothing like my face. The greenish tint has faded from my skin, the dark circles vanished from beneath my eyes. My cheeks are actually *rosy*, and the tiny zit I'd noticed popping up above my eyebrow has disappeared, leaving behind creamy skin the color of porcelain.

Mother starts talking again. Something about the Med Center's board of trustees being in crisis mode and working late, but I'm barely listening. I pull and pinch and tug at my skin, fascinated by the transformation. I bare my teeth and check my hair, but nothing else seems to have changed. My teeth are still coffee-stained, my hair still choppy. But my skin . . . my skin is perfect.

I snap the compact closed and cram it into my pocket. My fingers brush against something small and round. I frown and pull it out.

Ariel's tiny bottle winks from my fingers. I don't remember putting it in my coat pocket, but here it is. I turn it over, thinking of Ariel's perfect hair. Devon's flawless complexion.

"Magic serum," I whisper. If this were a fairy tale, the bottle would have come from an evil witch Ariel had met in the woods. It would be cursed. I'd eventually have to pay for my sudden transformation. In reality, I'm betting Ariel and

Devon found it in Koreatown the last time they were in Manhattan. Under my breath, I say, "Thanks for sharing."

Mother doesn't look up from the cell phone that's found its way back to her hand. "Did you say something?"

"No," I say. "Drink me," the label on the bottle reads. I flip it over, hoping Ariel wrote the name of the shop where she found it on the back. But there's just a scrawled number:

2/3

I stare down at the number and, for a long moment, I can't breathe. Ariel made me a scavenger hunt once. She'd ripped up pieces of paper and left them all over Weston, eventually leading me to a secret party in the basement of the boys' dormitories. On the back of every clue, she'd scrawled numbers just like this one—*1/10, 2/10, 3/10*—so I'd know I hadn't missed one.

My heart beats faster. I knew Devon and Ariel had been into something. Maybe the bottle was just a single piece of the puzzle. If this was the second of three clues, that meant there could still be two more. That I could find them.

But no—the clues are back at Weston. I squeeze my eyes shut, and I'm hit with a want so strong it nearly knocks me over. Why didn't I try harder to stay? Why do I always, *always* give up so easily?

Darren taps his knuckles against the steering wheel. Mother's fingernails click against her phone screen.

I think of empty beds, twisted sheets. Devon's hand lying across a pile of leaves. Ariel's hair floating below the surface of the water.

Our car pulls to a stop at a red light. Darren hums from the front seat as the engine idles. I glance out my window and notice a poster peering out at me from the coffee shop at the corner. It's for an anniversary gala at the Med Center in a few weeks. The posters are everywhere, commanding townies to help the hospital "Ring in Our 50th Year!" by donating whatever insane amount of money they'd need to donate to score an invite. I stare at the navy-blue outline of the hospital and study the silver-scripted words.

"What if I took more hours at the Med Center?" I blurt out suddenly. Mother lifts her head, and the hair falls away from her eyes.

"What are you talking about?" she asks. I glance out my window, looking for the anniversary poster, but it's gone. We're driving again.

"Could I stay at Weston if I volunteered for more hours at the Med Center?" I ask. Weston Prep and the Underhill Med Center have always had a symbiotic relationship. The Med Center donates money and sets us up with prestigious internships that look marvelous on a college application. And we provide them with unlimited unpaid labor. It's win-win. Every Weston student volunteers for the internship program at the Med Center, but I always took on as few hours as possible, not wanting to run into Mother. "I could come in every day. That way you could check on me."

Mother shakes her head. "Dean Rosenthal—"

"Rosenthal only kicked me out of school because you asked her to. If you made a phone call, I'd be right back in."

Mother studies me, eyes flashing, mouth a straight line. I feel like I'm being scanned, like she's downloading my brain and searching for nefarious motives.

I shift in my seat, uncomfortable with her scrutiny. She must find it infinitely frustrating to never know what I'm thinking. It wouldn't occur to her to just ask. To make me a cup of tea and sit down at the kitchen table to talk about all the things I'm afraid of, all the things I want out of life.

My heart gives a strange lurch, startling me. I thought I was too old to wish for the impossible.

"Is that what you really want?" Mother asks carefully. "To be a student at Weston again?"

I press my lips together. It's always been just Mother and me, but Mother was never really there, so mostly it was just me. Then I met Ariel and Devon, and everything changed. I learned how it felt to have people care about what I did and where I was. My phone is still filled with texts from both of them that I can't bear to delete. *Where are you? What are you doing? What do you think about . . . ?* How do you go back to being alone after that?

What I really want is for them to be alive. I want to be sitting next to them in study hall right now, passing gossipy notes and trying not to laugh out loud. I want to forget that there was a time they were secretive and cruel. I want everything to be like it was.

I curl my fingers around Ariel's mystery bottle. I can't have that. So I'll settle for figuring out why it was taken away.

"Yes." I shift in my seat, mirroring Mother's confident

posture. Hands folded on knees, shoulders straight, head back. "That's what I want."

Mother lets another moment of silence pass between us. A negotiating tactic, I'm sure.

"I want straight As," she says finally.

I've never gotten an A in my life, but sure, let's throw that into the mix. "Fine."

Mother smiles and, for a moment, it's almost like she's proud of me. My heart lurches again, but this time the feeling is easy to ignore. She's not really proud, after all. I don't think she's capable of that emotion. At least not when it comes to her only daughter.

"Darren," she says, "turn the car around."

Chapter Nine

Mother sends me back to the dorms while she "works things out" with Dean Rosenthal. I don't let myself think too hard about what that means.

My dorm is empty, the floors dusted with morning sunlight. Zoe will be in class by now, oblivious to the fact that she has a roommate again. She's lived in this dorm for almost a month now, but her movie posters are still rolled up and sticking out of boxes. She hasn't bothered plugging in the sleek, flat-screen TV sitting on top of her dresser. For the amount of crap she has, the girl lives like a monk. Why own a TV if you aren't going to watch it?

I push the door closed behind me. It whispers against the wooden frame, clicks into place.

"Come out, come out, wherever you are." My voice sounds oddly flat in the empty room. It doesn't echo back to me.

Ariel and I shared this room just one month ago. She

slept in Zoe's bed, and stored her clothes in Zoe's closet, and stared in the mirror on the back of Zoe's door to apply her lipstick. If she left some clue for me to find, it should be here.

I drop my luggage next to my bed and kick off my shoes. Zoe has long since muffled the last echoes Ariel left in this room. I can't feel her here anymore. I pull open the top drawer of her dresser and push the clothes aside. Zoe has hidden a tiny pocketknife with a pink handle beneath her rumpled uniform skirts and balled-up socks. She could get expelled for that. Next to it, a well-creased sheet of notebook paper, folded. My mouth quirks. Love note, I bet. I push the drawer closed again without touching either item.

Ariel wouldn't hide anything in her dresser anyway. I close my eyes and massage the bridge of my nose. *Think.* If this really is a scavenger hunt, there will be a method to where the clues are hidden. The bottle was in a bag of underwear she made me buy. Why?

Because she knew I wouldn't find it. I open my eyes and stare at the floorboards between my feet. Ariel knew I wouldn't go digging around for that bag of underwear. I didn't even want to buy it in the first place. She knew it would stay hidden in the back of my closet until . . .

"She died." I swallow, the words hanging in the air around me like floating bits of dust. She'd been planning on killing herself, then. Planning it for long enough to plant three clues for me to find. They never found a note with her body. Maybe she left this instead.

A wave of anger and pain rises inside me, but I push it

down. This actually makes things easier. It's like a riddle. Where else would Ariel think I'd never go?

I lift my head, my eyes settling on the closed door on the far side of our dorm. Only a handful of the dorms at Weston have private bathrooms. Mother pulled strings to get one for me. I haven't used it since—

The community bathrooms in the hall actually aren't that bad. Zoe hasn't even mentioned using our private bathroom, though I've seen her glance at the door longingly while trying to apply eyeliner in the mirror above her dresser. The last time that door was opened was when the EMTs rushed into the room with a stretcher and dragged Ariel's dead body out of the bathtub.

I open the door and flick the lights. Ariel's shampoo sits on the side of the tub, a ring of soap dried around it. A stiff washcloth hangs over the faucet. A single black hair tie sits on the counter next to the sink. It could have been hers or it could have been mine, and there's no way to tell for sure.

I wrap my fingers around the doorknob and focus on how cold the brass feels beneath my skin. Something buzzes in my ears, a sound like the flickering fluorescents in the hall bathrooms. I look up at the ceiling and remember we don't have fluorescents in here. Just a normal bulb hidden behind frosted glass.

Ariel's voice echoes around me. *Answer the question, Charlotte.*

And then mine. *Let him go.*

I swallow, tasting vomit at the back of my throat. It was

the last conversation we had. The last words we spoke to each other, and we didn't even speak them here. I feel betrayed. How does the room know? Who told?

I glance at the bathtub, and I expect a flash of memory: Ariel lying below the surface of the water, hair like tentacles stretched around her.

Instead, I see her as she was during that last argument. Her eyes bright and flashing. Her smile cruel.

Do you love him more than you love me?

I pull the bathroom door shut, and stumble back into the dorm. My breathing is thick, heavy. There's a line of sweat on my forehead.

My phone buzzes from my coat pocket, shocking me so much that I release a yelp and jerk around. Pain prickles up my neck. I dig my phone out and check the screen. One new message, from Mother:

Dean's office. Five minutes.

Mother is already standing outside Dean Rosenthal's door when I arrive, her black coat buttoned up to her chin. She casts a glance at me, and her eyes flicker back to her phone.

"It's been handled," she says, tapping the screen. She starts walking, nodding for me to follow. "Dean Rosenthal has requested that you bring your GPA up to a 3.0 by mid-terms, which are . . ."

"March twenty-eighth," I say. "Six weeks away."

Mother pushes through the heavy oak door leading into the hallway. Once it's closed behind her, she lifts her head.

"Of course you and I have a different agreement," she says. "Straight As. That was the deal."

I nod. "I understand."

"I want to see significant progress within two weeks," she continues. She squints down at her phone. "The hospital's anniversary gala is on the twenty-seventh. If you've brought your grades up by then, you can stay. If not, we'll revisit the idea of you going back to New York."

I press my lips together, careful to keep my face blank. Two weeks. I have a C or lower in every class, including fencing, my physical education credit. It's a ludicrous deadline. I could study until well past midnight, complete a dozen extra-credit assignments, and ace every single test, and I'd still be lucky to get a B average. It's like she wants me to fail.

Mother waits for me to answer, one eyebrow raised. Her expression is a challenge. I turn her terms over in my head. Maybe I'm looking at this wrong. Two weeks won't be long enough to make Mother happy, but seventeen years hasn't been long enough to make her happy, either. If it's obvious I'm going to fail, then I have no reason to worry about grades and classes and my stupid internship. I can focus all my time on solving Ariel's puzzle.

I force my lips into a smile. "Two weeks sounds adequate."

"You'll need to speak with the dean to get your updated schedule. She insisted that you take an earlier shift at the

Med Center this semester so you'll be less likely to . . . *forget* to show up." Mother lifts her eyes to my face, one eyebrow raised. "Your first shift is tomorrow at nine thirty. Be sure to check in with me after you finish."

She pushes the school doors open, hurrying down the steps to where Darren waits with the car, her high heels clacking against the stone. I watch through the glass in the door. She pauses and glances back at me, and, for a second, my reflection lines up with hers. We have the same long, straight nose, the same full eyebrows and high cheekbones. Only our eyes are different, mine brown instead of blue. I always thought we looked nothing alike, but reflections don't lie. We're so similar. It's astonishing.

Mother holds my gaze for a moment, and then she turns and slides into the car, the gold rose glinting from her lapel.

My hands are sweating when I walk out of Dean Rosenthal's office one hour later. I've smeared the ink on the new schedule she printed for me, creating a Rorschach test of room numbers and subjects and times. I crumple the schedule into a ball and shove it into the front pocket of my backpack. I hurry down the halls, footsteps echoing. It's nearing the end of third period. Teachers' voices sneak out through the cracks beneath their classroom doors.

". . . quadratic formula . . ."

"American . . ."

". . . *arigatou.*"

The bell rings, cutting the voices short. *Shit.* I walk faster, hoping to avoid the throng, but doors fly open and the hallway quickly fills with plaid-and-navy-clad students. They muscle their way toward the doors, shoulders wedged together. A few people glance back, staring at me unapologetically. I hear whispers and giggles. They must know about my near-expulsion. Weston is small, only about fifty students per year. News travels fast.

I duck my head, pushing my way past. The halls are always mobbed but today it's intense. I rise to my tiptoes and peer over dozens of glossy, perfectly coiffed heads. A line has formed, stretching through the double doors and into the quad, where it bottlenecks at the frozen-over fountain.

I squeeze through the other students and into the quad, finally spotting the source of the traffic jam. Three seniors perch on the fountain's concrete edge: Chloe Pearce, Molly Hendricks, and Vivian Marsh, widely considered Weston's most popular girls but only because Devon and Ariel never applied for the job. We used to hang out with them a little, but they were always second-tier friends. We'd go to their parties and we'd hold their hair back when they threw up, but we'd never let them have our secrets.

They look how you'd expect—hair dyed the same golden blond/brown, fake-tan-colored skin, stacks of brightly colored flyers clutched in thin yet toned arms. An iPod sits on the fountain next to their feet, connected to a tiny speaker blasting candy-coated hip-hop.

Molly tosses a stack of flyers into the air like confetti.

They flutter down to the sea of waiting hands, blocky black letters shouting the words "SENIOR BONFIRE" from their brightly colored pages.

The senior bonfire is a Weston tradition. It happens every year in the late winter, when the frozen ground has just begun to thaw but the nights still seem to stretch for days and days. The party begins before nightfall and lasts until the early hours of the morning, lit by a massive bonfire in the middle of the woods. It's the one party each year the teachers don't break up.

Molly and Chloe and Vivian start dancing on the fountain, hips gyrating in tandem. Voices become high-pitched and pointed. The beginnings of a migraine stretch through the back of my skull. I'm about to head inside when our school mascot, the Weston Warrior, steps out of the crowd and stops in front of the fountain.

Wait—not the usual Weston Warrior. *Jack.*

Jack wears the Warrior's metallic kilt and shiny blue cape. His chest is bare, and he's painted a glittery blue *W* on his skin. He holds a plastic sword and wears the helmet, too—silver with a white fringe. The whole thing is very Trojan man.

Chloe grabs his hand and pulls him onto the fountain with her. Jack dances like he does most things—enthusiastically, and with little skill. He body-rolls and runs in place and does jazz hands. He does the robot. Badly. If Ariel were here, she'd catcall and shout something dirty. *Show us some leg!* Okay, probably dirtier than that. But I just watch.

Jack's chest is red with cold beneath the glitter. He smiles and the skin around his eyes crinkles, which has to be the sexiest thing I've ever seen. Something in my chest flips. Time to go.

I'm at the school building and I have the door open and one foot inside, when—

"Charlotte!"

I turn and Jack is standing behind me in all his glittery, bare-chested glory.

"You think I didn't see you?" he asks, panting. He must've leaped off the fountain and pushed through the crowd to get to me before I went inside. Chloe and the others look lost without him, a solar system that's misplaced its sun.

I frown. "I'm sorry, do I know you?"

Jack flashes another eye-crinkling smile. "Ha-ha. Ian got sick." Ian's the fifteen-year-old who usually plays the Weston Warrior. The real costume includes a jersey to cover his skinny chest, but Jack made the right call by going without. It'd be a sin to cover those abs. "Chloe asked me to fill in at the last minute. What do you think?" Jack turns in place. "I make this look good, right?"

Yes, he does, but I force myself into kid-sister mode. I wrinkle my nose. "Stay at least three feet away from me so I don't get all glittery."

"No hugs, then?"

He comes at me with arms wide, like this is something we do now, and I flinch away from him on instinct, knocking into the person behind me. The roaring, laughing crowd around us goes on Mute, but only in my head. Jack blinks, and I swear I can hear the sound of his eyelashes passing through the air.

He rocks back on his heels like I pushed him. "Sorry," he says, and now I feel stupid for making things weird. He clears his throat. "So. I thought you were leaving."

"I came back."

"I see that."

"I quit quitting," I say, and now we're on solid ground. Meaningless banter. Our common language.

"Good for you," Jack says.

It's my turn to talk again. Jack waits patiently. I cross my arms over my chest. If I stand still for long enough, I might turn to stone.

Say something, I tell myself. *Say something. Anything.*

"Are you going to the bonfire?" I blurt out, nodding at the fountain where Molly, Chloe, and Vivian are still dancing. They keep snatching glances at us. I wonder if they think I'm going to off myself next, like Rosenthal does.

Oh God. Is that what Jack thinks? Is that why he's talking to me now, after we spent the last month avoiding each other?

"Yeah," he says. Something passes over his face, lighting him up. "Remember last year?"

I frown. Technically, the bonfire is supposed to be seniors only, but Ariel, Dev, and I snuck in last year. I spent the entire night nursing a drink that tasted like melted Jolly Ranchers while Dev and Ariel engaged in a fierce competition to see who could smooch the most random hotties. Ariel made me swear I'd never tell Jack she was there.

"What do you mean?" I try to keep my voice casual, but Jack raises an eyebrow, calling my bluff.

"Please, Charlotte. Do you think there's any chance I didn't know you all snuck in?"

"I didn't . . ."

"Ariel said she'd be in her dorm studying all night. *Studying*. Did you ever see her study for anything?"

"Do eyeliner tutorials on YouTube count?"

Jack straightens his cape. "Remember Colin Everly?" he asks, referencing some senior who graduated last year. I nod. "Well, Colin told me Ariel made out with half the lacrosse team that night. Is that true?"

"I spent most of the party by myself wishing I were anywhere else in the entire world, so I don't really remember." I glance down, pretending to smooth a wrinkle from my skirt. "Would you care if it was?"

Jack shakes his head, and a full smile unfurls across his face. He looks like he's considering a pleasant memory and not evidence of his dead ex-girlfriend's betrayal. "Nah. That was Ariel. I bet she looked good. With the firelight, and—"

"She looked amazing," I say, cutting him off. I was so jealous of Ariel that night. It seemed violently unfair to me, like her beauty could be held directly responsible for my ordinariness.

Jack cuts his eyes toward me. "That's funny."

"What's funny?"

"Just . . . Ariel said the same thing about you. She said the guys couldn't keep their eyes off you."

I wore jeans and a T-shirt that night, and I didn't even try to do anything with my hair. I was the most underdressed person at the party. It was embarrassing. "She's such a liar."

"Ariel lied a lot, but never about you." Jack's eyes shift downward, landing on my mouth. I'm suddenly very aware of every inch of space separating my body from all that bare skin.

I lick my lips, and his cheeks color. He becomes very concerned with the plastic sword hanging from his hips. His hands are covered in glitter, and staring at them, I feel a sudden flare of want. I picture those hands wrapped around my waist, smearing glitter over my skirt. He lifts me up, and I wrap my legs around his—

"Did she tell you she came to see me after you all got back?"

I swallow, pushing the daydream from my head. *Get it together, Charlotte.* "What are you talking about? She didn't sneak out." Ariel and I fell asleep on our dorm floor that night, drunkenly whispering as the room spun around us.

"Yeah, she did. She tapped on my window at, like, four in the morning. We snuck up to the river. You know the one near the highway?

I see water lapping against Ariel's legs, soaking the edge of her flannel skirt. "I know it."

"Right. Well, it was cold as hell. There was ice on the river, but she walked right in, like she'd done it a million times before. I don't even think she shivered. I waited on the shore, watching, while she just . . . stood there." Jack swallows, his Adam's apple bobbing up and down in his throat. "She swore to me that she didn't go to that bonfire, but she *reeked* of smoke. Do you remember how she used to do that? Lie right to your face?"

"I remember." The next words fall out of my mouth before I can stop them. "You really loved her, didn't you?"

"Yes." Jack answers so quickly that I know he can't be lying. "Ariel was a force. She was the reason they name hurricanes after people."

"She would have loved that line."

"That's why I never said it to her." Jack is still smiling, but then he looks at me and the smile fades. I can see the ring of gold around his pupils. The dusting of freckles on his left eyelid.

He shifts toward me, and suddenly we're close. I could touch his arm. Ariel would be so mad. I almost glance behind me, to make sure she isn't watching.

"Ariel never seemed like a real person," Jack says, his voice lower than it was a second ago. "Being with her was like taking a break from the world. But being with you . . . it was like the real world made better."

Every inch of my skin seems to vibrate. How long do you have to wait before you can steal your best friend's boyfriend? What if she's dead?

Is a month long enough? A year? How about forever?

In my darker moments, I used to think that was why Ariel

had done it. Death meant they could never break up. I could never have him. She'd be the one we loved the most, forever and ever.

"Charlotte! Hi!" The new voice is so unexpected and so sudden that it takes me a long moment to figure out where it's coming from. Chloe has appeared next to Jack, and her body is so tiny and compact that, at first, my eyes pass over her, like she's a mirage. Her golden highlights glow in the sunlight. Her fake tan doesn't look even a little bit orange. She blinks, and I swear I feel a rush of wind coming off her eyelash extensions. "Did you get a flyer?"

She thrusts a neon-pink flyer at me, lips spread wide over twin rows of white teeth. Ariel would notice the smudge of coral lipstick. She'd say something awful that sounded like a compliment in the moment and only hit later, when Chloe was replaying the conversation in her head. I don't say anything. I take the flyer, feeling stiff. Something has shifted, but I can't quite place my finger on it.

I look down to the flyer, and that's when I notice Chloe's hand. Casually resting on Jack's arm.

"Oh!" I say the word out loud, and I feel like such an idiot that I pretend to cough to cover it up. I blink and look away.

"It's next weekend!" Chloe hugs her body closer to Jack's arm. I want him to squirm away, to shake her off, but he just stands there, statue still, refusing to meet my eyes. "You should come! It would be so, *so* great to have you there!"

The exclamation points at the end of Chloe's sentences

have brought back my migraine. I lift a hand to my face and rub my eyes with my thumb and forefinger.

"Uh, yeah, I'll try," I say. I look at Jack again, but he seems very interested in a bit of thread coming loose from his cape.

A lump forms in my throat. I shift my eyes back down at the flyer, but I don't really see the words on the page. They switch places, tricking me. "I'll definitely try."

Jack glances back at the girls handing out flyers. "I should . . ."

"Get back to dancing," I finish for him. "Me, too. I mean, I should get to class. I'm not dancing." *For the love of God, stop talking.* "Um, see you later, Chloe."

She says something else, but I've already turned and stepped into the school building. The door slams shut behind me, cutting her off.

I breathe in and in, forgetting to exhale until the oxygen makes me dizzy. This is my own fault. I shouldn't bother with Jack, or with anyone. I don't need friends here anymore. I'm only staying long enough to find Ariel's clues, and then it's back to New York and good-bye to all of this.

As soon as I turn the corner in the hall, I ball the flyer up in one hand and throw it in the trash.

Chapter Ten

Jack has always been a joiner. When I told him I wanted to start an animal shelter, he went to Dean Rosenthal's office with me to talk her into letting us use the old garden shed. He made a petition when she said no, and got everyone in school to sign it. He volunteered to help clean out the old shovels and flowerpots and half-full bags of soil after she finally gave in.

We were alone one night, repainting the walls. I wasn't wearing any makeup, and I had my hair pulled back with a rubber band. My jeans were two sizes too big, and my T-shirt was from a math camp Mother had made me attend, and probably I wasn't wearing a bra because, let's face it, I don't actually need a bra.

But I glanced up at one point, when the sun had started to set and twilight had stretched out across the floor of the shed, all golden and soft. Jack was staring at me. His head was tilted and his eyes were narrowed, and he had this look on his face. This look I've never seen except in really good romance movies. Awe. He was looking at me like I was something holy. It was the first and only time I ever wondered if I was beautiful.

I did a bad thing. But I had my reasons.

I just thought you should know that.

Chapter Eleven

I spend the rest of the day searching. I look beneath Ariel's old desk in calculus, the only class we had together. She used to pass me notes constantly, not even bothering to hide them from the teacher. Unfortunately, the only thing beneath her desk is old gum. I check her favorite bathroom stall, the one where she carved our names into the door, and I search the alcove just past the library where we used to sneak cigarettes between classes. Nothing.

I skip dinner that night. Zoe isn't at the dorm when I get back, but she left a Post-it on my bed.

Welcome back, it reads in big, loopy handwriting. *Won't be home tonight. Don't wait up.*

It's 100 percent against Weston's rules to stay out all night, but whatever. I crumple the note into a ball and toss it, then I take advantage of Zoe's absence to search every inch of our dorm. I find an old lipstick and a few stray bobby pins, but no more mysterious bottles, no notes. I try the closet next, standing on my tiptoes so I can search the very back. Someone's stuck a cardboard box into the far corner. I grab it and pull it down, tossing the lid aside.

My breath catches. A beaded cocktail dress glimmers from inside the box. I run my fingers over the black lace and glittering gold beads. I was with Ariel the day she bought this. We saw it in the window of a vintage store, and Ariel stormed in and demanded the clerk get it down for her. The store's only fitting room was being used, so she stripped right there, in front of the blushing clerk, while I shrugged off my coat and tried to cover her up.

I lift the dress from the box and gently rest it against my knees. The lace is spiderweb thin. I worry it'll come apart in my hands.

It's beautiful, but it's just a dress. Not a clue.

During history class the next morning, I try to think of every place that was important to Ariel. I spend most of the period hunched over my desk, scribbling things down and crossing them out again.

"Miss Gruen?"

I look up too quickly, and pain shoots down my neck. I bite the inside of my lip to keep from grimacing. Someone laughs behind me, the kind of low laugh that's almost a release of breath.

I clear my throat. "Yes?"

Mr. Oakley raises an eyebrow. *Shit.* He must've asked a question. The backs of my ears grow warm, but I keep my face carefully blank. A clock stares down from the wall above the door, second hand ticking like a metronome. The other students sit, silent, around me. No one whispers the answer. No one tries to help. Their excitement over my impending embarrassment vibrates through the air like electricity.

I lift a hand, pretending to study my cuticles while I think. Zoe sits in the desk next to me. She lowers her head, and her black hair swings forward, cutting a sharp angle against her cheek. She's doodling something in her notebook, drawing a thick square around the words—

"'Ptolemy I Soter,'" I read out loud, shifting my eyes back to the front of the room. Zoe slaps her notebook shut, cheeks flaring. Mr. Oakley turns back to the whiteboard and scrawls my answer. Zoe scribbles something on a piece of paper and tosses it to me. I slide it onto my lap and read while Mr. Oakley has his back turned.

Cheating will get you booted again.

I grab my pen and add: *So will staying out all night.*

I toss the note onto Zoe's desk and turn back to my own notebook. Last year, back before she became a fencing star, Zoe used to hide behind her hair and speak only in old movie quotes. I think I liked her better that way.

I tap my pen against the side of my desk as I reread my short list:

Bathroom

Devon's dorm

Woods

Med Center

I've already drawn a thick, angry line across the word "bathroom." I pull my pen through it again, just to drive the point home. That leaves three places. I drop a spot of ink onto the page next to "Med Center" and slowly darken it with my pen. Ariel, Dev, and I all did the internship together last semester, though we spent more time whispering in the supply closet than actually interning. Ariel might have hidden something there. I have my first shift next period.

I hurry out of class as soon as the bell rings, making it onto the bus into Underhill seconds before the doors slide closed. I take a seat near the back, dropping my bag on the floor between my feet. I suppose it's weird, how we leave school to do shifts at the Med Center in the middle of the day.

A few Weston students perch on the edge of their seats near the front of the bus, talking in thin, high-pitched voices as we crawl through the trees toward town. They're under-classmen, probably freshmen. I recognize one of the girls from CNN. Aurora or Audrey or something like that. She's the senator's daughter, I think.

She turns and sees me sitting at the back of the bus. Her eyes go cartoon-character-wide, and she whips her head back around, leaning in close to her friends. I can't hear her whispering, but I don't need to. I know what she's saying.

See her? That's the one. She knew the suicide girls. She was their friend.

A second later, they all lift their heads and look at me. I

slouch down in my seat and stare pointedly out the window to keep from meeting their eyes.

The bus rumbles to a stop in front of the Underhill Medical Center fifteen minutes later, its automatic doors screeching open. I wait for the other Weston girls to leave, and then I grab my bag and climb from my seat, shivering against the sudden rush of winter air. I pull a scarf out of my bag and wrap it around my neck, not caring that the Med Center is only a few yards away. I ball my hands into fists and stick them in my coat pockets.

The hospital looks like it was built here by mistake. It's a mountain of glass and steel towering above the leafless trees and dead grass. It belongs in Manhattan or Chicago, not a Podunk town in Upstate New York. Light ripples off the wall of windows, seeping into the dull gray sky around it. Everything about it is modern and cold and state of the art. It's my mother, transformed into a building.

I head inside. There's a sudden rush of warm air, a thick smell of antiseptic, the muffled hum of voices. Carpeting swallows my footsteps as I move from the entry to the main hall to the lobby, wood-paneled walls around me.

You need a badge to get through the main doors, but I lost mine months ago, so I give my name to the woman working the reception desk.

"The volunteer coordinator will be with you shortly," she says, pointing me to the waiting area.

I settle myself into a stiff wingback chair. The lobby has

always felt more like a hotel than a hospital. A wall of windows overlooks the surrounding woods, and there's a fountain in the far corner spurting a trickling stream of water over a bed of mossy rocks.

I close my eyes and smell cigarettes—the expensive French ones Devon occasionally bummed from Zoe. I feel sleepy and loose, like I'm pink-wine drunk. Devon and Ariel persuaded me to steal my mother's keys and sneak in here after hours one time because Devon thought there would be painkillers hidden in the cupboards. But we only found tongue depressors and floss and brochures for volunteer programs. We cut the pictures from the brochures and glued them to the tongue depressors and spent the rest of the night performing increasingly lewd puppet shows and laughing until wine came out of our noses.

"Charlotte?"

I flinch and open my eyes again. Amelia Potter, the Med Center's volunteer coordinator, stands in front of me, wearing crisp white scrubs and black tennis shoes. She's pulled her black hair into a tight bun, making her face look long and pointed.

"Your mother mentioned you'd be starting up again today." She smiles in a way that tells me she hates me and all other kids whose important parents get them second chances they don't deserve. So at least we're getting off on the right foot.

"Yes." I stand and pull my bag over my shoulder. "Thanks so much for letting me come back after—"

Amelia waves my apology away, but her expression doesn't change. "As long as you're willing to put in the work this time, I'm happy to have you back. Come with me."

She turns on her heel, walking at a brisk clip. I follow her through the familiar maze of hallways, past rooms filled with patients and doctors and expensive-looking equipment. The Med Center is huge. There are a million places Ariel could've hidden something. I don't know where to begin.

Amelia stops in the middle of the hallway, sneakers squeaking against the tile.

"Go ahead and get changed," she says, nodding at a door to her left. "I'm sure you remember where we keep the scrubs. And make sure you wash your hands for exactly two and a half minutes using soap and the hottest water you can stand."

"Yes, ma'am," I say, heading into the locker room.

"Make sure to scrub under your nails!" she calls as the door swings shut behind me.

I change quickly and store my clothes and bag in one of the metal lockers lining the walls. The locker room seems like an unlikely hiding place, but I check the rest of the lockers and open all the cupboards, digging behind stacks of fresh scrubs and a box of extra trash can liners. Nothing. Frustrated, I quickly wash my hands, cringing under the scalding water as I stare at the clock on the wall above the sinks, watching the second hand tick slowly past.

After I'm done, Amelia leads me to the Med Center's free clinic. Filmy curtains hang from the ceiling, sectioning the room into half a dozen areas, each containing a narrow hospital bed and a jumble of complicated-looking machines.

"We'll start you off slow today," she says. "Just stop by each cot and change out the patients' pillows, clear away the bedpans, and make sure there are enough linens in the cupboard. Think you can handle that?"

I nod and Amelia pats me on the shoulder, telling me to come find her when I've finished. I get started, pulling linens out of cupboards and checking bedpans and fluffing pillows. It takes about ten seconds for me to remember why I stopped showing up for these shifts. Without Ariel and Devon around, interning at the Med Center is mind-numbingly boring. There's no one to make jokes or tell stories with. Just cupboard after cupboard of scratchy hospital linens, and bedpans that always smell faintly of piss and bleach, and glassy-eyed patients asking if you want to be a doctor when you grow up.

A few other students from school wander through the room, performing their own tasks, but I duck my head whenever they come close. They probably recognize me, but they're polite enough to walk past without pointing and staring, like the girls on the bus.

"Can you get me some more gauze from the supply closet?" a nurse in pink scrubs asks after I've been working for almost an hour.

"Sure," I say. I head to the closet in the hall and grab a few rolls of gauze, then hurry back. The nurse thanks me and leans over a cot near the windows. A man lies there, a thick layer of bloodstained bandages hiding his face.

"What happened to him?" I ask.

"We aren't really sure," the nurse explains, unwrapping the fresh gauze. "He's a John Doe. Someone dropped him off a few weeks ago. Looks like he was badly injured in a fire, but he hasn't regained consciousness yet, so we haven't been able to confirm anything."

She cuts a length of gauze from the roll. "If he doesn't come out of this soon, we'll need to transfer him to long-term care."

I kneel next to his bed and pull two fluffy pillows out from the shelf beside him. The nurse eases him forward, and I slide a new pillow behind his back. I turn to grab another.

There's a flicker of movement outside the window. I spot it from the corner of my eye and jerk my head around on instinct. Nothing there.

The nurse looks up from the machine she'd been studying, eyebrows furrowed. "Is something wrong?"

I stare out the window for a beat longer. The bushes are still trembling, but it could just be the wind. Or an animal. My skin itches, though. I feel like I was being watched. Like the woods themselves were tracking my movements.

"Nothing's wrong," I say, sliding the second pillow behind the patient's back. "I just thought I saw something."

Chapter Twelve

I'm outside Mother's office when my phone beeps. I fish it from my backpack.

Jack's name flashes across my screen. *Can we talk?*

The words crawl over my skin like ants. I wonder if Chloe looks through his phone, like Ariel used to. If he had to delete this text as soon as he sent it. I used to love the mystery of it, how I had to destroy his messages, like a spy in a movie, as soon as I read them. How his words only existed in my mind. Now it just makes me feel guilty.

I stick the phone back into my bag without responding and knock on the door.

"Come in," Mother calls, her voice muffled. I open the door. She glances up from the stack of papers she's holding, a ballpoint clenched between her teeth.

"Charlotte?" she says, removing the pen. I frown, taking in the mess of her usually pristine office. A stack of files sits on the corner of her desk, spilling ragged-edged papers across the shiny surface. A few of the books on her shelf have toppled over, and her most prized possession—a sleek black samurai sword given to her by a Japanese businessman—sits crooked in its stand. It looks like it's going to fall over.

I step into the office, closing the door behind me. Her closet hangs open, a white lab coat dangling from the door-knob. A local news program blares from the tiny flat-screen TV sitting on the bookshelf next to her sword.

"... *the fire spread fast. So far, there's no word as to what caused the initial* ..."

"Is this a bad time?" I ask, tearing my eyes away from the screen.

"Oh no, it's fine." Mother clicks the television off and removes the lab coat from the door so she can push it closed. "The board is going through a bit of a disaster at the moment and—"

"Still?" I interrupt.

Mother blinks. "Pardon?"

"You said they were having some kind of crisis yesterday in the car."

"Did I? Anyway, take a seat. I wasn't expecting you for another ..." She glances at the clock above the door and frowns. "Is that the time?"

"I can come back later," I say, backing toward the hall.

"Sit." Mother slips into her lab coat, nodding at the chair in front of her desk. "How was your first day?"

"Fine." I shift uncomfortably on the stiff leather chair. "Normal."

"Amelia took care of you?"

"Yes."

"That's good." Mother frowns. "Your hair looks better. Did you even it out last night?"

"I washed it," I say, tucking a strand behind my ear.

"Is that all?" Mother walks to the other side of her desk and sits. Her fingers are smudged with ink, and she's left black prints on her coat. I stare at them for a long moment. My mother is never disheveled. She's never out of sorts. The crooked samurai sword stares down at me like a warning.

I start to rise from my seat. "Are you sure you don't want me to—"

"I spoke with that college counselor I was telling you about the other day. Petra, remember? Anyway, she mentioned a few study programs we could get you enrolled in before you take the SATs again this spring. Your scores last year were atrocious . . ."

I drop back into my seat as she talks. Mother knows I don't want to go to college. I've told her a dozen times.

"Obviously, you've missed admissions for this September," Mother says. "You were supposed to get your application in by the end of January."

I squirm. This chair is ridiculously uncomfortable. I reach for the knobby thing that controls the lumbar support.

"Petra seems to think you have a good chance of getting

in somewhere decent next fall. Apparently, taking a gap year is in fashion . . ."

The chair sinks to a foot above the ground. I release a grunt and nearly knee myself in the chin. Mother presses her lips together, the muscles in her neck tightening.

"Sorry," I say. I twist the knob to get the chair to rise again.

"Did you eat breakfast today?" Mother asks. I don't answer. She stands and crosses the room before I can protest, pulling her purse off its hook on the back of the door. She digs around inside and removes a protein bar, which she holds out for me.

I stare at the bar like it might bite. "I'm fine."

"You're not fine. You're not eating again, and it's affecting your concentration." She shakes the bar. *"Eat."*

I still don't reach for it. You probably think I have an eating disorder, but that's not it. I just don't like being told what to eat. When to eat. I get enough of that in the rest of my life.

Mother closes her eyes. "You're not leaving here until you take this, Charlotte."

I groan but lean forward anyway, pulling the protein bar from her fingers. "I'll eat it on the bus," I lie.

I make it back to school just in time for lunch. Daily announcements crackle over the loudspeaker. The girls' soccer team is headed to nationals. Kelly Wexler and Roger Graham were named presidential scholars. Evan Whitney was admitted to the MIT summer science program.

The list goes on, but no one claps or lifts their head or

even seems to hear what's being announced. Some of the other students talk while they eat, but most are hunched over books and notecards, memorizing lists of elements or long-dead presidents while they munch on broccoli. The announcements hang over them like threats.

Do better, try harder, study more . . .

Jack and Chloe sit next to each other at a table across the room. He hasn't texted me again, and I doubt he'll try to talk to me here, in front of her. I watch them from the corner of my eye as I push a chunk of chicken around on my plate. He says something, and she throws her head back, laughing loud enough for the entire cafeteria to hear. I cut the chicken into teeny-tiny little pieces. She's wearing his track jacket, the blue one with WESTON printed in silver letters across the chest.

"Why do you wear this?" I asked him once. We were in the quad last year, just the two of us. I leaned over and pinched his jacket sleeve between two fingers, the fabric slick to the touch. "You aren't even good at track."

"Ouch," Jack said, pressing his hand over his heart. "She wounds."

"Ha-ha," I said. I was still holding his jacket, and he turned too quickly and the sleeve tugged up over his arm, my fingers trailing along the skin between his wrist and his elbow.

It felt exactly like that thing that happens when you shuffle your feet across carpet and then touch someone. Static electricity. I could feel every hair on my body standing on end. Every inch of my skin hummed.

When I looked up again, Jack was staring at me like he'd never seen me before. His breathing had deepened, his eyes sparked, and then he stood too quickly, made an excuse about being late to study hall, and was gone.

That was the last time we touched.

My cheeks burn at the memory. I shift my eyes back down to the shredded chicken sitting next to the perfectly balanced portions of broccoli and quinoa on my plate. Weston only serves gluten-free, macrobiotic food. I can't quite bring myself to lift it to my mouth and chew. Mother's protein bar still sits at the bottom of my backpack, probably squished between some books. Before leaving the Med Center, I grabbed a bag of chips from the vending machine and ate those instead. They tasted wonderfully artificial.

Chloe laughs again. "Jack, stop it!" she squeals.

I stand and dump my lunch into the trash, uneaten.

I make my way to the locker room and start changing into my fencing uniform: a puffy white jacket, metallic-gray lamé, and lace-up boots. I have a minute until class starts, so I poke around, wondering if Ariel might've left something for me here. The girls' locker room wasn't on my list, but there's no harm checking.

I pull Ariel's old locker open, but it's empty, a coat of dust on the metal shelf where she kept her sports bra and tennis shoes. Devon's locker still has her padlock dangling from the latch, but I know the code: *33-8-17.* The lock falls open in my fingers.

Devon's locker is far from empty. Her gym bag lies on the

floor, filled with clothes and shoes that are starting to stink. I wrinkle my nose as I poke through it, but there's nothing out of the ordinary. I turn my attention to the metal shelf and find a bottle of face cream, a pair of goggles, a small red notebook.

I pull the book off the shelf and flip it open. Row after row of numbers line the pages: *4:30.02, 4:05.03, 4:02.40, 3:58.69, 3:42.40* . . . Devon swam the 400-meter freestyle for Weston's swim team. This must be where she recorded her times.

I study the last set of numbers she scribbled down: *3:42.40*. That can't be right. I was never a swimmer, but Devon talked about it constantly. The summer before our senior year I used to sit at the side of the pool, stopwatch in hand as she cut through the water, arms smooth and strong and straight. She was trying to take five seconds off her time so she'd be a contender for the state record—which was 4:44.40. I remember shouting that number at least a dozen times when she finally made it. She leaped out of the pool and wrapped me in a hug, neither of us caring that she soaked my clothes all the way through.

I shake the memory out of my head, and refocus on the numbers scrawled in her notebook. It took her all summer to cut those five seconds, but this list makes it look like she was dropping time steadily: twenty-five seconds here, sixteen seconds there. Her last time was a full minute faster than what it was last summer.

"That would be a record." I pull out my phone and look

up the world record for the women's 400-meter freestyle. It's 3:57.07—almost fifteen seconds longer than Devon's last recorded time. Devon would have been winning medals and attracting college scouts. But she barely swam at all during those last few months. It was like she got bored of it.

A locker door bangs open. I flinch and shove the book into my gym bag, pushing Devon's locker closed with my elbow. Zoe stands at the end of the aisle. She's already dressed in her fencing gear, but it doesn't look bulky and awkward on her. She could be walking down a runway.

"You have nice shoes," she says, smirking.

I look down at the clunky gray fencing boots. "What?"

"Those black strappy ones you hide in the back of your closet." Zoe makes an okay symbol with her fingers. "Very nice."

"You went through my things?"

"You went through mine first."

It takes me a long moment to remember what she's talking about. The pink pocketknife. The love note. "I was looking for something of Ariel's," I explain. "I didn't touch your things."

"Whatever. Stay out of my shit." She turns, slamming her locker door shut. The sharp crash echoes through the room, making me flinch.

I have a sudden flash of a memory as I watch her walk away: Zoe sitting in the corner of the quad, hunched forward so that her long hair hid her face. She was watching something on her phone, and she had her headphones in so she couldn't hear the crowd of upperclassmen a few feet away, making fun of her.

I bet no one makes fun of her now that she's nationally ranked. I bet they compliment her eyeliner and let her cut in front of them in the lunch line, hoping to get on her good side. Like talent is something that can rub off on them.

I walk into the gymnasium with my helmet under one arm. Long, narrow mats stretch across the width of the room. The word "piste" pops into my head. The mat is called a piste. I may have skipped half the practices last semester, but I haven't forgotten all my fencing training. The rest of the class has already paired up, two girls to a piste. I stop next to an empty mat, partnerless.

Coach Lammly sweeps into the room. She's built like a French bulldog—tiny with muscular arms and small, pointed ears. She wears her dark hair short and slicked back against her head.

She raises an eyebrow as she walks past me. "Equipment, Gruen!" she barks, pointing to my helmet. I look around the room. Every other girl already has her helmet on.

I tug mine over my head.

"You're going to need a saber, too," Coach says, winking. A few of the other girls chuckle. I suddenly remember why I hate fencing. I cross the gymnasium, to the far wall where we store the practice sabers in large metal lockers. Behind me, Coach turns to address the class.

"Good, I see you've all found a partner," she says. I tug a

locker door open and pull a saber off its metal hook. Right. One needs a partner to fence with. *Crap.*

"I'd like you to focus on your footwork today, particularly your advance, retreat, and lunge. Some of you have progressed on to the saber flèche"—Coach Lammly's eyes flicker over to Zoe—"and that's fine. Just make sure you focus on your positioning as you practice. I don't want to see any sloppy lunges in here."

Coach leans back and then shoots forward, knee bent, landing in a perfect lunge. "See where my feet are? That's proper form."

She straightens and glances at me again. I've stopped beside the same empty mat, hoping she won't notice that I'll be practicing my footwork solo. No such luck. She jerks her head at the last piste on her right, where Zoe stands.

"Miss Gruen, your partner is waiting."

I'm suddenly glad for the clunky fencing helmet. At least I know the rest of the class can't see the blood drain from my face. I don't bother checking the gymnasium to make sure every one else already has a partner. Of course they do. No one wants to fight Zoe. I force one foot in front of the other, until I'm standing on the piste across from her.

She tilts her head to the side, her expression unreadable beneath the black mesh. "I was partnered with Coach every other day this week," she says. "Now I have to babysit."

"I could surprise you," I say.

"Doubtful."

Coach blows her whistle. "On-guard position, ladies."

Zoe falls into a perfect on guard: feet spread, knees bent, saber held at a slight angle before her face. I mimic her, but my arms feel too long. I crouch lower, and my legs awkwardly jut out from my body. My saber sways in my hand. Zoe holds hers rod-straight.

It doesn't matter how you do, I tell myself. But then I think of those girls laughing when I forgot to grab my saber, the condescending sound of Zoe's voice. *Doubtful.* Is this how it's going to be now that I don't have Ariel and Devon to watch my back? Because that's pretty pathetic.

Coach blows her whistle again, one sharp note. All around us, girls start moving. Boots pad and thump against the mats. Metal clashes with metal.

Zoe stays still.

"Footwork, ladies!" Coach barks.

I shuffle forward—front foot, then back foot, leading with my heels. Maybe I don't have to do *well*, but I'd like to get through this without looking like a complete idiot. I don't remember much from the half dozen classes I actually attended. I think Coach said something about alternating the length of your steps. I take short, quick steps, then long, slow ones. Zoe retreats easily, saber still straight in front of her helmet. Okay, this isn't so bad, but I can't keep chasing her down the piste. I have to actually *do* something.

I lunge, and she flicks her wrist to the side, blocking my saber with the edge of her blade. I start to pull back, and she taps me on top of my helmet. Point Zoe.

"Fantastic parry-riposte, Zoe," Coach shouts.

"I thought you'd done this before," Zoe says, her words muffled by her helmet. My cheeks flare. So much for not looking like an idiot.

"Can we just get this over with?"

"If you say so." Zoe advances. Her movements seem too quick. Her front toes barely brush against the ground before she raises her back heel, her entire body slinking forward with animal grace. It's almost like she's floating.

I stumble away from her, forgetting my footwork completely. My balance is off, my back leg cramped and awkward, my front leg jittery. I nearly trip over my own too-large feet.

"Gruen, you look sloppy," Coach shouts.

I grit my teeth together. I can do this. It's *fencing*, not dismantling a nuclear warhead. And Zoe may seem supernatural, but she's not—she's just a girl. I keep my front and back heels parallel and gently lift my toes. Back foot, then front foot, then back foot. Zoe cocks her head. She looks like a cat considering a mouse before eating it.

She lunges, and I parry too late, my blade cutting through nothing but air. The tip of Zoe's saber presses into my chest. Two points. I try to recover and get tangled in my own limbs. Zoe flicks her wrist, slapping her blade against my upper arm. Three points. Two more strikes and I'm out.

I tighten my grip on the saber, and the handle groans beneath my gloved hand. This is ridiculous. No wonder no one else wants to spar with her. It's like fighting the wind.

I hear Ariel's voice in my head. *Can we keep her?* Jealousy flares through my chest. I imagine Ariel watching this, embarrassed for me. Poor little Charlotte. So nice. So mediocre.

Zoe shuffles forward. This time I see her advance as a series of tiny movements. It's like she's moving in slow motion. She cocks her knee before taking a step. Her shoulder twitches as she starts to raise her saber. The noises around me fall silent. I no longer hear the other girls breathing, or the click of metal hitting metal. Without thinking, without making any kind of a plan, I kick my back leg out and lunge forward, jabbing at Zoe's chest with the tip of my saber. The blade bends as I hit my mark. I got a point. I've never gotten a point before.

Zoe's shoulders tense. She advances, and I lift my saber a second before she brings hers down on my shoulder. A voice whispers at the back of my head, *Parry-tierce*. I don't have time to marvel at myself for remembering the term. Zoe lunges. I bring my sword across my chest and metal slaps on metal. *Parry-quarte*.

"Much better, Miss Gruen," Coach calls. I hesitate for a second, the compliment warm in my chest. Zoe darts forward. I feel the prick of her saber through my layers of protective clothing. I raise my saber and Zoe parries, her blade tapping the top of my helmet.

"You're out," she says, falling back. She whips her saber to her side, the blade whistling as it moves through the air. I shuffle backward, trying to remember what I usually do with my arms when I'm standing. My own saber feels like a lead weight in my hand.

Zoe studies me like I'm some new organism she doesn't understand. "Let me give you some advice," she says. My entire body tenses. Sweat pools between my fingers and my heavy fencing glove.

"Yeah?" I say. "And what's that?"

"Leave," Zoe says. "You don't belong in this class, in this school. Do yourself a favor and go home before you end up like your friends."

Her words slam into me. *Leave.* I open my mouth, but Zoe turns and stalks across the gymnasium before I can say a word.

Chapter Thirteen

The rest of my classes pass in a blur of quadratic equations, Japanese vocabulary, and intense discussions on the themes of *Ulysses*. I have vivid memories of raising my hand, reading chapters, answering questions. But I don't feel like I was there for any of it. I existed in a shadow world, watching myself play the part of high school girl.

Meanwhile, Zoe's voice plays on a loop in my brain. *Do yourself a favor*—I shake my head, pushing the words away.

I still haven't turned in my *Brave New World* essay, so Ms. Antoine sends me to the library to work on it. The room, usually filled with cramming students, is nearly empty. I push open the heavy doors and drop my books at the nearest table. They thud against the wood, the sound echoing off the walls.

Our library is a little famous. It's been featured on about a million best-of lists and blog posts, their headlines all reading something like "20 Libraries Every Book Lover Has to

See to Believe" or "100 Libraries to Visit Before You Die," which is a little morbid. Brass chandeliers dangle from the arched ceilings. They were originally made for candles, but the school updated them. Electric lights flicker behind their yellow panes, illuminating a marble floor and row after row of gleaming wooden bookcases. Long study tables stretch across the width of the room, each outfitted with dozens of top-of-the-line laptops that look out of place against the backdrop of wood and marble.

I pull a laptop toward me and key in my password. I open a Word document and stare at the blinking cursor, trying to come up with something to write about. I purse my lips and type a few words into the Internet browser: *Brave New World essay themes*. I check over my shoulder to make sure no one's watching my dubious study methods, and then press Search.

Thousands of results pop up, and my eyes glaze over as I scan them. "Freedom vs. happiness in *Brave New World*." "Discuss the importance of the World State's motto." "Is it possible to manufacture happiness . . ." I rub my eyes with the palms of my hands, groaning out loud. I don't know how I'm supposed to write an essay about this. I couldn't possibly be impartial—if someone offered me a drug that would make me blissfully happy, I'm pretty sure I'd take it. It'd be like steroids for your emotions.

Steroids. The word flashes through my head in neon. I sit up, blinking, and pull my backpack onto my lap. I dig around inside until I locate Devon's tiny red notebook. I flip it open.

The numbers scrawled across the page seemed impossible. But if Devon was on something . . .

Blood pounds in my ears, blocking out the sounds of students turning pages and tapping their pencils against their desks. The mood swings. The cruelty. The secrecy—it all fits.

I stick my books into my bag and duck out of the library. Ms. Antoine will be pissed when she finds out I skipped, but I can't just sit here trying to focus on a stupid essay when this new info is rattling around inside my mind. This is the first lead of any kind I've gotten since coming back to Weston. I have to find out if I'm right.

I head into the quad. Icy air creeps up from the frozen ground and rubs its face against my ankles. I tug my sleeves over my hands, shivering. Frost winks from the windows lining the enclosed courtyard. I hurry down the cobblestone path, past the windows, and through the dormitory door, face ducked to keep anyone from recognizing me if they happen to look outside.

The door falls shut with a soft click. Devon's dorm is the first room on the second floor. I take the steps two at a time and round the corner, so focused on being quick that I don't prepare myself for what I'm about to see.

It hits me like a punch to the gut. I stop in the middle of the hallway.

Her message board still hangs from her door, same as when she was alive. It's one of those half-corkboard, half-wipe-board things. The corkboard holds all her old stuff: the cardboard *D* covered in chunky glitter, photographs of me and Ariel, dried flowers from one of her old boyfriends. I move forward until I'm directly in front of it. I run a finger along the edge of a photograph, letting the sharp corner dig into my skin.

Me and Dev and Ariel in the woods, tribal-print blanket spread below us, vodka hidden in plastic water bottles with the labels peeled off. Ariel is lying on her back, hair tangled and wild around her, dress hitched up to show off her long, pale legs. Devon flips off the camera, dark eyes narrow and bored. She's pulled a floppy felt hat low over her forehead, casting half her face in shadow. I'm the only one smiling, which means Jack must've taken the photo. I'm leaning forward, grinning like a fool. My hair is long and sun-kissed, almost white-blond. It curls lazily around my bare shoulders. I'm wearing Devon's leather halter, my hands spread wide in front of me to hide my exposed midriff. I look beautiful in this picture, almost as beautiful as Devon and Ariel. I look happy.

I close my eyes, and there's Devon's voice in my ear: *You're skinny as all hell. Show it off.* I think I threw her halter into one of my suitcases. The leather is probably creased and wrinkled now.

I turn the doorknob. It creaks open beneath my hand.

Devon's room is a time capsule. I heard her parents are stuck in an airport in Tokyo, which is why they haven't been back to collect her things yet. She was always neat, the kind of girl who never left anything out of place, whether it was a stray hair tie, or a stack of color-coordinated books, or her bloodred silk duvet. I step into her room and push the door closed behind me. The walls muffle all outside noises. Everything goes still.

The air still smells like her—she wore Flash by Jimmy Choo, the scent all pepper and flowers. Spicy and sweet. I consider opening a window so I don't have to smell it, but the thought of the scent being gone forever makes something inside me clench. No window, then.

I move around the room with my hands clasped in front of me. I don't want to disturb anything. Her bed is neatly made, the duvet tucked in at the corners, her black-and-gray pillows freshly plumped. I pull open a dresser drawer and feel another sharp pang as I stare down at Devon's uniforms, folded and stacked in rows. I run my finger along the edge of one of her skirts. She took them all to a seamstress to have the hem taken up two inches. The bottoms of the skirts barely grazed the tops of her thighs.

I grin. Devon was taller than Ariel and me, but her skirts still looked like handkerchiefs. I remember holding one up in her dorm room, joking that it wouldn't even fit over one of my legs. Ariel said it was scandalous, which made Devon that much more proud of herself. My smile fades with the memory. I slide her dresser drawer closed.

Stop, I tell myself. I'm not here to reminisce. I move over to her desk. I pull open the bottom drawer, and a row of hanging file folders slides toward me. I drop to my knees to sort through them. They're arranged by year, and then by subject. From what I can tell at first glance, it looks like Devon saved every single assignment she ever completed.

"Psycho," I mutter fondly. Steroids don't affect school-work, so I close the drawer and try her closet instead. I'm not sure what I expect to find back here, maybe another Victoria's Secret bag, this one filled with identical vials of the serum, all neatly labeled. I shuffle through dark coats and brightly colored ballet flats and a couple of brown-and-gold Louis Vuitton suitcases. But the shelves are empty except for an unopened bottle of red nail polish.

Russian Roulette, it's called. I start to put it back on the shelf and then change my mind and slide it into the pocket of my skirt.

"Come on, Devon. Help me out here." I drop to my hands and knees and peer into the shadows beneath Devon's bed, but there's nothing there, not even a dust bunny. My dorm seems to breed dust bunnies. I find them in every corner, under every piece of furniture. I frown, trying to picture Devon on her hands and knees, sweeping beneath her bed. The picture doesn't hold. Devon doesn't do housework. Her family's had the same maid since she was a baby.

I try her bedside table and find a folded piece of notebook paper with nothing written on it. An empty tin of mints.

Go home before you end up like your friends, I think. I can't even figure out what *happened* to my friends. Why does everyone keep expecting me to end up like them?

I sink onto Devon's bed, lowering my head to my hands. My theory about Devon being into some kind of scary performance-altering drug seems stupid now. She wouldn't have taken something that dangerous and then gotten bored with swimming the second it started working. She wouldn't have killed herself over it.

And, besides, I took the serum, too, and I'm exactly as ordinary as I always was.

I try to inhale, and my chest hitches. It feels like my nose has closed up, like the air I'm trying to choke down is too hot, too . . . thick. My head aches, and my chest burns, and . . .

A sob bubbles from my lips, breaking the perfect stillness of the room. I close my eyes, and then I'm lying on Devon's bed and her pillow is beneath my head. I don't want to go to my dorm. I shouldn't have come back here. I don't want to deal with this school without Dev and Ariel. How am I supposed to attend a party without Devon to help me perfect winged eyeliner? Without Ariel whispering that the guy in the corner is checking me out? How am I supposed to take a test without my friends to help me make flash cards and quiz me all night? Who's going to bring me a celebratory box of macarons from that amazing bakery in town?

The thought of doing this alone makes me ache. *I can't, I can't, I can't.*

Dev's parents will be here any day to claim her things. They'll move everything out of this room and pack it into boxes and store it away somewhere. I'll never see it again. I press my hands flat against Devon's duvet cover, focusing on the silky-soft feel of the fabric beneath my fingers. After that, Devon really will be gone, and any chance I had of unraveling her and Ariel's mystery will disappear with her. I'll be here alone. Forever. I close my eyes, desperate to think about anything else.

My cheeks are wet when I finally fall asleep.

Laughing voices echo through my head. I'm in the woods, Ariel and Devon racing ahead of me. I call for them to wait, but they're too fast. They're like gazelles dancing through the trees, their legs impossibly long, their feet not quite touching the ground. I'll never catch them.

I know I should give up, but I just pump my legs harder. My feet get caught on twigs and brush. I stumble and scrape my knee on a rock, but I push myself up again, running faster. I can't let them get away. Not this time.

Just when I know I can't run any farther, I see it—a shadow waiting beneath the trees. My chest clenches in relief. *Ariel.* I knew she wouldn't leave me behind. But when I reach the shadow, I see that it's not Ariel. It's Jack.

"Stop looking for them," he says in a voice that sounds like my mother's. "You already know the truth."

"What are you talking about?" I ask. He tilts his head toward me, and I see that his face has been burned. Skin drips from his cheeks. His eyes are bloodshot.

"You're the one who broke them," he says. "You're the reason they left."

Chapter Fourteen

I wake up in Devon's room the next morning, dried tears crusting my eyes, my mascara staining her pillow. Girls laugh and giggle in the hall outside the dorm. I groan and fumble for my cell so I can check the time. I'm late. If I don't hurry, I won't make it to class before first bell and—whoops—no more second chance.

I consider letting it happen. I could stay here through first period and, within the hour, I'd see Mother's car parked at the curb, waiting to whisk me off to a different kind of life. I could forget about Devon and Ariel, and whatever they got themselves into. Everything would be so much easier.

You don't belong in this school, Zoe said. *Leave.*

I stand, straightening my skirt in front of Devon's mirror. My complexion still looks perfect. Creamy and pale and flawless. I press my index finger into my cheek and

pull at the skin below my eye, searching for shadows or dis-
coloration. But there's nothing. I could be Photoshopped. I
bare my teeth. They're perfectly straight from years of
braces, but coffee-stained. Mother keeps trying to get me to
use some professional-grade whitener, but I hate the way it
makes them tingle. I turn my head to the left. And then to
the right. I pinch a lock of blond hair between two fingers.

"Better," I say, letting the hair drop back into place. Two
days ago, it looked like I'd gotten in a fight with a lawn mower,
and my hair wouldn't lie flat unless I loaded it down with
industrial-strength gel. But now it's transitioned into edgy.
The unevenness looks intentional.

I turn away from the mirror, taking one last look at Devon's room. Sunlight slants in from the window, painting
everything gold. The smell of pepper and flowers still hangs
in the air. I fluff Devon's pillow and turn it so that the side
covered in mascara stains is to the wall, and then I pull my
bag over my shoulder and step out the door.

". . . before I have to be in physics, so let's make this
quick."

The voice echoes down the hall, followed by the dull
thud of a door swinging shut. I swear under my breath and
duck into the staircase alcove. Footsteps pad against the car-
peted floor, moving closer.

"You think Coach will be okay if we just leave the flowers? Or should we write something?"

"I know what I want to write."

A pause. Then, "You probably shouldn't."

"Why not? It's not like she can do anything to us now."

Two girls stop in front of Devon's door. I lean past the wall, studying the backs of their hair: one short and black, cropped to just below her ears, the other blond, curly, and twisted in a tight braid. Amber Hadley and Sarah Shield, JV members of Devon's swim team.

Sarah—the blonde—kneels. She places a bouquet of white tulips wrapped in tissue paper on the floor in front of Devon's door. "Should we say something?"

Amber picks up the marker attached to Devon's wipe board and scrawls a *B* across a bit of empty space. "Like what? You want to pray?"

Sarah lifts her shoulders in a jerky shrug. "No. But maybe we could say that we hope she's finally found peace. Or something."

Amber draws an *I*. "I don't hope that."

"Jesus. She *died*, Amber."

Amber doesn't turn around. She pulls the marker across the wipe board in a big, fat *T*. "Yeah? Who cares? I'm not going to pretend I liked her just because she offed herself."

"Amber—"

"No, seriously. Remember when she flushed Kelly's bra down the toilet? Or when she said you were an embarrassment to the team and should just quit? And what she did to Hattie . . ."

Amber doesn't finish the end of her sentence. She draws

a *C*, the marker squeaking against the wipe board. Sarah finally figures out what she's writing and swats her on the leg.

"Don't," she says. I expect Amber to argue, but she just puts the cap on the marker and drops it, letting it swing from the string connected to the board. She wipes her cheek with her hand.

I ease back around the corner. I don't need to hear any more. I slip my shoes off and carry them down the stairs, my bare feet silent on the carpet. I wait until I'm in the quad to put them on again. Icy grass crunches beneath my toes.

I've heard stories like this before. Earlier this year, Dev got suspended for a week for hazing this girl named Hattie Goldberg, a freshman on her swim team. Or, she would have been suspended if Daddy hadn't made a phone call and gotten her sentence lowered to an afternoon in detention. Dev told everyone it was no big deal, but Hattie never came back to Weston. No one talks about her anymore.

Devon wasn't a bad person. She had a dark sense of humor. She liked to push boundaries. If she sometimes went too far, it wasn't because she was trying to hurt anyone. It just never occurred to her that there were people who weren't as strong as she was.

A week after Ariel died, Devon snuck into my dorm in the middle of the night. She woke me up by pressing her hand over my mouth. So I wouldn't scream.

"I need your help with something," she whispered. She seemed raw and empty in a way I'd never seen her before. Devon had always been too much. Too loud. Too intense. Too smart. Too beautiful. That night, standing over me, she was none of those things. She was a shell.

But Ariel had just died. We were both shells.

I followed her outside, into the dark, through the woods. The trees seemed wilder in the moonlight. Feral. I felt like they were reaching for me, following me, whispering. Devon clearly knew exactly where she was going. She hummed under her breath as we walked, a single, low note. I pretended the wings flapping above me belonged to birds instead of bats.

Devon stopped in front of a cave I'd never seen before.

"It's in there," she said, staring into the perfect darkness beyond the cave's entrance. "Want me to go first?"

I resented the implication that I wasn't brave enough to go into a dark place without her to protect me, so I walked right past her and into the cave. Something rustled in the trees behind me, and I flinched and whirled around, tripping over my own feet. Devon was next to me but nearly invisible in the shadows. Her eyes reflected twin pinpricks of moonlight.

I remember thinking her eyes looked strange. Like there was nothing behind them.

"It's fine," she said, touching my arm with the tips of her long fingers. "There was a rabbit."

Maybe I should have turned back then. My instincts were screaming for me to leave. But, remember, I was still in shock. I felt everything either too strongly or not at all. I didn't trust myself. And Devon, my sister, was standing beside me.

The darkness of the cave seemed to pulse. Seemed to breathe. I took another step forward. Rocks clawed at my toes, and twigs scratched the arches of my feet. Shapes floated out of the darkness like things rising from deep water. I saw the rocky sides of walls, the uneven ground, the yawning black stretching farther and farther into nothing.

Then the moon slid out from behind a cloud and illuminated a shaggy black pelt. I watched it rise and fall once before I understood what I was seeing. A stray dog.

The dog leaped out of the cave and clamped down on my hand and wrist. I screamed and fell backward, hitting the ground so hard that pain shot through my tailbone and left my head spinning. The dog didn't let go.

"Devon!" I screamed. I expected her to leap in and help. Swat at the dog with a spare stick or throw a rock at it. But she hesitated, eyes narrowing like she couldn't understand what was happening.

Hot blood wound down my arm. My bones felt split in half.

In reality, Devon had only paused for a fraction of a second. But it felt like I waited hours for her to lunge forward and grab the dog by the scruff of his neck. She dug her fingers into his dirty fur and pulled him off me—easily. Sweet relief flooded through my hand as the dog released his teeth. Devon lifted the dog and tossed it aside, like it was a stuffed animal. Like it didn't weigh over a hundred pounds. I remember thinking of mothers hauling cars over their heads to save trapped children. Something about how adrenaline and fear add up to super strength.

The dog hit the ground with a whimper and scrambled back to its feet. It had something wrong with its paw—it was limping.

"It was hurt," Devon explained, studying me with those strange, empty eyes. "I thought you could help—"

I pushed myself to my feet and grabbed her arm. "Come on," I said, dragging her back into the woods before the dog could attack again.

I washed the blood off my hands in the bathroom, squeezing and opening my fist a few times to make sure nothing was broken. My bones were fine, but the dog had torn through the skin between my index finger and my thumb. There's still a thick, gnarled scar weaving down my palm.

I stare at the scar now, noticing the way it looks pink in the light of the sun. Barely healed. You might think I stopped talking to Devon after that. Or that I yelled at her for being so thoughtless. That I told someone she needed help.

I didn't do any of those things. At the time, I couldn't imagine losing Devon so soon after losing Ariel, and it didn't even occur to me to let someone else into our private world. What happened was weird and scary. But it was between family. I kept the memory of that night inside me. Down deep, in the dark places I didn't have to look at.

At the time, I had to believe that Devon had never meant for me to get hurt. She had led me to an injured animal, and maybe she hadn't thought about what the consequences would be, but she hadn't done it on purpose. It was part of her grief. A reaction to what happened to Ariel.

I move my thumb over the raised, ugly skin, cringing at a phantom twinge of pain.

Of course, I could have been wrong.

Chapter Fifteen

Three more texts from Jack over the next two days.

I thought things weren't going to be weird between us?

Remember that time Ariel was convinced she saw Beyoncé in town and she made us follow her around for an hour, but it was just some girl?

Message received. I'll leave you alone.

Delete, delete, delete.

Jack's car is parked outside the Med Center the next day, and he's hunched in the front seat, warming his hands by the heater. I freeze inside the sliding glass doors, torn between wanting to run away and wanting to stand here and drink him in. He's wearing his track jacket again, the same one he draped around Chloe's shoulders in the cafeteria, and his hair is windswept, his cheeks pink from the cold. He looks like he should model athletic footwear.

I will not get inside that car. But I don't know if I'm promising this to Ariel or Chloe or myself. I walk forward, and the Med Center doors whoosh open. I duck my head, walking toward the bus stop and trying my best to pretend I don't notice him.

A car door slams shut. "Charlotte, wait!"

His voice unglues me. I know I shouldn't wait, but my feet stop moving all on their own.

"Traitors," I whisper down at them. Jack jogs up next to me, his long legs crossing the distance between us much too quickly.

"I thought you were going to leave me alone," I say.

"So you have been getting my texts?" He runs a hand back through his hair, leaving it adorably mussed. I stare at it for a beat and then imagine Chloe pulling her fingers through it, telling him he looks hot. I shift my eyes to the ground.

"Let me give you a ride home?" he asks.

Don't get into the car, don't get into the car, don't get into the car.

"Sure," I agree.

We climb into his car and buckle our seat belts. It's awkward, being so close. Being alone. I want to cover my ears with my hands so I don't have to hear Jack clear his throat, or sniff, or breathe. I drop my arm on the armrest—then flinch when Jack reaches for the gearshift, almost touching me.

He gives me a look but doesn't say anything. "You've been avoiding me."

"You avoided me first," I point out. It's unfair. Jack kept his distance after Ariel's body was found, but it's not like he wouldn't take my calls, if I'd made any. He waited two weeks. (Did he have an instruction manual? What's the appropriate amount of time to wait before calling up your dead ex-girlfriend's best friend?) I'm the one who wouldn't answer the door, who pretended I didn't hear him calling my name. I ignored his texts and notes and attempts to catch my eye in the cafeteria.

Jack pulls the car out of the Med Center parking lot and onto the main street.

"I wanted to call you," he explains. "Right after it happened, you were the only one I wanted to talk to. It was just too weird, with the funeral and everything. Her family kept inviting me over for dinner. They wanted to talk about how much we all loved her, and all I could think was, 'I wish Charlotte was here. Charlotte loved her more than anybody.'"

I can't picture Jack with Ariel's family. Her artist father who pretended to love Ariel more than anything else in the world, and then lost interest the second his fingers started itching for a paintbrush. Her crazy religious mother, who spent most of her time praying for Ariel's salvation.

"That sounds like a fun evening," I deadpan.

"You have no idea." Jack shudders. "They kept calling each other 'babe,' but the way they said it was like an insult. 'I noticed you didn't take the trash out, *babe*.' 'I was going to get to it later, *babe*.'"

I cringe. "I forgot they did that."

"Yeah. I think they wanted to understand what happened. Why she . . . But I didn't know what to tell them."

"She wouldn't have wanted them to know anyway. She hated them."

Jack levels his eyes at me. "I know that. I knew her, too."

I look straight ahead, but I can still see his profile from the corner of my eye. His straight nose. His unnaturally long eyelashes. His hands gripping the steering wheel. I shift in my seat, suddenly aware of how warm it is in this car. I switch off the heater and turn to face the window.

This was a mistake. All it's doing is reminding me of what I can't have.

"I just wanted you to know that I didn't . . . not call because I didn't want to." Jack clears his throat again.

"And now you're with Chloe." I only say it because it's the meanest thing I can think of.

Jack's fingers tighten around the steering wheel. "My dad thought it might help me move on. Someone new and all that."

I try not to make a face. According to Ariel, Senator Jack H. Calhoun Sr. believes that exercise cures mental illness and a hard day's work can take you anywhere. He's the kind of man who grabs life by the tail and smiles at strangers. He doesn't seem like a bad guy. He just doesn't like dark, complicated things. And he never understood why his only son was dating someone like Ariel, who was both.

"I bet your parents love Chloe," I say. I fog the passenger window with my breath and play tic-tac-toe on the glass. Perfect, uncomplicated Chloe.

"They haven't met her yet," Jack says. "They want me to bring her to dinner."

Dinner at the Calhoun house is serious. Ariel was only asked once, and she and Jack dated for over a year.

"Lucky girl," I say.

We stop at another traffic light. Jack is silent, and I know that he's watching me. I keep my eyes on the window so I won't look at him. I trace an *O* in the condensation. And then an *X. O. X.*

Jack leans toward me, his seat belt pulling against his chest. "You have something . . ."

He touches my hair and everything inside me goes still. I feel my entire body shifting toward him, like a flower turning toward the sun. He pulls his hand away, his thumb grazing the curve of my ear, and I have to bite my lip to keep from gasping out loud. His skin is smooth and warm, and there's a callus on his thumb because he holds his pen wrong.

"Leaf," he says, showing me the small brown leaf he plucked out of my hair. He opens his fingers, letting it flutter in the space between us.

* * *

That night I place the leaf beneath my pillow, like a kid with a tooth. I heard somewhere that doing this affects your dreams, and I want to dream of Jack. Jack's smile. Jack's hands. Jack's voice.

But I dream of the woods again. Shadows and laughter and running. Searching for the two people I can never find.

Chapter Sixteen

Mother insists that we meet for breakfast before my next shift at the Med Center. She's already waiting in a booth near the back of the cafeteria when I walk in, nose wrinkling as she sips her coffee. The Med Center isn't known for its culinary excellence.

"Amelia had good things to say about you," she says, placing her mug back on the table as I slide into the seat across from her. "She said you've been doing well at the clinic."

I stare down at the soggy veggie omelet she ordered for me. Mother never compliments me. I have no idea what to say in response.

Finally, I come up with "Yeah."

Mother unfolds her paper and flips to a story near the middle. She's reading the *Underhill Daily,* a fourteen-page newspaper that rarely covers anything more scandalous than a tag sale at the library. I stare at the back page.

"Did you get bored with the *Wall Street Journal*?" I ask, nudging a red pepper with my fork to make it look like I'm eating.

"She's rarely so impressed," Mother continues, ignoring me. She turns a page so quickly that it rips in half. "Apparently, you're showing a lot of initiative."

I chew on the inside of my cheek. That's two compliments in less than thirty seconds. A record. "Um, thank you?"

Mother glances at me over the top of her paper. "Are you going to eat that or play with it?"

That's more like it. I stab the pepper with my fork and put it into my mouth.

"You're looking so thin," Mother says, shaking her head. She takes another sip of coffee and turns back to her paper, completely ignoring her own fruit plate. "Your English teacher mentioned that you got an A on your latest essay," she continues. "'The Destructive Nature of Man, as Depicted in *Brave New World*.' Interesting topic."

I'm so shocked by the news that I'm getting an A on something that it takes me a moment to process my mother's third compliment of the morning. For a fraction of a fraction of a second, I'm the daughter she always wanted. "Did you read it?"

"I skimmed the thesis statement," Mother says, narrowing her eyes at something in her paper. For a long moment, she doesn't say a word. I scoot forward in my seat, trying to catch a glimpse of what she's reading. She turns the page.

"Do you really think it's the nature of genius to move toward its own destruction?"

I open my mouth to respond and then realize—"Wait. Ms. Antoine hasn't handed our essays back yet."

"She sent me an e-mail."

That brief flare of pride vanishes. "You're e-mailing my teachers? You don't trust me to hand in assignments now?"

Mother lifts an eyebrow, not bothering to explain herself. I make a face that she doesn't see.

"My point is that you seem to be improving." She selects a single grape from her salad and holds it between two fingers, inspecting it for a moment before popping it into her mouth. "I'm impressed. I wasn't sure you were serious about bringing your grades up."

"Does that mean I can stay at Weston?" My voice sounds casual enough, but I can't stop tapping my fork against my plate. I don't even realize what I'm doing until I tap too hard, sending a rubbery mushroom skidding across the table.

Mother folds down the top half of her paper and stares pointedly at my fork. I set it on the table next to my plate and fold my hands in my lap.

"You still have a week before the anniversary ball. We'll see," she says. "I'm headed out of town for a few days. My plane leaves this afternoon."

"Today?"

"Just after lunch," she explains.

I don't know why she's bothering to tell me this. Mother's

always jetting in and out of town, usually without a word to me. Just a month ago, she left for close to three weeks and never bothered to tell me where she was. It's the main reason I live in the Weston dorms instead of her tiny, hospital-adjacent apartment.

"Where are you going?" I ask.

Tight smile. "The board needs my help. It appears we've misplaced an important asset, and I need to see if I can locate it. I'll be back for the anniversary ball, but I may not see you again before then. I'll forward you my itinerary when I'm back in my office."

I resist the urge to reach for my fork again, just to have something to do with my hands. "Why?"

Mother shrugs. It's a stiff, sudden movement that tries and fails to look casual. "In case there's an emergency."

I press my lips together. Mother has always said that "emergency" was just another word for "poor planning." "What kind of asset—"

"It's not important." Mother folds her newspaper and places it on the table next to her coffee. She taps her fingers against the tabletop—*index, middle, ring, thumb.* It's an old habit, leftover from her days playing the piano. Her instructor used to make her practice scales, even when she wasn't sitting in front of her instrument. She still does it when she's thinking. Or nervous.

"I have to make a meeting," she says. "I'll call you when I get back to town." She presses her napkin to her lips, somehow managing not to smudge her lipstick, and stands.

She hovers next to my chair before leaving. "Do me a favor and stay on the Weston grounds for the next few days, when you aren't at the Med Center."

"Sure," I say, not really meaning it.

"I'm serious," Mother says. There's an edge to her voice, and I'd call it fear if I didn't know her so well. "I'm aware that you and your friends used to wander through the woods together, but it's not safe now that you're on your own."

I pick up my fork again and tap it against the side of my plate. She's never worried about my safety in the woods before.

"Charlotte," Mother says. I nod, which isn't technically a lie. I have to search the woods for Ariel's clue. Nothing is stopping me from doing that.

She gives me a look as she pulls her purse over her shoulder, and then sweeps out of the cafeteria without offering any further explanation.

I slump in my booth. I have a few minutes before my shift starts, so I reach across the table for her cup of coffee. She only took a few sips—it's practically fresh. My eyes wander to her discarded newspaper as I drink. I pull it toward me.

The local papers occasionally run stories about the Med Center and the work it does for the community. But I scan the headlines, and there's nothing in the paper about the hospital. The most interesting story is about some forest fire in the woods not far from here. I turn to the middle of the paper and scan the short story. *Fire at a juvenile detention center . . . no known survivors . . . have yet to account for every offender . . .*

I stare at the black-and-white photograph next to the story, letting my eyes blur until I can't tell which black blob is smoke and which is fire. My two best friends just committed suicide, and my mother's worried that I'm going to be attacked by an escaped prisoner from a juvenile detention center three hours from here. Dean Rosenthal and everyone else in this school seems to think I'm about to off myself, too. But not my mother.

I tighten my grip on the paper, and it crinkles beneath my fingers. This is just like her. To focus on some unlikely, problem far away and completely ignore what's happening right in front of her nose.

I drop the paper on the sticky table and take another sip of her coffee.

I push aside the plastic curtain separating an empty cot from the rest of the clinic. There's usually a line of patients with broken limbs and deep cuts and bad burns trooping through the clinic but today it's quiet. A nurse named Gene gives an older woman stitches on a bed next to the door. Our only other patient is the anonymous burn victim lying in the cot next to the windows. Amelia is transferring him to long-term care tomorrow.

I check the cupboard next to the empty cot to see if there are enough sheets and pillowcases, and make a note of what I need on the tiny pad of paper I carry in my back pocket.

A voice drifts in from the hallway. ". . . but what if we did some sort of memorial? Everyone could wear a white rose to the bonfire."

"I still think it's tacky. She was Kyle's ex-girlfriend. He's probably *devastated*. Think about it, Viv. Wouldn't you be *devastated*?"

Footsteps approach. I look up as Molly and Vivian walk into the room. They're both in navy-blue scrubs, like me, and Vivian carries a stack of pillows and sheets. They look strange without Chloe sandwiched between them. Like a puzzle missing its final piece. I have a sudden, crazy impulse to pull the privacy curtain in front of me and hide until they go away, but I don't move quickly enough. Molly spots me and her eyes widen.

"Charlotte. Hi." She speaks slowly, like she's talking to a toddler. Her eyes flick to Vivian, widen even further, and then move back to me. I resist the urge to groan. Does she think I can't see her? "How are you *doing*?"

"Fine," I say. "Who died?"

"Mary Anne Simmons," Vivian cuts in, itching her nose ring. The tiny gold loop in her left nostril is the only thing that gives her an edge over Chloe and Molly. "It happened, like, three weeks ago. There was some freak accident at this place she was volunteering. She was a senior last year. I don't think you knew her."

"Yeah, your crew didn't really hang with Mary Anne," Molly adds. Her face reddens as she realizes that "my crew" is also dead and no one's wearing white roses at the bonfire for them. She glances at Vivian for help.

"She hung with Kyle Gibbons and Cecily Monroe and those guys." Vivian twists the nose ring, and I try not to cringe. I don't think she realizes she's doing it. "Jocks, mostly. Ariel thought they were dull."

"Right," I say. I vaguely remember Kyle following Ariel around at some party last year. Whenever his back was turned, she caught my eye and yawned dramatically.

Vivian pulls open a cupboard and starts stacking pillows, her back to me as she works. Molly flashes me the kind of awkward smile usually reserved for distant relatives at family reunions. Polite but strained. I guess that means our conversation is over. I grab my notebook and double-check to make sure I've noted everything I need.

"Are you coming tomorrow night?" Molly asks. I figure she's talking to Vivian, so I don't answer. After a second, Molly clears her throat. "Um, Charlotte? Are you coming tomorrow night?"

I lift my head. "What?"

"To the senior bonfire?" Molly shifts her weight from one foot to the other. "Chloe said you were thinking about it. It's tomorrow at nightfall. I was just wondering if you'd decided yet."

I glance at Vivian and notice that she's stopped putting away pillows. Vivian and I used to hang together at parties when everyone else was getting drunk and stupid. Ariel and Dev were good at a great many things, but holding their liquor was not one of them. After they passed out, Viv and I would make food runs and persuade the boys to let us play

Mario Kart. We'd take bets on who Chloe would end up sucking face with.

But she never called after what happened to Ariel. None of them did.

"I'll think about it," I say. Molly flashes me a wide smile and pulls a crumpled yellow flyer out of her pocket.

"Here," she says, thrusting it at me. "In case you didn't get one the other day."

I take the flyer, my eyes traveling over the thick black letters. SENIOR BONFIRE! FRIDAY! AFTER DARK! The exclamation points promise a night of gleeful firelit fun.

Vivian flashes me a smile that almost looks genuine and starts toward the door. "See you tomorrow, Charlotte. Or not. Whatever."

I spend the rest of the day going over every place on my list again. I check inside every drawer and closet and wardrobe at the Med Center. I head back to Devon's dorm, but her parents have finally collected her things. The door hangs open, the room empty.

The only place I haven't managed to search is the woods. It's always been off-limits, and the school increased security a few weeks before Devon's suicide because of the forest fires. Burly rent-a-cops prowl the grounds during the day, and their flashlights flicker through the trees after nightfall.

I'm pretty sure I can sneak past them. Devon did, and I know every path and tree in the woods, same as her. We've been wandering around in its darkness with Ariel since sophomore year. But I'm too nervous. Being caught out of bounds means automatic expulsion and, for the first time, I'm wondering if coming back to Weston wasn't such a terrible idea. I'm starting to get used to being at the school without Ariel and Devon.

I get an A on a physics assignment, my first A. I stare at the red-scrawled letter for nearly a minute, trying to remember what I did differently this time. I usually read the chapters twice, and then work out the problem sets at the end. But this time I just scanned the chapter, and the information stuck in my head. It was easy. I fold the worksheet and tuck it inside the back cover of my textbook instead of throwing it away.

Chloe invites me to sit at her table during lunch. She makes Vivian and Molly scoot over so I can sit next to her, and she compliments my hair, saying I look "chic, like a French girl."

That afternoon, I answer three questions correctly during history, more than any other student in the class.

I have fencing again on Friday morning. Genie Wilson hurt her ankle and has to sit out, so I get paired with her old partner, Kay Marsh. Zoe goes back to sparring with Coach Lammly.

Kay is taller than almost every other girl in class. I'm closing in on six feet, so that puts her only an inch or two shorter than me. Strands of sandy-blond hair peek out from beneath her helmet. She whips her saber in front of her body and drops into on-guard position. I mirror her and, for once, I don't feel awkward or clumsy. I sit low in my lunge, my legs strong beneath me.

Coach Lammly blows her whistle.

Kay advances, her sword a blur. I parry, blocking a thrust to my right, and then sweep my saber across my chest to block a second blow. I flick my wrist and riposte, tapping the flat of my blade against Kay's helmet. Point me.

Kay recovers and hits me with two quick thrusts. The tip of her blade slaps my arm, and then jabs into my chest before I manage to recover. Two points to Kay. *Damn.* I slow down, watching the way she moves. She isn't as good as Zoe. She's all attack and no strategy. If I keep her reacting, she's bound to make a mistake.

I fall into retreat. Kay advances, pushing me back toward the end of the piste. She thrusts, and I parry-tierce, then riposte, tapping her shoulder with my blade. We're two to two now. She lunges and I parry-seconde, moving my blade down and out. I throw my arm up, and she dances back into retreat. I think I hear her swear, her helmet muffling the sound. She lifts her arm to thrust, and I catch her in the ribs. Point me. Three to two.

Kay thrusts once, twice. I block both, then shuffle forward with a feint. Kay parries, and I catch her on her exposed left side. Four to two. One more point and I win.

Kay lunges, catching me on the chest with the tip of her blade. She pulls back too quickly, and I bring the flat of my blade down against her shoulder. Five points. I win.

I've never won before.

"Looking good out there, Gruen," Coach Lammly calls. "If you keep improving like this, you might actually get to compete this year."

My mouth quirks, then stretches into a full smile. I haven't smiled like this since before Ariel died. It feels . . . strange. My lips pull tight at the corners, like they might crack. Competition is something my mother understands. I can almost picture her sitting in the stands, not cheering—probably not even watching too closely. But there.

The thought follows me back to my dorm. I move through my routine on autopilot, still replaying my win as I drop my bag onto the bed, and tug off my shirt, then grab my plastic caddy full of shower supplies. I think of the final swipe of my saber, the winning point. I walk into the bathroom and kick the door closed behind me.

It isn't until the shower is on, the scalding water running over my scalp and down my shoulders, that I realize what I'm doing. I'm standing in the exact spot where Ariel took her last breath. It's the first time I've taken a shower here since the night she died.

I look down, watching the water pool between my toes before trickling toward the drain. I wait for the memories to crash into me. Ariel's hair floating beneath the surface of the water, her voice repeating the words of our final argument. *Do you love him . . .*

But there's nothing. She's not here anymore.

I turn the faucet, and the steady stream of water sputters off. I climb out of the shower and wrap a towel around myself, using my palm to clear the condensation from the mirror. My face reflects back at me: glossy hair, clear skin. I lean closer to the mirror, peeling my lips back from my teeth. They're straighter, whiter, unstained. I chomp them together twice, like I'm testing whether they're real.

I don't look like the Charlotte that Ariel and Devon knew anymore. I'm different. Better. And it's not just my appearance—my classes feel manageable for the first time since I started at Weston. My fencing is improving. I'm eating lunch with the most popular girls at Weston.

Maybe my old friends were holding me back.

The thought feels like a betrayal. I reel away from the sink and spin around, pressing my back into the cold porcelain so I don't have to face my reflection anymore. Apparently, all it takes is one good day to make me forget how Ariel used to make me laugh whenever I got a bad grade. How Devon used to fix the game whenever we'd play MASH, so we'd all end up with the lives we wanted.

Chloe and her friends might let me sit at their lunch table and invite me to parties, but they'll never be like Ariel and Devon. They'll never be family.

A tear leaks out of the corner of my eye. I brush it away, hating myself for my willingness to forget them. I need to remember why I came back here. To find Ariel's clues. Solve the mystery of what happened to her and Devon.

My strange dream echoes through my head. I see Jack staring at me, and I hear laughter echoing through the trees. *You already know the truth.*

No, I think. I'm not the reason they killed themselves. There's something else. Something I'm missing. I slam my fist against the sink, and I swear I hear the porcelain crack beneath my fingers. I flinch, but it's still intact when I look down at it. *Obviously.* I'm not strong enough to break a sink in half.

The flyer Molly gave me peers up from the bottom of my trash can. I threw it away last night, sure that nothing could compel me to brave the senior bonfire alone. Now I lean over and pluck it out of the trash, flattening it against the side of the sink. It'll be dark, and the entire senior class will be there, but the bonfire might be the only chance I get to search the woods.

I run a finger over the blocky black letters. Water drips from the showerhead and hits the porcelain tub behind me. The sound echoes off the bathroom walls, hollow and haunting.

Chapter Seventeen

Branches reach across the darkening sky. They sway in the wind, sending shadows dancing over my feet. I step into the woods, and voices travel through the trees to greet me. They boom and laugh and shout. Beckoning.

I pick my way over sticks and twigs and rocks, unsteady on my heeled booties. I hadn't realized it would be this dark tonight, or that there'd be so many people here. It's going to be damn near impossible to properly search the place, especially if Ariel's next clue is as small as the bottle she tucked in with my underwear.

Anxiety rises in my chest, but I push it back down. There's really only one place Ariel would have left something for me. We had this cove we liked, where the trees made a canopy of leaves overhead, blocking the sky. We hid secret notes under the rocks that littered the ground and scrawled our names on the trees and christened the ground with spilled wine. I'll sneak over later, when everyone else is drunk and sloppy.

I tug the sleeve of my sweater past my knuckles, fighting the urge to shiver. It's too cold to be out without a coat, with snow still melting under the trees and ice coating the packed-dirt path. But tonight the cold doesn't bother me as much as usual. Orange light flickers through the trees. People spread blankets around the bonfire, and crouch on fallen logs and rickety lawn chairs while a song with a heavy bass line thuds around them. People weave away from a table that holds cans of soda and a bowl of punch. Usually someone brings a keg, but because of Devon's death, we have teachers chaperoning the party this year. They don't seem to notice the silver flasks being passed from hand to hand.

I hover at the edge of the trees, wondering what to do next. I never had to worry about attending a party alone when Ariel and Devon were alive. It didn't matter what the event was, or who was dating who—we were each other's dates, always. It feels weird to be standing here with no one. What do other people do at these things?

I spot Zoe near the edge of the clearing with a few others—girls with clunky glasses and loose-fitting clothes and edgy haircuts. *Geek chic.* I turn in place, scanning the crowd for anyone else I know. I don't recognize Molly until she swivels around, lifting her hand in a wave. She's drawn thick kohl liner around her eyes and yanked her hair into a tight bun that pulls at the skin around her forehead.

"Charlotte! You came!" Molly throws an arm around my

shoulders and spins me to face the rest of her crew. Suddenly, Jack is standing over me, staring with inappropriate intensity considering that Chloe is hanging from his arm.

"Hey," I say, and he nods with just his chin. A new song starts to play, all gravelly voices and lusty chords. It's sex made into music. The space between Jack and me seems to pulse. Firelight dances across his perfect face, elongating his nose and chin and making his eyes look almost black. Every bone in my body turns to dust.

I quickly turn my focus on Chloe so that I don't collapse onto the ground in a heap of skin and blood. Oh—

Chloe got a haircut. Her bronzy-blond locks stop just below her ears, the edges spiky and uneven against the nape of her neck. Just like mine. I have to remind myself to close my mouth.

"Don't be mad." Chloe wrinkles her nose, pinching a lock between two fingers. "I didn't mean to play copycat, but your hair looks *so* cute. I couldn't help myself."

"It's okay," I say without thinking. My brain is several paces behind. The most popular girl at Weston has copied the choppy, awful haircut I gave myself after Ariel committed suicide. I know it's been looking better, but still. I hacked it off with a freaking *plastic razor.*

I glance back at Jack. He's still looking at me, transfixed by something happening with my lips. I run my hand over my mouth, and he shifts his eyes up again.

Chloe looks at my mouth, and then at her boyfriend. She tightens her grip on his arm. "*Jack*, tell Charlotte I'm not being creepy. Imitation is the sincerest form of flattery."

"What?" He pulls his arm out of Chloe's hands, and she punches him playfully on the shoulder. He's looking at me again, and this time he seems to be distracted by the portion of collarbone framed by the V of my sweater. He raises his eyes to mine.

"Is that new?" he asks. Chloe turns to me like she, too, is fascinated by the timeline chronicling my ownership of this sweater. I feel naked. *Is that new?* Come on, Jack. What kind of guy asks about a sweater?

"Um, no," I say. "It's pretty old."

Molly taps Chloe on the shoulder, and Chloe turns around. I use the sudden distraction to raise an eyebrow at Jack over the top of her head. You'd be amazed at how much you can say with an eyebrow. Jack and I used to communicate with them almost exclusively. He'd wiggle his eyebrows at me across the classroom when Mr. Oakley said something inadvertently dirty during a lecture on the bubonic plague. He'd lift both eyebrows in mock surprise when I dominated during a round of flip-cup.

Now my eyebrows are saying, *What the hell is wrong with you?*

Jack shrugs. Unlike eyebrows, shrugs are infuriatingly vague. He looks at my collarbone again, and I honestly can't decide if I want to slap him or stick my tongue down his throat. Clearly, this sweater was the wrong choice for tonight.

Chloe turns back around, and I force my mouth into a fake smile. "It looks really good," I say. "Your hair, I mean. Suits you much better than me."

"That is *not* true," Chloe says. She shouldn't be so nice to me. I basically just screwed her boyfriend with my eyes. She and her friends should be spreading vicious rumors about me right now. They should be filling my conditioner with Nair and stealing my underwear after gym class. But Chloe just smiles and shakes her head. A shiny blond lock falls across her forehead, and it couldn't look more perfect if she'd planned it.

I turn to the other people in the group, searching for anything to help me change the subject. My eyes drop to the white rose pinned to Molly's shirt. Kevin and Vivian stand beside her. They're wearing flowers, too.

"Those are for your friend, right?" I search my memory for her name. "Mary Anne?"

Vivian lifts a hand to her rose. "We're actually wearing them in honor of all the students we've lost over the last year," she explains, tracing a petal with her finger. "We were just talking about them."

"No other school in the area has had so many deaths," Chloe chimes in. "Isn't that strange? It's like Weston is cursed."

I let my eyes go unfocused, and Chloe's face becomes a blurry mess of shapes and colors. I want to go back to talking about my bad haircut or my sweater or how Chloe and Jack keep touching each other or *anything* to keep us from discussing this. Chloe wants to know why Weston has so many more deaths than other schools? It's not like it was an accident. Devon and Ariel took their own lives. Suicide tips the scales.

Chloe keeps on talking, but I stop listening. It's easy—like hitting Mute on a remote control in my head. Is this what things are going to be like from now on? Awkward conversations with girls I don't even like. Gossip and fake smiles and long stretches of silence, all of us trying to come up with something to say.

"Charlotte?" Jack's voice is a lighthouse steering me out of the fog. I blink, refocusing on his face. He finally seems to have figured out which parts of my body are appropriate to stare at while in the presence of his girlfriend because he's looking at my eyes, and some of the fiery intensity has drained from his gaze.

I exhale. Okay. I can handle this.

"Hey," Jack says, waving his hand in front of my face. "Still in there?"

"Sorry," I say. "Spaced out. What were you saying?"

"Just that some of us were thinking we could drive up north, to the juvie center where Mary Anne used to work. Maybe leave flowers for her or something."

"You knew her?"

"Yeah." Jack frowns, like I should have known this. "We were in French Club last year."

"You don't take French."

"You don't have to study the language to be in the club."

"I didn't know that," I say in a perfect politely curious tone. I give myself a mental high five. Nobody who overheard this conversation would think that I'm calculating the inches between Jack's lips and mine. That I'm trying to figure out a casual way to run my finger along the back of his hand.

"Anyway," Jack says. "You could come with us."

I picture the three of us in the backseat of some car: Chloe sitting on Jack's lap, my leg pressed against his. He wants to go back to the way things were when Ariel was alive. Making eyes at each other behind his girlfriend's back. Sending texts she's not supposed to see.

"There should be enough room. Kevin has a car," Jack says. Kevin turns at the sound of his name, sloshing the sticky red contents of his Solo cup onto my boots. I leap backward, but not before punch soaks through the pale brown leather.

"Kevin obviously won't be *driving* the car," Jack mutters. Chloe swears, and Vivian smacks Kevin in the arm.

"How much booze did you put in there?" she snaps. He shakes his head, unable to focus on her face.

"*WhatdidIdo?*" he mumbles.

"It's fine," I say, shaking the punch from my boot. "I'm going to see if there are napkins near the punch bowl."

"You want me to come with?" Chloe offers. I try not to visibly cringe.

"Don't worry about it," I say, backing away. "I got it."

I turn before Chloe can come up with some other reason to follow me through the party. I couldn't give a shit about these boots, but I'm happy for an excuse to get out of this conversation. Jack can't honestly think I'm going to trail along after him and Chloe, like I used to trail along behind him and Ariel. Living in Ariel's shadow was one thing. It was Ariel. She was worth it. Chloe's just another blond girl wearing too much lip gloss.

I weave through the crowd and disappear into what I assume is the line for drinks. Coming here was a mistake. I need to duck away from this crowd and check the cove as quickly as possible. Then I can go home.

I glance over my shoulder to see whether Chloe's still watching.

"Worried your doppelgänger followed you?"

I turn toward the voice and spot Zoe standing next to the punch bowl. She stares at me over the lip of a red Solo cup, and then her dark eyes flicker to the group behind me. "Don't worry. She's staying put."

I grab a cup and ladle some of the sticky, sugary concoction into it, just to have something to do with my hands. Zoe pulls a plastic water bottle out of her pocket and tips it into her drink. I raise my eyes.

"Vodka," she whispers, stealing a glance at the teachers. They're huddled together on the other side of the bonfire, looking like they'd rather be anywhere else in the entire world.

"I didn't know you drank," I say. Zoe sneers and puts the bottle away.

"Why? Because I'm Asian? You think I have some tiger mom following me around to make sure I stay in line? That's *Chinese* mothers, FYI. My mother's French."

"I meant because you're an athlete," I say. "Don't they get all bent out of shape about underage drinking in the Olympics?"

"Oh." Zoe flashes me a fast smile. It reminds me of Ariel's smile—there and then gone, like you'd imagined it. She takes another drink of punch. "You're probably right. Sure you don't want any?"

"I'm heading back to the dorms."

"Really? Doesn't Chloe want you to be the new Heather?"

I frown. "What?"

"From the movie *Heathers*?" I shrug, and Zoe cocks an eyebrow. "Seriously?" she says. "You've never seen *Heathers*?"

"I don't watch a lot of movies," I say, turning down the path that leads to the dorms. Time to put this disastrous experiment in social interaction behind me.

"You've been different since you got back," Zoe calls after me. I stop and turn around. Zoe is studying me, like she's looking for a clue. "It's almost like you're somebody else."

"Yeah? Who's that?" I ask. Zoe looks into her drink and shrugs. It's a vaguely French movement that seems to involve her entire body.

"Ariel," she says. "Or Devon."

I'm flattered, but Zoe didn't say it like it was supposed to be a compliment. I think of what she told me after our fencing match. *Go home before you end up like your friends.*

"I don't see anything wrong with that," I say.

Zoe raises an eyebrow. "Noted."

I glance at Chloe's group again. Vivian says something, and Molly laughs, spraying the ground with soda.

"You can do better than them," Zoe adds. "I overheard them talking in the bathroom and, apparently, the great and popular Chloe is losing status with the underclassmen. They all think it was slutty to go after Jack so soon after everything with Ariel. Vivian had this idea that they should cozy up to you. She thinks people will stop gossiping if it looks like you approve."

Zoe takes another sip of her drink, looking extremely pleased with herself. I wait for this new information to hit me. For the pain or hurt or anger to explode through my chest, making it necessary for me to mumble some excuse and run away. But Zoe's words have no effect. It feels obvious, even a little boring. Of course Chloe and her friends are using me. It's the Weston way.

"Why are you telling me this?" I ask.

"Honestly?" she says. "I thought maybe you'd cry."

I resist the urge to "accidentally" knock her drink over. "Sorry to disappoint."

Zoe smirks. I walk away before she can say anything else, mentally calculating how long it'll take me to make it to the clearing in the dark. Out of the corner of my eye, I see Jack separate from Chloe's group and start toward me.

Shit, shit, shit. I walk faster.

He follows me without saying a word. We walk away from his friends, to the edge of the party, silently, like this was our plan all along. Two hundred thousand questions flash into my head at the exact same time. *Is Chloe watching? What are we doing? Would Ariel . . . ?* It feels like standing in the middle of Times Square, trying to choose one message

from the myriad. Everything is flashing lights and screaming voices.

Then I step out of the clearing and into the trees, and
everything inside my head goes still. Jack follows, wordless.
I lead him off the familiar path and into the deepest dark. I
know this part of the woods by heart. I hear his shoes crunch-
ing over dead leaves. His slow, even breathing grows heavier
the farther we move away from the light of the fire. We're
alone now, but I don't turn around. We are Orpheus and
Eurydice traveling out of Hades. If I look back, he'll vanish.

My feet carry us to our place, the one Ariel, Devon, and I
never shared with anyone else. Her laughter still hangs in
the air here like a physical thing. It spiderwebs through the
tree branches. It gets stuck on my face as I duck into the clearing. I take a deep breath and turn around.

Jack's eyes are two hot coals in the darkness. His body
radiates heat. I'm suddenly glad for the clouds covering the
stars, the tree branches sending deep shadows over the cove.
How could Ariel stand to look at him? It's like staring into
the sun.

"Hey," he says. In the darkness, his voice is everywhere.
It seeps below my skin and wraps around my bones.

"Don't," I whisper. But my voice is so quiet that maybe I
just think it.

Jack takes a step closer and, if we were anywhere else, I'd
move away from him. I'd respect the two feet of space we
always keep between us.

But we're standing in the woods—*my* woods—in the cove that Ariel always said was magic. I don't move. I tilt my chin, daring him to come closer.

His eyes travel over my chin and my lips, my eyes, my forehead. He stares at me like it's the first time he's ever been able to look at me before, and maybe it is. He takes my chin in his hands, moving my face toward his. His fingers leave trails of fire on my skin.

I close my eyes, but that just makes it worse. Jack smell. Jack face. My heart beats so fast it hurts.

You're wondering if I slept with Ariel's boyfriend.

If that's why she killed herself.

Well. I didn't. I fell in love with him. If you don't understand why that's worse, then you've probably never been in love. Or had a best friend.

"Should I stop?" Jack asks.

I swallow. For a second, it feels like Ariel's here. Like she's watching. She waits at the entrance to the cove, a wry curve to her lips.

Do you love him more than you love me?

I push her away and press my lips to Jack's. Because I can.

She isn't real, I remind myself. *The real Ariel is dead.*

Chapter Eighteen

Do you love him more than you love me?

That was how my last conversation with Ariel began. She showed up at the shelter after hours, after I was supposed to clock out, because she knew I'd be cleaning up and feeding the animals and double-checking that everything had been taken care of. She surprised me, and I flinched and whirled around.

"What did you say?" I asked, keeping my face neutral so Ariel wouldn't know how badly she'd scared me. "What are you doing here?"

Ariel stopped at a cage holding a kitten, this tiny tabby with brown-and-white fur and a wet pink nose. He was smaller than my hand, his eyes barely open. Ariel dragged her fingers over the bars of his cage, and he shrank away from her, trembling. Ariel never understood why I liked animals. She complained that they smelled like piss and that even the nicest ones bit her. I said it was because they could tell she hated them.

"Jack," she said, her eyes flicking to me. "My boyfriend, remember? Or, I guess, my ex-boyfriend now."

My heartbeats blurred together in a solid thrum of vibration. *Ex-boyfriend. She said ex-boyfriend.* I smiled, like we were talking about anybody. Like I didn't care. "So you finally broke up with him?"

"He broke up with me, actually," Ariel corrected. "Because of you."

"No," I said, too fast probably. This wasn't how it was supposed to happen. We'd agreed. Ariel opened the cage with a click.

"Don't lie to me, Char." She pulled the door open and reached inside, running a single finger down the kitten's back. He mewed. "He just told me. He took me to that bench near the library and told me that he can't be with me anymore because the two of you are in love." Ariel looked around the shelter. "He said you fell in love here, actually."

This wasn't how it was supposed to happen. I'd told him to wait. Ariel would get bored and dump him—she always did—and then she wouldn't care whether I dated him or not. She wasn't one of those girls who got all bent out of shape if you went after her ex. She treated boys like tissues. Disposable. Interchangeable.

But it was different if he dumped her. Then I took something that was hers.

"Ariel . . . ," I started, but she shook her head.

"It's okay. I'm not mad, silly." She reached inside the cage and pulled the kitten out. She cradled him in her cupped hands and made a hushing noise as she continued to stroke the downy fur along his spine. "It's understandable. You're much closer to what Daddy and Mommy Jack had in mind, I'm sure. I can picture you sitting at that huge dinner table, all dressed up in pearls and Chanel." She tilted her head to the side. "Do you daydream about that?"

I didn't answer, but I didn't have to. "Of course you do," Ariel said. "You dream about being perfect for them, making them love you like a daughter. Then you'll finally get the loving family you always wanted." Her mouth a cruel line. "You think Mrs. Calhoun will let you call her Mom?"

For a long moment, we didn't speak. Ariel cooed at the kitten and I watched her. The kitten looked afraid. His eyes—barely open a second ago—were suddenly wide. He squirmed in Ariel's hands, but she held so tightly.

"Ariel, be careful," I said. She looked at me curiously, like she'd forgotten I was there. She tightened her fist around the kitten's belly, and he mewed louder. He swatted at her hand with his tiny, furry paw.

"You didn't answer my question," she said. "Do you love him more than you love me?"

I reached for the kitten, but Ariel moved away from me, holding her hands behind her back so I couldn't reach him. The kitten clawed at her. He must've broken skin because blood dropped to the floor behind her. Ariel didn't react. I don't think she noticed it.

"Let him go," I said. I tried to move past her, but she shoved me. I stumbled back, slamming into a row of cages lining the wall. I smacked my elbow against a heavy padlock attached to one of the cages and pain zipped up my arm. A dog started barking.

"Answer the question, Charlotte."

"Jesus, Ariel, you're going to hurt him." I grabbed her arm and yanked. Her hand popped open and the kitten fell to the floor. He landed on his feet and shot across the room, shivering.

Ariel stared down at her arm. My fingers left red marks on her skin. "I can't believe you did that."

"What's wrong with you?" I could barely contain my rage. The kitten was still mewing, his voice small and helpless. He was hiding beneath a row of empty cages. It was going to take forever to coax him out. "Just get out of here."

"Charlotte—"

"I don't love you," I said, because I knew she wasn't going to leave until I answered her stupid question. "Are you happy now? I don't even like you most of the time. You're a bitch. No, you're worse than that. You're a monster."

Ariel studied me. I looked for something in her eyes. Remorse, or sadness or guilt or anger. *Anything.* But they were beautiful and empty. Hollow. It was like looking at a doll.

Ariel turned on her heel and stalked out of the shelter. That was the last time I saw her alive.

The next morning, I found out there had been a fire at the animal shelter. Every single animal inside had burned to death. Ariel wasn't in any of her classes that day. I thought she'd felt too guilty about what she'd done. That she couldn't face me.

Then I found her in the tub.

Chapter Nineteen

I wake the next morning with Jack's kiss still painted on my mouth. Like lipstick I forgot to wash off before going to bed. I lift two fingers to my lips and let them linger there. Remembering. My fingers taste like salt and fire.

I roll over in bed, pulling my phone off the side table. We're meeting again this morning, nine o'clock, same place. It's Saturday, so we don't have classes, but I have a shift at the clinic at ten thirty. I already find myself coming up with excuses to cancel. I wonder if they'd believe I have the flu . . .

I push back my comforter and crawl out of bed, careful not to let the mattress springs creak. I don't want to wake Zoe. I pull open a drawer, cringing at the soft scrape of wood.

I frown. My clothes aren't where they're supposed to be. They're still in the drawer, of course, but they're all wrong. My favorite jeans sit on top of my school uniforms, but I know they were at the bottom of the drawer last night. A top

I vividly remember shoving into a corner of the drawer is now nicely folded.

I glance at Zoe's sleeping body. She must've gone through my things again.

"Bitch," I whisper. Her eyelids flutter, but she doesn't wake. I make a mental note to read her stupid love letter later. I tug on a pair of jeans and a sweater and duck into the hallway, pulling the door closed behind me with a barely audible click.

The morning is crisp. There are already a few security guards out, but they're mostly milling around the site of the bonfire, looking for stragglers who didn't make it home after the party. I slip past them easily.

I jog through the woods—just enough to get my blood flowing without making me sweat. I feel oddly energized, like I could run a marathon or climb a mountain. The air tastes like spring, and birds coo in the distance. It feels like I'm living inside a greeting card.

I reach the spot early, and Jack isn't there, so I collapse against a tree. Sunlight tickles my face.

Something rustles through the bushes. I open my eyes a crack. "Jack? Is that you?"

There's no answer, and the rustling goes still. Must be a squirrel. I'm about to close my eyes when something blinks at the corner of my eye, like a beacon. *Look at me*, it seems to say. I squint.

A bright yellow brick sits at the edge of the cove, next to a growth of weeds and dead grass.

That doesn't belong here, my brain tells me. Ariel and I

came here practically every day. I know every tree, every twig.

I take a step toward it and kneel to get a closer look. Someone has painted the rough surface of the brick in small, even strokes. I run my fingers over it, and a thrill of excitement shoots through me. Bananarama, the shade is called. I was with Ariel the day she found it. She plucked it off the counter with two fingers.

"Do you think this will make me look like I have gangrene?" she asked, shaking the bottle.

"Not unless you paint your whole hand," I told her. Ariel shrugged and slipped the polish into her pocket without paying for it.

I lift the brick and turn it over, and there, half covered in dirt, is a stiff white business card. Ariel's familiar, slanted handwriting whispers across it.

Follow the yellow brick road.

A small, desperate cry breaks the stillness of the cove, and it takes me a moment to realize the sound came from me. I lift a trembling hand to my mouth, and the brick topples back to the earth, bottom side up. Ariel's strange message stares up at me.

Follow the yellow brick road. Below the words, down at the corner of the card, she's scrawled a number: *1/3.*

I jerk my head up, eyes searching. I take a step forward, and then another one. It's like my legs know where to take me. I hurry through the trees, following paths once made clear by Ariel's feet and Devon's and mine. Until—

There. A banana-yellow brick peers out from beneath a bush to the side of the path. My heart hammers in my chest, and my breath comes fast and hot. I drop to my knees, grabbing the brick with both hands. My fingers tremble as I turn it over. Another business card, Ariel's handwriting slanting across it.

Follow the yellow brick road.

I smile.

I know the game now, so I keep moving, stopping only to kneel and examine more yellow bricks, each one urging me farther and farther into the woods. There's no trail to follow, no human footsteps leading us through the brush. It's just trees and bush and shadow. Animals coo and scurry. Goose bumps climb my arms as I hurry farther. Farther.

I know where Ariel's leading me long before I see the red-brick path cutting through the trees. Suddenly, I want to turn and head back to the cove, forget I ever saw her stupid note and yellow bricks. This doesn't feel like a clue anymore. It feels like Ariel's messing with me, just like she used to when she was still alive.

I move through the woods, toward the path. A breeze ruffles my hair, but I barely feel it. I stop at the edge of the bricks.

The old animal shelter waits at the end of the path, ragged strips of caution tape still dangling from its front door. Its soot-darkened walls have caved in, making the small building tilt to the left. Blackened glass litters the grass surrounding the structure and old beams jut out of the roof. They remind me of broken bones sticking out of skin, and I look away, shuddering. The air still carries the smell of smoke.

A yellow brick lies at the end of the path, to the left of the yawning hole where the door once was. I doubt anyone else would notice it. It's smudged with soot and dirt, the banana color barely visible beneath the black. I kneel and wedge my fingers around the brick, carefully easing it out of the ground. There's no note this time. The brick blocks a small, shallow hole. Inside the hole is a phone.

My heartbeat becomes a low, steady thrum. I pull the phone out of the hole. It's not Ariel's. Ariel's phone looked like her—there were always sparkly cases, and rhinestones and backgrounds displaying adorable photos of her and Jack tangled together. This phone is generic and off-brand. I turn it over in my hand, fingers shaking. The screen is cracked and some of the paint has chipped off, but otherwise it could be new. I find the power button and press down.

It won't work, I warn myself. But then a bright light flashes on and fades as a home screen appears. A warning flashes— 10 percent battery. I bite down on my lip, grinning. Okay, so it works. What now?

I check recent calls, but there aren't any. Voice mails— none. Text messages—none. E-mails—none.

"Dammit, Ariel." I close out of her in-box with a quick, violent jab of my thumb. I open the notes app, but it's empty. I dig my teeth harder into my lip.

What. The. Fuck. Why leave me a phone with nothing on it?

There aren't many apps on the screen, so I go through them one by one. Nothing's written in her calendar—I search back and forward a year, but she hasn't made a single entry. She hasn't downloaded any other apps or games. I open her photos folder—and there it is. A single picture.

I click on the icon, and a close-up of Ariel zooms onto the screen. I've never seen this photo before. It's cropped in close on her face, her eyes and mouth taking up practically the entire screen. A single tear clings to her cheek.

"Ariel doesn't cry," I whisper. As far as clues go, this is pretty shitty. She isn't doing anything, just staring into the camera like an idiot. I'm about to close out when I notice the red dot at the bottom of the screen. It's not a photograph. It's a video.

I press Play, and Ariel's face begins to move. She looks down for a beat, and then flicks her eyes up again, staring at the camera through the fan of her lashes. The gesture twists something in my gut. I've seen Ariel do that move countless times. The coy downward glance, the flirty flutter of lashes. At first she only used it on boys, but it quickly became second nature. It was the easiest way for her to play up the charm, get someone to give her whatever she wanted. I shake my head at the screen. She probably didn't even realize what she was doing.

"*Charlotte*," Ariel says, her voice barely louder than a breath. "*If you're watching this . . .*"

The image freezes, then jerks, jumping forward in the video. *Shit.* The phone must have water damage after all.

". . . *fires*." Ariel's eyes have grown wide. She clears her throat and shakes her head maniacally, sending a red curl across her forehead. "*. . . destroyed the woods they . . .*"

Another jolt on the screen, and the video leaps forward.

"*. . . monsters . . .*" Ariel presses her lips together, her eyes hard. *"Can't feel anything . . . I'm numb."*

The video pauses again. Then shudders. Then freezes. Ariel's face alters in small ways—her mouth turns upward, an eyebrow twitches. I hear snippets of voice, but no words.

Then the video stops. The Play button appears on the bottom of the screen.

I swear under my breath and start it again, hoping for better quality. But the video plays in the same jolts and starts, Ariel's message just as nonsensical as before. *Fire. Monsters. Numb.* I close out of the video and click on the e-mail icon. I can send it to myself. Even if the phone has water damage, the file should still be good. I start a new e-mail and click on the icon to attach the video file. The screen freezes. It goes black.

"No." I jab the Power button, then I hold my thumb down to get the phone to restart. Nothing happens.

Whatever clue Ariel left for me is gone.

Chapter Twenty

Ruined. I finally find a second clue, and it's ruined.

I want to throw the phone against a tree and watch it shatter. What kind of idiot leaves a phone with important information on it *outside*? I wish she were still alive so I could ask her what the hell she was thinking.

Voices echo through the trees, telling me the security guards have finished at the bonfire site and are coming closer. I study the phone, frowning. I could try charging it. Maybe it isn't water damaged after all—maybe it just ran out of batteries. It's some cheap brand that I've never heard of, so I doubt anyone at this school will have the right charger. I pull my own phone out of my pocket and look it up online. I find the charger easily, but the only website that sells it has it backordered. Annoyed, I click the link to buy and then slip both phones into my pocket and duck through the woods toward school.

I don't go back to my dorm. Zoe will be there, and I don't want to see anyone right now. Instead, I stalk through the empty school halls. I don't feel angry, exactly. There's a better word for this electric energy crackling through my veins. *Adrenaline*. I want to run and jump and scream. I want to hit something.

I stop in front of the door to the girls' locker room, and, suddenly, I know exactly what to do. I push the door open, my footsteps echoing off the concrete walls and floors. Row after row of metal lockers stare out at me, as though they're on the verge of speaking. I go to my locker and turn the combination until it pops open beneath my fingers. I pull my fencing gear on and stick my bag inside, clicking the lock shut.

Technically, anyone involved in a sport is allowed to use the gymnasium outside of school hours. Still, I feel like I'm misbehaving. I flick a switch and the overhead fluorescents buzz on, casting the gymnasium in an unnatural white glow. The quality of light feels different now that I'm the only person here. Colder. It crackles against my skin.

I walk to the far wall and remove a practice saber from the metal cabinet. I tighten my grip around the handle. The weight feels good in my hand. I fall back into a lunge, whipping the saber in front of me. The emptiness around me seems to pulse closer. It's like the walls are watching.

I can't quite explain what happens next. It would be one thing if I were athletic, if I had a history of taking out my anger and frustration with sports. But I've never done this before.

I lunge forward, my feet moving easily through patterns Coach has drilled into my head over the years. I never really listened, but something in my body held on to the lessons, because my footwork is perfect. I parry and lunge and retreat. The blade whistles through the air. I feel like I'm dancing. Like I'm flying.

I don't know how long I keep this up. It feels like hours, hours of my feet performing complicated routines, hours of my arm whipping and stabbing and slicing. Sweat plasters my hair to my forehead, and my muscles burn, but I don't stop. I don't want to stop. My heart slams against my chest and blood pumps in my ears. I don't think about the mystery bottle or Devon's notebook or Ariel's ruined video. I think about turning my left heel and pivoting on my toe, twisting at my wrist instead of swinging from the shoulder. Keeping my movements controlled. Sharp. Contained.

A shadow separates from the doorway, and I freeze, my blade trembling.

"Who's there?" I call. I lower my sword and take a step forward.

Zoe stands near the open door, watching me.

"Hey!" I shout, but she turns and disappears into the hallway without a word.

I spend my shift at the Med Center in a daze. I fluff pillows and check charts and answer the phone, but I'm still in the woods, still clutching Ariel's cracked cell phone with both hands. Her voice is a song that won't leave my head. A melody I only know half the words to.

Fire. Monsters. Numb.

I open a patient's linen cupboard and then close it again without seeing what's inside. Questions swirl through my head, and if I don't keep moving, they'll multiply and grow. Ariel expected me to find the video before discovering the "drink me" bottle in our dorm. The video was supposed to be my first clue. Maybe it explains the serum and why she wanted me to drink it.

I stop at the supply closet in the main hall to stock up on sheets and pillows and bedpans. I can't stop seeing Ariel's wide, red-rimmed eyes, her mouth frozen in a grimace. Goose bumps crawl up the backs of my arms. It didn't seem like she was talking about the serum. She looked scared. Like she was trying to warn me about something.

Fire. Monsters . . .

A door at the end of the hall swings open, and Jack steps out. Seeing him feels like pressing a reset button—my brain goes mercifully blank. I hug a stack of sheets to my chest and touch my lips with one finger.

"Jack?" I call, and he turns. "What are you doing here?"

"Physical," he says, his brows knitting together. "The track season just started."

He isn't smiling. It isn't until that exact second that I remember I was supposed to meet him this morning before breakfast. *Shit.*

My brain isn't blank anymore. It's crowded with guilt and

clues and the memory of a kiss in the dark. Jack starts down the hall without looking back. I hurry after him, tangled sheets unraveling from my arms.

"Wait. Talk to me," I call. Jack stops walking. He runs a hand through his hair, leaving it mussed and falling over his ears.

"Now isn't a good time."

"I didn't mean to blow you off this morning," I blurt. "I just got . . ."

"Distracted?"

"*Yes.*"

"Kyle saw you in the woods," Jack says. "What were you doing if you weren't coming to meet me?"

I open my mouth, then close it again when I realize I'll have to lie. My chest turns to ice, and a crack splits it down the middle—cutting me in two. One half belongs to Ariel and her secrets. The other belongs to Jack.

I swallow. "I can't—"

"Don't lie to me." Jack curls his hand into a fist. I wait for him to do something reckless—like punch a hole in the wall, leaving his knuckles cracked and bleeding. But the anger drains out of him before that can happen. His arm falls to his side. "Ariel, I just—"

I feel like I've been slapped. "Ariel?"

Jack blinks. "What?"

"You called me Ariel."

"No I didn't." But he did, and he knows it. I see her name reflected in his eyes, waiting on his lips. Jack tightens his jaw. I thought I had all his expressions memorized, but I can't read this one.

A horrible thought whispers to me: *Is this how he looked at her?*

"It doesn't mean anything," he says. But he's wrong. It means there was a moment when Jack thought I was his dead ex-girlfriend. Just now, for a second, Ariel and I were the same.

The ice in my chest thickens. I can practically hear it groan and crack. I don't want to be split in two. I don't want to be mistaken for a dead girl.

I stick the sheets onto a tray in the hall and take Jack by the elbow. "Come with me."

"Where?"

I glance down the hallway to make sure no one's watching us, and then I open the supply closet and shove Jack inside, pulling the door closed behind us.

I can't see Jack, but I feel him in the darkness. Warmth radiates from his skin. His breath smells like spearmint.

"I'm not Ariel," I say.

"I know that." His voice is barely a whisper. "Charlotte—"

I press my lips to his. I want to taste my name in his mouth. I want to steal the warmth from his skin.

We kiss until our lips are raw and our hands can't find new places to explore. Jack is heat and muscle and want. He presses me against a shelf filled with bedsheets. Something rattles, tips over, and falls to the floor. I feel a hard jab at my back and I gasp, but Jack covers my mouth with his, muffling the sound. His hands find my waist, tugging me closer.

I've watched Jack kiss Ariel so many times. On her mouth, on her cheek, on the top of her head. Once he kissed every one of her fingers. Like they were precious.

I always imagined what it would be like if he ever kissed me. He would taste like rain, I thought. His skin would be rougher than I imagined, his hair softer. I was right about all that, but I never stopped to think about how *I* might feel.

Heat gathers inside me like a storm, swirling around shame and guilt. The pain and pleasure complement each other, like salty and sweet. I kiss Jack so hard that my lips start to hurt, but it still isn't enough. I can't get close enough to him.

"I missed you this morning," he says, his mouth moving against mine.

"Me, too," I murmur. Every inch of my body itches, needing to touch him. To be touched. His lips trail down my neck and over my collarbone. His fingers slip past the waistband of my scrubs. I close my eyes, leaning into him. I weave my hands behind his head and bury my fingers in his hair. I want him closer. I want him—

I go cold.

I pause, my face inches from Jack's. It's like someone has flipped a switch, shutting off everything inside me that can feel. All that hurt and heat is gone. I'm empty.

I press my mouth into Jack's, but his lips are just lips. His hands on my waist are just hands. *No.* I want this. I *want* to want this. I just feel weird because it's Jack. Because I've wanted him for so long.

But deep down I know it's something else. Something's wrong.

Jack pulls away from me. "Are you okay?"

I nod, and then realize he can't see me in the dark. "I'm great."

"You don't seem into this."

"I am," I say, but my voice sounds weird. Jack hesitates.

"Look," he says after a moment. "This might seem soon, but I want you to come home with me. For dinner with my parents. This Monday night."

"What about Chloe?" I ask.

"I broke up with Chloe." Jack finds my hand in the dark and squeezes. "I want to be with you, Charlotte. Only you."

These words do what Jack's kiss didn't. My heart flips. My knees feel weak. *You love him*, I remind myself, and a flicker of warmth sparks to life in my chest.

"I'm there," I say.

"I should go," he says, kissing me again. "Class."

"Yeah."

He looks like he might say something else, but then he shakes his head and lowers his hand to the doorknob. "We shouldn't leave at the same time."

"I'll wait."

Jack kisses me one last time, on the forehead, his lips lightly brushing the skin just above my eyebrows.

You want him, I remind myself. You've always wanted him.

Then he's out the door and down the hall, his shoes making a shuffling sound against the tile.

Chapter Twenty-One

I can't sleep that night. My skin hugs too tightly to my bones. My muscles itch.

I replay the moment in the supply closet with Jack. My fingers in his hair. My mouth pressed to his mouth. Everything was heat and want, and then—*nothing*.

I've never felt anything like that before. It wasn't even an emotion. It was an absence of emotion. A void.

My bed is a slab of concrete beneath me. I roll onto my back, arms stretched above my head, too-long legs taking up so much of the mattress that my feet dangle off the end. I feel like I'm about to rip a seam. I shift onto my side, knees pulled to my chest, arms curled beneath my head. I press my eyes closed. I can feel my heart beating in my closed lids. *Ba-bomp. Ba-bomp.*

I think of twisted sheets. Empty beds. Voices giggling in the dark.

I crawl from my bed and slip out of the dorm. I hold the doorknob until the latch settles against the frame, and then release it without a click. The hallway is painted the color of midnight. I close my eyes, and I swear I can hear the sounds of a dozen girls breathing behind their heavy wooden doors. That's impossible, though. The walls are thin, but they aren't that thin. I'm imagining it.

A girl rolls over on her mattress, making the springs creak. Another whispers *don't* in her sleep. Someone coughs.

The sounds are deafening.

I move down the hallway and stairs and out the door, like a shadow. Frost winks from the grass. The air smells like snow. I'm not wearing shoes, but that doesn't seem to matter. I don't feel cold in my thin sleep shorts and tank top. I bounce in place to get the blood moving through my veins. Then I start to run.

Rocks dig into my heels. Twigs scratch my ankles. My breath floats in front of my face, cloud-thick and gray. *Ten more minutes*, I think. I'll just run until I tire myself out and then I'll drop back into bed, legs burning and body drained.

But ten minutes turns into twenty turns into forty. I run faster. Harder. I stop keeping track of the time. I run in circles so I'm never too far from the school.

Trees whip past me, branches swaying in a breeze I don't feel. Stars glimmer overhead. I let my mind travel through my body, searching for pain or fatigue. Nothing. My muscles sing.

The stars fade and then vanish. The moon dips below the tree line. Birdsong thrills through the air.

Ten more minutes. The sun peeks over the distant hills, turning the sky pink and purple and gold. Finally, I stop.

For a long moment, I stand, frozen, beneath the trees, waiting for exhaustion to catch up to me. For my legs to spasm and my chest to seize and sweat to break out on my lower back. I wait, but it never comes. I ran all night, and I don't feel the least bit tired.

Turning, I start the walk back home.

Chapter Twenty-Two

We pair off again during fencing on Monday, one on one. A quick glance around the gym tells me everyone else already has a partner.

"You're with me."

I turn toward the voice. Zoe stands behind me, sword propped on the ground next to her. Her body is made of points and edges.

"Goody," I mutter.

We take our places on the piste. Zoe drops into an easy lunge, sword held straight before her. I felt large and clumsy the last time we fought, like my limbs weren't the right length for this sport. I feel different now. Zoe might be small and fast, but I have better reach. A little strategy could keep her from getting within striking distance.

I fall into position and lift my sword.

Zoe darts at me without waiting for Coach to blow her

whistle. The way she moves looks wrong. It's too fast, for one thing, and jerky in a raw, animal way. Her blade cuts through the air, and I parry on reflex, metal clinking. She dances back, the balls of her feet barely touching the ground. It's like she's floating. Like gravity can't hold her.

I've seen Zoe fight a dozen times before, but never like this. Never like she meant it.

Something in me tightens. I want to beat her. Just once. I want to show her who really belongs at this school. I move my weight to my front foot, flexing my toes inside my boots. Zoe stabs at me, and I duck to the side, her saber whispering past my helmet. She lunges, jabbing at my chest, and I bring my sword down in a swift arc, knocking her blade aside. Surprise flickers across her face, but it's gone in a second. She tightens her grip on her saber.

She flicks her sword. I leap back, but the edge of her blade catches me on the wrist. Point Zoe. I dart forward, jabbing her hip before she can retreat. Point me. Zoe lunges. I knock her blade away, then tap her on the shoulder in a perfect parry-riposte. She swears, her voice so low I barely hear it through her helmet. She lunges again, and this time she hits me in the chest.

The lights beat down on us. A film of sweat gathers between my forehead and helmet. It's easier to attack than defend. I need to force her into retreat. My feet move automatically, like someone else is controlling them. Zoe's fast, but I can match her. I advance, forcing her back two steps. Three. She alters her footwork, taking a short step and then a long one to keep me from guessing what she'll do next. It doesn't work. It's like I see every move before it happens.

We're at the end of the piste. The wall is right behind her. Nowhere left to go. I shift my weight to my back foot, preparing to lunge—

Zoe leaps forward and then back again, using the momentum to propel herself off the ground. She has one foot on the wall behind her, then two. She races up the wall, and then she's above me, helmet inches from my own, feet windmilling over her, as if gravity is an amusing concept. I swing, but my sword catches nothing but air. She lands—like a cat—on the piste behind me.

Coach is blowing the whistle and people are shouting. There are no flips in fencing. Not even showy, impossible ones. Zoe cocks her head, ignoring them all.

It's a dare.

My heartbeat becomes a steady thrum. Zoe turns her wrist, whipping her sword at my side. I jerk my saber down and out, knocking it away. Zoe lunges, and I fall back. Our sabers clash together, then spring apart, the blades blurs of silver. Zoe gets a hit in low on my blade, knocking the sword from my grip. It clatters to the ground a few feet off the piste, leaving me unarmed.

Normally, this would count as a penalty, and the match would pause to allow me to grab my sword. But we're not really fencing anymore, and Zoe doesn't hesitate. She slashes at me like she's holding a broadsword instead of a practice saber.

Time slows. I flip into a low backbend—knees bent, one hand propped beneath me, the back of my head inches from the floor. My body moves in a fluid way, like there aren't bones and muscles holding me together any longer. Zoe's blade whips through the air above my nose.

My legs are springs. I arch my back—*jump*—and then I'm on my feet again. Whispers erupt, and I have just enough time to realize that I did something impressive before Zoe's on me, stabbing and swinging. I leap to the side as she strikes, missing me. She stumbles forward, grunting. She's losing energy.

Stunned silence fills the room. Coach Lammly's whistle hangs from her lower lip, forgotten. My sword is two feet away. Zoe lunges and I spring back onto my hands, my body an arc. I could never do a handspring, not even when I used to take gymnastics in middle school, but now I'm tumbling over myself—practically flying—my shoulders strong, my feet never touching the ground. It feels like I've been off the ground for a long time.

I slide to the floor, falling into a perfect split. My saber winks from the ground. Zoe lunges, and I reach. My fingers wrap around the hilt as her blade whips toward me. I throw my sword over my head, just managing to block her blade. Metal screams. I push Zoe off and swing my arm to the side, catching her hip with my blade. Point me.

If we were still fencing, I'd have just won.

Coach Lammly fumbles for her whistle and blows—two quick bursts.

"Enough," she says, incredulous. She blinks, like she's just come out of a daydream. "Locker room—both of you. I'll be in to . . . to discuss this in a moment."

Scattered applause echoes through the gym as I stand, peeling off my helmet. Someone catcalls and a couple other girls laugh nervously. They don't seem to know how to respond.

I turn toward Zoe, but she's already stalking across the gymnasium, moving faster than I imagined her short legs could carry her. I follow. The students who'd been watching turn back to their partners, shrugging. Show's over.

I step into the locker room, letting the door slam shut behind me. Zoe yanks her helmet off, her face beet red, her hair glued to her forehead with sweat. Her chest rises and falls as she struggles to catch her breath. I lift my hands in front of my chest, worried she's going to attack again. She doesn't.

Instead she says, "You took the serum, didn't you?"

Chapter Twenty-Three

I stare at Zoe's lips, certain I heard her wrong. She holds her saber like it's a real weapon, like she might drive the whip-thin blade through my body with a flick of her wrist.

I suck a breath in through my teeth. "What did you—"

"Shut up." Zoe shifts her eyes to the side, pressing a finger to her lips. She stalks the length of the room, peering down each row of lockers.

Satisfied, she turns back around. "We're alone." She crosses her arms over her chest. Waiting.

Out with it, Charlotte. "How do you know about the serum?"

One of Zoe's thin eyebrows arcs upward. "So you did take it."

"You took it, too? Did Ariel give it to you?"

"Ariel?" Zoe's eyes narrow into slits. "You got the serum from Ariel?"

"Where did you think I got it?"

Zoe studies me. It takes an eternity for her to answer. "We got it from Mr. Byron," she says, referring to Weston's school nurse. "He told us it was a vitamin supplement."

"We?"

"Ariel, Devon, and me." Zoe sits at the edge of a wooden bench and folds her hands in her lap. "Byron's assistant came and found us on the first day of school and told us we'd qualified for some new program. All we had to do was take the serum and record any changes we noticed. Like a drug trial. I figured it was zinc or vitamin C. I didn't even feel different at first. And then . . ." Zoe trails off, looking into space. "My skin cleared up, like, overnight. I thought it was this new face wash I'd been using, so I didn't put it together right away. But then my fencing started getting good. *Really* good. Coach was talking about college scouts. The Olympics . . . That's how I know you took it. A week ago, you were a terrible fencer."

I ignore the insult. Instead, I think of Devon's notebook, and the columns of record-breaking swim times scrawled across the pages. It wasn't steroids—it was the serum making her better. And my hair, my skin—it all fits. "So it's some sort of miracle drug?"

"That's what I thought, too."

A chill that has nothing to do with the temperature creeps over my skin. "What do you mean, 'thought'?"

Zoe doesn't look at me. She folds the cuff of her sleeve, then unfolds it again. "Ariel started acting strange after about two months on the serum. Distant."

"Ariel was always distant."

Zoe shakes her head. "Not like this."

I think of Ariel's red hair floating below the surface of the water, her blank eyes staring at the ceiling. "You think the serum did something to her."

"*I* didn't. Not at first. I didn't know Ariel that well. I figured she was disturbed, that she got into a fight with her boyfriend. Or you. It didn't occur to me that the *vitamin supplement* the school nurse gave us might've caused her to . . ." She swallows, unable or unwilling to finish her sentence.

"So what changed?"

"Devon showed up at my dorm a couple of weeks ago, freaking out about some girl on her swim team. Hayley—"

"Hattie Goldberg." The name slips out of my mouth by accident. I press my lips together, like that might keep the rest of the story from coming out with it. I don't want to remember Hattie, but I don't exactly have a choice. She's locked in my head much as I wish I could forget her. Blood blossoming across the surface of the pool. The sound of laughter bouncing off tile walls, growing sharper, turning into screams.

Zoe stares at me. "I've only heard rumors."

"Devon broke Hattie's arm." I stare down at the toes of my boots so I don't have to see the expression on Zoe's face. "She'd been holding her under the water after practice. Hazing her, sort of. Hattie couldn't breathe and she tried to fight, so Devon broke her arm."

I don't mention that I was there, in the stands. One of

Hattie's bones tore through the skin on her wrist, spilling blood into the pool. It spread so fast, like a drop of food coloring hitting water. One second the pool was clear, and the next it was cloudy and red and girls were screaming. I don't tell Zoe that I thought Hattie was dead. I thought Devon had killed her.

Devon and I stood together after, while we waited for the ambulance with the rest of the swim team. We were shoulder-to-shoulder, me in my uniform, Devon still wearing her dripping swimsuit. She turned to me, and there was a kind of emptiness in her normally vibrant brown eyes. She said it had been easy. Like snapping a twig.

"That makes sense," Zoe says. "The serum makes you stronger, I think. Last week I was trying to close a window in the locker room, and the glass just *shattered*. I had to call the janitor to fix it." She looks up at me, sheepish. "Devon never told me what really happened with Hattie."

Anger flares through me, but Zoe didn't break anyone's arm and Devon's dead, so I don't know where to direct it. "What *did* she tell you?"

"She thought there was something wrong with her. Her emotions were messed up."

I frown. "Messed up?"

"She said it was like they were behind a thick layer of glass, and she could see them, but she couldn't feel them."

Bullshit, I think, disgusted. She just didn't want to take responsibility for what she did, for the ugliness inside her. But then Ariel's video crackles to life in my head. *Can't feel anything,* she whispered into the camera. *I'm numb.* Did she record that video before she burned down my animal shelter? Or after?

One of them claiming they did something terrible because they felt numb was easy to dismiss. But both of them?

"Devon thought it was the serum," Zoe continues. "She talked to Mr. Byron about it, but I guess he blew her off, so Devon wanted to sneak into his office and go through his things. She thought there'd be files or something explaining what he did to her. I didn't want to go with her, so she said she was going to go on her own. That was two weeks ago."

I count the days back in my head. "Right before she committed suicide."

"I didn't believe her then. But now . . ." Zoe stares down at her hand. She stretches out her fingers and then curls them into a fist. "It started happening to me, too, exactly like Devon said it would. I feel . . . different. Empty, sort of. It's like I'm—"

"Numb," I finish for her.

Zoe's head snaps back up. "Is it getting you, too?"

The bell rings, making Zoe and me flinch. I'm suddenly very aware that we're having this conversation in the girls' locker room. That we still have to explain the incident in the gym to Coach Lammly.

The door behind me slams open, and students stream into the room, talking and laughing. I catch Zoe's eye and she jerks her head, motioning for me to follow her down an empty row of lockers.

"Listen," she whispers when we're alone again. "We could sneak into the nurse's office together. See if there's—"

"But you said Devon already looked."

"I said she *wanted* to. She died before she could tell me if she ever got in, or found anything." Zoe studies me. There's something strange about her eyes. Like they're not connected to the part of her body that feels and thinks and worries. "They really didn't tell you about any of this?"

I'm considering coming clean about Ariel's video and the final, missing clue, when something occurs to me. "That's why you volunteered to be my roommate, isn't it? So you could spy on me?"

"No." Zoe's jaw tightens. "I mean, sort of. That's why I moved in with you at first. I thought Devon and Ariel might have told you something they didn't tell me, but you were pretty clueless, so I left it alone. Then you almost got expelled and when you came back . . . well, you were different."

"So you started going through my things?" I say this too loud, and the muffled conversations around us go quiet.

"Keep your voice down." Zoe moves closer, and I shuffle away from her, slamming into a row of lockers behind me.

"Is that why you told me to leave?" I ask.

"I was doing you a *favor*," Zoe says through clenched teeth. "Devon *died*, Charlotte. Just like Ariel died."

This room feels small all of a sudden. The walls are creeping closer.

"What are you saying?" I ask.

Zoe shakes her head, irritated. "If you left when you were supposed to, you might have been okay. But now . . ."

"You think we're going to die? That this serum is going to make us commit suicide?"

Zoe meets my eyes, unblinking. "I don't know what I think. But we're not safe."

"This is crazy." I turn toward the door. Screw Coach. I need to get out of here. I need to think without Zoe and half of the Weston fencing team staring at me.

"Charlotte, wait." Zoe grabs me by the wrist. "This is happening whether you believe it or not. You could be next."

I jerk my arm out of her grip, and her fingernails leave thin red lines on my skin. "Leave me alone."

I stumble out of the locker room in a daze. People crowd the hallway, but I can't separate their individual voices from the blood pounding in my ears, the air humming around me. I have calculus next period, but I walk right past the hall leading to class and push through the doors to the quad, dropping onto a stone bench.

Sunlight filters through the trees, illuminating the blue veins stretching across my wrists. I trace the spidery lines with one finger.

We're not safe, Zoe said. *You could be next.*

"She's wrong," I whisper. But I can't deny that I'm changing. My skin and hair are healthier. I'm doing better in all my classes. I'm suddenly the best fencer in school.

And two days ago, Jack kissed me and I felt nothing. I thought there was something wrong with me. But what if . . .

I spread my fingers and then tighten them into a fist, watching my veins fade and bulge. I imagine I can feel the serum moving just below the surface of my skin, seeping into my blood. Changing me.

I slam my fist into the bench, and the stone splinters beneath my hand.

Chapter Twenty-Four

Jack's family limo pulls into the roundabout in front of school, headlights flashing.

I pick a piece of lint off my dress and straighten my headband. I went for a classic look tonight: black shift, single strand of pearls, low heels. I check my reflection in the glass door to make sure my hair is still lying flat.

Normally, I'd be nervous that I chose the wrong thing to wear, but not tonight. It's unnerving. I've spent the last hour trying to feel anxious or afraid or a little bit timid. But it's like the emotions have been deleted from my memory.

I pinch my palm, reveling in the flare of pain. I can still feel things. I'm just psyching myself out. Like when you're certain you're about to get sick so you imagine you have a sore throat and a stuffy nose.

Footsteps thud down the staircase. I turn, and Jack stands behind me in a slim-fitting charcoal suit, paired with a creamy white shirt. He doesn't wear a tie, and he's left the top buttons of his shirt undone at the collar, allowing a triangle of skin to peer through. His cognac-colored shoes and belt gleam under the dim lights.

"You look beautiful." Jack leans in and kisses me on the cheek.

I feel . . . *something.* It's not quite the weak-in-the-knees, stomach-flip, light-of-breath rush of emotions I used to feel whenever I saw Jack. But that's just because we kissed. Because he's mine now. It's natural that I wouldn't be giddy anymore.

"You, too. Lovely as a summer day." I straighten Jack's collar, and he smiles with the left side of his mouth.

"Shall we?" He offers me his arm and then leads me through the double doors and down the steps to the waiting limo. A man in a stiff black suit opens the back door, revealing an interior of sleek leather, tinted windows, and walnut trim. We slide inside, and Jack produces a key from his pocket. He unlocks a cabinet beneath his seat, removing a miniature bottle of champagne.

I wrinkle my nose. "I'm not getting drunk on the ride to your parents' house."

Jack pops the cork, and fizzy gold liquid spills over the mouth of the bottle. He catches it with his tongue.

"Trust me, you're going to need this to get through a night with the Calhoun family." He wipes his mouth with the back of his hand and offers the champagne to me.

"Oh really? What horrible things are they going to subject me to?"

"I don't want to frighten you . . . but there might be baby pictures involved."

I don't laugh, and Jack's smile dims. To cover, I lift the bottle to my lips to drink. *I didn't laugh because the joke wasn't funny*, I tell myself. But Zoe's warning circles my mind. *You could be next.*

I shake my head, and the words pop like bubbles. I weave my fingers through Jack's and squeeze. He looks at our clasped hands and then up at me, grinning.

For tonight, at least, I'm not going to worry about the serum.

The limousine pulls off the main highway and turns down a tree-lined road. There are few houses here and they're set so far back from the street that you can barely see them. I catch glimpses of white brick and climbing ivy, but otherwise, there's only meticulously trimmed bushes, and the odd Lexus SUV.

The limo stops at a tall, wrought-iron gate. The gate creaks open.

"This is where you live?" I ask as we pull toward the house at the end of the drive. It's old and Victorian, but impeccably maintained. Arched bay windows stare out from the front of the home like eyes, and intricately molded cornices crown the door frames. A portico juts out from one side, the porch lined with white columns.

"It's like the Addams Family mansion, isn't it?" Jack says.

It does look creepy in the twilight, with the bare trees towering around it. But beautiful.

I tip the last of the champagne into my mouth. "Maybe," I say, swallowing. "If the Addams Family suddenly came into a lot of money."

The driver lets us out at the front door and we make our way inside, handing our coats to Roseanne, the maid Jack's family has had since he was little. The front hallway features a carefully curated blend of gilded mirrors, crystal chandeliers, and marble statuettes. Jack leads me around the corner, into the main sitting room.

Oil paintings hang from the walls, and ornate carpets cover the gleaming hardwood floor. A velvet settee sits at the far corner, flanked by walnut side tables holding identical Tiffany lamps.

I take it all in. It's like walking into a dream I only half remember. Ariel described all this to me. I closed my eyes while she re-created this room, down to the brass birds engraved on the fireplace pokers and the tassels hanging from the silk pillows. I listened to her talk, and I wanted to be here so badly that I could taste it on my lips like salt. But now . . .

I force my mouth into a smile. "Wow," I murmur, turning in place. "It's like we're in a play."

"I know." Jack scratches the back of his neck. "My mother attended the Oscar Wilde school of interior design."

"I heard that!" a voice calls from the other room. Mrs. Calhoun herself rounds the corner a second later.

I don't know what I expected Mrs. Calhoun to look like—
Ariel just said she was a snob—but I can safely say that the
woman in front of me is the opposite. She's tiny for one
thing—I don't think the top of her head clears my chin—and
she looks, well, *normal*. She's dressed casually, in dark pants
and a camel-colored sweater with delicate gold bracelets
twinkling from her birdlike wrists.

"Some people have no sense of style," she says, shaking
her head at Jack before pulling him into a hug. Jack smiles
with his whole mouth when he's with his mother, like a little
kid showing all his teeth.

"Missed you, too, Ma," he says, planting a kiss on the top
of her head. She pulls away, turning her attention to me.

"And you must be Charlotte," she says.

I offer my hand. "It's a pleasure, Mrs. Calhoun."

"Nonsense. You'll call me Babs." Babs waves my hand
away and goes in for a hug.

Physical contact usually sends a shrill, sharp feeling zip-
ping over my skin, like electricity. I go stiff during every hug
or handshake or kiss on the cheek. But hugging Babs is easy.
Her body is small as a girl's. Her sweater feels soft beneath
my fingers. Cashmere.

I'm still hugging Babs when a man walks into the room
and claps Jack on the shoulder. "There he is!"

Jack stands up straighter. "Sir," he says, shaking the
man's hand. And then to me, "Charlotte, this is my father,
Jack Calhoun Sr."

Jack Sr. offers me his hand, but it's a moment before I reach out to shake it. I've seen photographs, of course, but it's still strange to see Jack and his father together. They look exactly alike, down to the dimples in their chins and the way their smiles tilt too far to the left.

"Wow," I blurt out, and Jack Sr. releases a roaring laugh. Jack smiles, too, but he still looks stiff.

"We get that a lot," Jack Sr. explains. He drops one hand on my shoulder and the other on Jack's, leading us from the room while Babs follows a step behind. "Now, Charlotte, I'm afraid Jack neglected to mention how beautiful you are."

"That's not true," Jack cuts in. "He's trying to get me in trouble."

Jack Sr. winks at his son. "I guess my memory isn't what it used to be."

We make our way into the dining room, Jack Sr. and Babs sitting across from each other at the ends of the table while Jack and I settle in the middle.

"He's going to spend the entire night flirting with you," Jack explains under his breath as he pulls out my chair. "He isn't being creepy or anything. It's just leftover politician charm."

"It's fine," I whisper back. Jack lets his hand linger on my back for a moment longer than necessary. I wait for the tingle of heat, the flurry of emotion. But it just feels like a hand. My smile stiffens as I slide into my chair.

"It's great to have you here, Charlotte." Jack Sr. says. "You'll have to tell your mother hello for us when you see her next."

"Jack and I have been very impressed with the work she's done at the Med Center," Babs adds, smiling. "She's such a visionary."

"My mom's on the board," Jack explains.

"Oh, right," I say. I think I knew that.

"Will you be attending the gala this weekend?" Babs asks.

"I'm not sure," I say, thinking of my mother's deadline. I might be in a car back to Manhattan by then. "Maybe."

Roseanne stops beside Babs and pours a glass of wine. Babs thanks her and then turns back to me. "Are you interested in medicine as well, Charlotte?"

It's such an easy question that my mind goes completely blank.

Empty, I hear Zoe say. *Numb.*

"Start with an easy question, why don't you?" Jack Sr. roars, laughing. Babs smiles politely.

"What do you like to do for fun, dear?" she prods after a moment.

"Um," I say, but I can't come up with a single thing. *I like to look for clues my best friend left behind before committing suicide,* I think. *You met her once, remember? You hated her.*

"Our Jack is the star of the track team, from what I hear," Jack Sr. cuts in when I don't answer. "Babs and I are looking forward to his first meet. We might have to paint our faces blue and silver!"

"I'm sure the papers would love to get a photo of that," Babs says.

"Why not? I'm proud of my son."

I smile politely, wondering where Jack Sr. gets his information. I've been to Jack's track practices. If he isn't the worst person on the team, he's a close second.

Jack reaches for my hand under the table. "Charlotte likes animals," he says. "She opened the animal shelter last year. I told you about it, remember?"

"Impressive!" Jack Sr. booms. Everything he says is a boom or a crash. He's like a human cannon.

"Thank you," I say, and Jack squeezes my hand. He thinks I'm nervous, but I'm not nervous. I'm nothing.

Babs and Jack Sr. politely change the subject to some woman named Mrs. Rodenheim and how it's such a shame that she won't be handling the Performing Arts Society gala this spring. After a moment, Jack leans toward me.

"Knock, knock," he says under his breath.

"Jack—" I glance at his parents, but they don't seem to be paying attention to us.

"Just answer the door," Jack says. I look down at my lap, pretending to straighten my napkin.

"Okay. Who's there?"

"Orange."

"Orange who?"

"Orange you glad I brought you to this incredibly boring dinner?"

I swat his leg with my napkin. "It's not boring."

"It is so boring. But I'm glad you're here."

I lift my eyes to Jack's face. I used to fantasize about

meeting his family. I knew I could do better than Ariel. I could make small talk and wear the right thing and laugh at Jack's mother's jokes. I could make them love me. It was the one way I could beat Ariel. The one way I was better than her.

Now that I'm here, I can't seem to muster the energy. I could write the rest of this night myself—the compliments on a splendid meal, the casual talk of college and summer jobs, and the careful avoidance of tricky subjects. It's like watching an elaborate dance. I have the sudden urge to shout something lurid, just to see if I can get them to miss a step.

I wrap my hands around my fork, my knuckles turning white. Why is this happening now? I'm so close to getting everything I wanted.

A flash of red hair appears in the hall, vanishing the second I turn my head. I stare into space for a long moment.

It wasn't Ariel, I tell myself when nothing appears. *Ariel's dead.*

"Everything okay?" Jack asks. I shift my eyes back to his and fake a smile. I never used to be able to do that, but it's easy now, like I grew new muscles the day I swallowed the serum.

"Fine," I say. "Where's the bathroom?"

Jack points down the hall, and I excuse myself. My knees shake as I stand, which is strange because I still feel so calm. I stop walking once I'm out of sight of Jack's family and lean my head against the wall, closing my eyes. My knees knock together, telling me something's not right. My body's out of sync with my mind. This is wrong.

I open my eyes and there's another flash of red hair. Ariel laughs, the sound breathy and cruel. I turn and stare down the long, dark hallway. No Ariel. The hallway ends in a set of glass doors that open onto a lush backyard mostly hidden in shadow. It's snowing. White flakes drift down to the earth. They seem to glow in the light of the moon.

I walk down the hallway and push the doors open. I'm always cold, but I don't feel cold tonight. The air is warm as bathwater. The snow kisses my skin. I stare over the white-frosted lawn, my breath forming icy clouds. Some animal left paw prints in the snow. Logically, I know it must be a raccoon, or a neighbor's dog. But they look like they belong to a wolf.

A memory surfaces. I think of Ariel sprawled across our secret clearing, her lips sticky with wine.

"In our next life, let's be wild," she said, staring up at the sky. "Let's be wolves."

"What about your boyfriend?" I asked.

Ariel turned her head toward me, her eyes dull and drunk. "Don't be silly, Char. Boys don't fall in love with wolves."

I kneel, staring down at the nearest paw print. There's ice crusted around the edges, making the snow hard.

Let's be wolves, Ariel said, and my first thought was of Jack. I couldn't imagine being a wolf if he was a boy. Why be a wolf when you can be a person? When you can be in love?

I smell Jack coming before I hear him. He smells like rain and pine trees and something else. Something I can never quite put my finger on. It's weird, isn't it? That I can smell him down the hall, through closed doors? I should be disturbed.

The door behind me creaks open and then closed.

"Hey." Jack kneels on the ground, rubbing his hands together for warmth. "What are you doing out here?"

"I'm not feeling well," I say. It's not exactly a lie. I'm not feeling anything, so I can't be feeling *well*, can I?

Jack presses the back of his hand against my forehead. "You're a little hot. You think it's a fever?"

"Maybe."

"We could have rescheduled, you know."

"I know." I try to smile, but it feels wrong. Like how someone might smile if they'd only ever read about it in a book. "I wanted your parents to like me."

Jack kisses me on the cheek. For a second, the scent of rain and pine trees overwhelms me. "They'll like you because I like you."

"I like you, too," I say. Jack kisses me again, his lips light against my own. He lingers in front of me, his nose touching mine.

"Sorry," I say, pulling away. "I just really don't feel well."

"Wait here," Jack says, standing. "I'll see if Dad can call the driver and get you a ride back to school."

Jack goes inside, leaving me alone in the snow. I run my fingers along the paw print. It feels hard and slippery to the touch. Like glass.

Let's be wolves, Ariel said. Zoe must've been right after all. The serum really is changing me. Because if Ariel asked me again, I wouldn't hesitate. I'd exchange my skin for fur, and I wouldn't spare a single thought for the boy I used to love.

Chapter Twenty-Five

Zoe's already asleep when I get back to the dorm. I hesitate at the door, watching her chest rise and fall beneath her comforter. A lock of black hair sticks to her cheek, fluttering each time she exhales.

I kneel beside her. I used to plug Ariel's nose when she was sleeping. She wouldn't be able to breathe and would wake up gasping and swatting at my hand. I doubt Zoe and I are close enough for that.

I jostle her shoulder, and her eyes pop open. She groans, blinking.

"Well?" she asks, and it's like we're finishing the conversation we started in the locker room earlier today. Like no time has passed.

I pull my headband off and shake out my hair. "I'll sneak into the nurse's office with you," I say, tossing the headband to the floor. "But we need to get the key."

Zoe nods into her pillow. "I have a plan for that."

"And we have to hurry." I don't say *because it's happening to me, too*, but I don't have to. Zoe's eyes travel over my face. Her lips curl into something too mean to be a smile.

"Not a problem," she says.

Zoe tosses a ring of keys onto my table the next morning at breakfast.

"How did you get these?" I ask, picking them up. Only three people have access to the nurse's office—Dean Rosenthal, Mr. Byron, and Byron's assistant, a sophomore named Sam or Simon or something else that starts with an *S*.

Zoe slides into the chair next to me. "Superpowers," she says. I raise an eyebrow. "*Fine*," she adds with a groan. "Byron's assistant has a thing for me. All I had to do was ask."

I hand the keys back to her. "I feel like we're in a Bond movie."

"I'm not a Bond girl. I'm a femme fatale. Like Rita Hayworth."

"I don't know who that is."

Zoe stares at me for a beat, her gaze withering. "You can't possibly be serious."

"When do you want to do this?" I ask, ignoring her shock.

Zoe shakes her head, and mutters something under her breath that sounds like "Americans." She snags a piece of bacon off my plate, standing.

"Now," she says, nodding for me to follow her. I grab my tray of otherwise untouched food and cross the room, dumping it in the trash before ducking through the double doors. Dusty sunlight pours in through the windows lining the walls. The door falls shut behind me, muffling the cafeteria noise. Zoe raises a finger to her lips, and we walk down the hallway in silence.

"Byron never gets in before nine," Zoe explains once we're too far from the cafeteria to be overheard. I pull my cell phone out of my pocket and check the time: *8:43.*

I angle the screen so Zoe can see. "Cutting it close."

"You said you wanted to hurry."

I put the phone back into my pocket. "Fair."

The nurse's office is down a flight of stairs, on the basement level. There are narrow windows just below the ceiling looking out onto grass and rocks and people's feet. The floors haven't been polished in a while, and the paint on the walls looks dull. No one would dare call the basement level shabby, but it's not as lavishly maintained as the upper floors, either. It feels like a subtle hint that coming down here denotes weakness. Those who dare to get sick at Weston don't deserve gleaming wood and fresh paint.

Zoe removes the keys from the pocket of her plaid skirt. She dangles them from one finger.

"Nervous?" she asks. I raise an eyebrow, and she snickers. "Yeah, me neither. Too bad. I bet being nervous makes you sneakier."

There was something about the way she said that word.

Nervous. Like she already knew the answer was going to be no.

"Do you feel anything anymore?" I ask.

The corner of Zoe's thickly lined eye twitches. She cuts both eyes toward me. "I'm trying to figure out how long I have left till . . ." She draws a finger across her throat and makes a vulgar noise. I cringe and look away.

"You don't know that the serum made them commit suicide," I say. "Correlation doesn't equal causation."

"Thank you, doctor." A bell rings somewhere above us, the sound echoing down through the ceiling. Zoe squeezes her shoulders toward her ears and releases them again. "What about you? Dead inside yet?"

Part of me wants to ignore her, like she ignored me. But I'm tired of trying to figure this out on my own.

"It kind of . . . flickers," I say. "Sometimes I'm fine, but then . . ." I think of being in the supply closet with Jack. Feeling so complete, then so empty.

Zoe stares for a moment. Something flashes in her eyes. It could be emotion, or else just a trick of the dim lights. "Yeah," she says finally. "It was like that for me, too. For a while."

We stop in front of the door to Mr. Byron's office. Zoe fits a key into the lock. It clicks open.

There's enough sun streaming in through the ceiling windows to illuminate the space, so I don't bother switching on the light. The room is fairly standard as far as nurse's offices go—bookshelves to the left, computer to the right, two narrow cots in the middle. There's another door on the other side of the computer desk, probably a closet or a bathroom, and a replica of a human skeleton stands between the two cots, one arm curved over its head in a strangely enthusiastic wave. A poster showing how to do the Heimlich maneuver hangs on the wall behind it.

I close the door with a soft click. "What are we looking for?"

Zoe sits in front of the computer and drops her hand onto the mouse. The screen blinks to life. "I don't know. Clues."

"Thank you, Sherlock."

Zoe swivels around in her chair, saying something in French that sounds suspiciously like an insult. "I'm not a spy," she says. "I don't know how to do this. Why do you think I wanted you to help me?"

I glare at her. "What's that supposed to mean?"

"*Please.* You think the rest of us didn't know that you, Ariel, and Devon snuck out practically every night? The dorm walls aren't that thick, genius. The other girls thought you were involved in some sort of drug ring, but I figured you just liked to explore places you didn't belong." Zoe raps her knuckles on the back of her chair. "I don't have that kind of experience. Before the serum, I was just a nerd with a sword."

"We weren't involved in a drug ring," I say. But given Ariel's reputation, I can't blame whoever started the rumor. I pinch the bridge of my nose, thinking. "Let's start at the beginning. Tell me what happened when you first came down here."

"When Byron gave us the serum?" Zoe purses her lips. "Byron's assistant, Simon, found me in first period and handed me a note saying I was supposed to come to the nurse's office. Ariel and Devon were already here when I got down."

"Anyone else? Besides Byron, I mean?"

Zoe starts to shake her head, then stops. "Wait—Dean Rosenthal was here, too, but just for a second."

I raise an eyebrow. "The dean was here?"

"She was on her way out the door. I passed her in the hall."

"Do you think she knew what Byron was doing?"

Zoe shakes her head. "She never said anything to me about it, so I don't know."

I lean against Byron's desk, the wood digging hard into my hip. "What about consent forms? Did they talk to your parents?"

Even as I'm saying it, I realize—Devon and Ariel had their birthdays over the summer.

"No need," Zoe adds, confirming my suspicion. "I turned eighteen in September."

"So they chose you three so they wouldn't have to deal with parents." I drum my fingers against the desktop. "That makes sense, I guess. And you just took the serum once, right? You didn't come down for a second dose or anything?"

"Just once. We had a follow-up appointment a month later, but after that, Mr. Byron told us we didn't need to come in again. He said the supplement had left our system, and

that the effects hadn't been as dramatic as they'd hoped."
Zoe shrugs her lazy shrug. "I thought that meant it hadn't
worked."

I nod. It sounds to me like Byron was trying to cover a
mistake.

"Try looking for health records." I lean over Zoe's shoulder, staring at the computer screen. "If he had you come in
for a follow-up appointment, maybe he took notes about
what he found."

Zoe clicks on a document icon on the computer and
scrolls down to a folder labeled "Student Records." She clicks
again, and a dialogue box pops up.

Password?

"Do you know it?" I ask.

Zoe scrunches up her nose. "No, but Mr. Byron's the kind
of guy who'd write it down on a Post-it. Look around."

She lifts the keyboard and looks beneath. I pick up a
pad of paper and flip through it, but every page is blank. Zoe
swears in French and starts paging through a word-a-day
calendar.

"Should we—" Zoe pauses. "Do you hear that?"

I listen. I hear the clock ticking from above the door,
and the shallow sound of Zoe's breathing. And then—

Footsteps. Someone's coming down the stairs.

Zoe grabs my arm.

"Hide," she whispers. She pushes her chair back and
ducks below the desk, curling herself into a ball. I yank open

the door next to the bookcase—it's a closet, thank God. I crouch beneath the row of hanging coats, my arms wrapped around my knees. A key scrapes against the lock.

I'm still pulling the closet door shut when a light switches on. *Shit.*

I leave the door where it is and scoot beneath the coats. Mr. Byron hums to himself as he steps into his office. He's old, his skin deeply wrinkled, his hair graying. I study him through the crack in the door, wondering if he's the mastermind behind the serum. If he's the reason Ariel and Devon had to die.

He looks up abruptly, and his eyes flicker to the open closet door. For a fraction of a second, he stares right at me. I curl a fist near my mouth to muffle the sound of my breathing.

Don't see me, I pray. *Please, please don't see me.*

Mr. Byron shrugs off his coat and starts toward the closet. His footsteps vibrate through the floor, making the door tremble. One by one, my nerves prick to life. I shrink farther into the closet, waiting for him to open the door . . .

He drops his coat over the desk chair, inches from where Zoe's hiding.

I exhale silently, my body slumping in relief. Something jabs into my back.

Frowning, I reach deeper into the closet, my hand groping against the wall before finding a small leather briefcase. I hesitate, my eyes shifting back to the door. The low humming tells me that Mr. Byron is still bustling around his office, oblivious to the girls hiding under his desk and inside his closet. As quietly as I can, I pull the briefcase onto my lap and open it.

The briefcase is empty. Its walls are lined with thick, spongy foam, and six hollowed-out spaces tell me that whatever had been stored inside is long gone now. I trace the spaces with one finger, imagining six tiny serum bottles nestled in the foam. They would just fit.

I can no longer hear Byron humming in his office, or footsteps, or anything over the blood pounding in my ears. Six bottles. Even if three of them went to Ariel and Devon and Zoe, and one went to me, that would mean there are still two doses of the serum that haven't been accounted for. *At least* two more doses. There could be more briefcases, more bottles. There's no way to know for sure.

The closet door swings open, and I flinch, biting back a scream. The briefcase topples off my lap and hits the floor with a thud.

Zoe narrows her black eyes. "What are you doing? Let's *go*."

Chapter Twenty-Six

"Is he gone?" I crawl out of the closet and push myself to my feet.

"He went to the bathroom, I think. But he'll be back soon." Zoe glances longingly at the computer. "Damn. If we had a few more minutes, I know we'd find something."

"We did." I pick up the briefcase, letting it fall open so Zoe can see the spaces in the foam.

Her eyes go wide. "You think that was for the serum?"

I snap the briefcase closed. "If it was, then at least two doses haven't been accounted for."

A door opens and closes somewhere in the basement, the sound echoing down the hallway. Zoe crosses the office silently and pushes the door open a crack.

"Still clear," she says. "But we should get out of here before he comes back."

I shove the briefcase into the closet, and we sneak out of the office, down the hall, and up the stairs. Zoe doesn't say another word until we've reached the main floor. The corridors are already crowded with students making their way to the first classes of the day. We must've missed the bell.

"Should we go to the dean?" I ask in a low voice.

Zoe shakes her head, hooking an arm through mine. "I have an idea," she says, steering me away from the throng of people.

"Hello? We have homeroom."

"We're not going. Think about this: How did I figure out you'd taken the serum?"

"I kicked your ass at fencing and you made a lucky guess?"

Zoe tightens her grip, making all the little tendons in my elbow pinch together. "*Exactly*. If we want to know where the rest of the serum went, we just need to figure out if there are any other Weston students kicking ass. Easy, right?"

We stop in front of the school library. A brass chandelier winks behind the glass doors.

"The latest sports scores are all listed on Weston's website," I point out. "We don't have to skip class—I can check them on my phone during first period."

Zoe peers through the glass doors, probably looking for Ms. Stotchky, the librarian. "We're going to need a lot more than that. Weston is a good school—it's not surprising when we win things. We need to find someone who was mediocre and isn't anymore. And I don't think we should limit our search to sports. We should look at anyone who's shown a sudden improvement in anything, from academics to . . . personal hygiene."

"Caitlyn Lee got a nose job."

Zoe scowls. "This is serious. Are you in?"

There are only a few days left before the Med Center gala. Mother will be back in town soon, and if she finds out that I've skipped another class, I'm done here. Forever.

But this is why I came back, I remind myself. Staying at Weston shouldn't matter anymore.

I nod and follow Zoe through the heavy library door and over to one of the study tables near the back of the room. The towering stacks of books block these tables from view, and Ms. Stotchky would never wander far enough from the front desk to catch us here without a pass. I drop my stuff onto a chair and slide a laptop across the polished wood table, hitting the track pad with one finger. The screen blinks to life, Weston's website staring back at me.

"I'll start with the recent stuff and work back," I say, sliding into a chair. "You start old and work up. We can meet in the middle. Sound good?"

Zoe slides into the chair next to mine. "Let's do it."

We work in silence. I click on the link marked "Recent Stats" and start reading through our sports scores. "Boys' Basketball Beat Dalton High 50–19." "Girls' Squash Beat Browning 7–0." "Varsity Wrestling Placed in the Regional Qualifier."

The results go on like this for pages and pages. My eyes glaze over as I try to find a pattern. After a while, I click over to the "News" section, where we list recent academic achievements. It's not much better. "Weston Wins Best Delegation at Princeton Model Congress." "*Weston Weekly* Selected Best in Show by NSPA Student Press." "Monica Donovan Named USEF Junior Equestrian of the Year." Etc., etc., etc.

I close my eyes to give them a break from the glare of the computer screen. Stats and headlines flash across my closed lids. *Best, won, placed, scored.* We win again and again and again. That's the only pattern I see.

"Find anything?" Zoe asks after we've been at it for hours. Or what feels like hours. I shake my head, and she sighs. "Me neither. Everyone at Weston is already the best. It's ridiculous." She closes her laptop and leans back in her chair. "What's that phrase? This is like trying to find a needle in hay?"

"Haystack," I correct her. She wrinkles her nose.

"That makes no sense. Who goes around dropping needles in hay? When was that ever a problem?"

"I don't think—"

Zoe suddenly sits up straight, her eyes widening. *"Oh."*

She stands and starts sticking notebooks into her bag.

"Are you leaving?" I ask.

She glances back at me, like she'd forgotten I was still sitting there. "I . . . well, I think I have an idea—but I'm not sure if . . . No. I need to check something out first."

"But what—"

"I'll talk to you later," she says, hurrying into the stacks. I stand and, for a second, I consider chasing after her and forcing her to tell me what just happened. But she's already gone. Sighing, I sink back into my chair, my eyes shifting to the glowing computer screen on the table in front of me. The headlines blur together. I close my eyes. I can't stand to look at them anymore.

Like finding a needle in hay indeed.

I go to a few of my afternoon classes, hoping Zoe will be in our dorm when I get back. No such luck. The only thing waiting for me is a padded envelope with a Japanese return label. I drop my bag onto my bed and rip the envelope open. A tangle of black wires falls out.

It's the charger I ordered for Ariel's mystery phone. *Finally.* I dig out the nondescript black cell from the rip in my mattress where I'd been hiding it and plug it in.

"Come on," I mutter, pressing my thumb into the power button. I stare at the black screen. Seconds tick by. Nothing happens.

I hit the power button again, and the phone makes a beeping sound, but the screen stays blank. I wait a few seconds, and then try again—the same thing happens. Something inside the phone seems to be working, but water damage is keeping the screen from functioning properly. *Damn, damn, damn.*

I briefly consider throwing the phone against the wall, but that's not going to make Ariel's video play. I press it between the palms of my hands, a string of profanity echoing in my head.

It beeps again—more insistently this time—and I jerk my head toward the screen before realizing the beep came from my phone, not Ariel's. Groaning, I dig the cell out of my pocket and check the screen.

Jack. *You around? Meet me after practice?* It's after four. Track practice only lasts for another twenty minutes or so. I cast one last glance at Ariel's malfunctioning phone, but there's nothing I can do with it now.

Be there in 5, I type back, grabbing my coat.

It's too cold for the track team to practice outside, so they're in the gymnasium today. Hurdles stand at intervals around the track while Jack and his teammates line up at one end, crouched in low lunges as they wait for the coach to blow his whistle. I duck through the doors and up the stairs, finding my usual spot in the bleachers. Jack sees me and nods, his hands propped on either side of his front foot.

I smile and wave. I haven't been to one of Jack's practices since before Ariel died. I keep expecting her to push through the double doors and drop onto the bench next to me. My smile suddenly feels fake. I dig my cell out of my pocket so that I have something to do with my hands.

I pull up a browser and search for "cell water damage fix." The coach blows his whistle, and the gym is filled with the sound of squeaking sneakers and panting. A hurdle or two smacks to the ground, but I don't bother looking up. I scroll through the results on my phone. Everyone seems to agree that I'm screwed. *Water damage can't be fixed. Buy a new phone. Good luck with that.* Triple shit.

The coach blows his whistle again. "Looking good, Calhoun!"

I glance up and see Jack panting and high-fiving his teammates. Maybe my brain is skewed from studying stats and records all morning, but that seemed fast. And when did Jack ever beat someone at hurdling?

A sick feeling floods my stomach.

The coach has the hurdlers line up again. Jack crouches into place, his hands to either side of his front foot. He stares straight ahead, eyes narrowed in concentration. I scoot to the edge of the bench, both hands gripping the wood beneath me.

The coach blows his whistle again.

The hurdlers are off. Jack clears the first hurdle, and the second. I've never seen him leap like that before. There could be springs attached to his sneakers. Back when Ariel and I used to watch practice, he was always the slowest runner. It took him twice as long as everyone else to get around the track.

Now he pulls ahead of the others easily, and then he's jumping over the fourth hurdle and the fifth, never slowing, never showing any sign of fatigue. His back foot clears the top of the hurdle by several inches. Is that *normal*? It looks strange. Superhuman. I consider looking up pictures of other hurdlers online, but I can't tear my eyes away from Jack. He has one hurdle left, and then he's jogging to a stop and the coach is blowing his whistle. The others have barely made it halfway around the track. He's won again. He never wins.

I think of the six empty spaces in the foam walls of the briefcase. Six doses of serum. A snatch of conversation whispers at the back of my head.

You think we're going to die?

I don't know what I think.

I curl my fingers around the edge of my seat. Jack glances up at me again and winks, but I can't bring myself to smile or wave or do anything but stare.

Jack took the serum. Jack is going to die.

Chapter Twenty-Seven

I head for the boys' dorms instead of waiting for Jack at the locker room. He's always surrounded by teammates after practice. I need to talk to him alone.

I huddle in the trees outside his window, shivering, as I wait for a light to flick on. I used to come here at night with Ariel. She'd knock on Jack's window and slip him a note or a good-night kiss while I hovered behind her, waiting to walk her back to our room so she didn't have to brave the woods alone. I'd pretend I didn't hear them whispering and giggling. I'd tell myself I wasn't jealous. Now it's just me and I'd give anything to have her standing beside me. I wrap my arms around my chest, bouncing impatiently on my toes.

A light switches on, glowing gold between the slats in Jack's blinds. I rise to my tiptoes and knock on the cool glass. The blinds move, and Jack's hand appears to push them aside. He frowns when he sees me.

"Hey!" he says, grunting as he pushes the window open. "I thought you were going to meet me after practice."

"I . . ." Someone laughs inside his room. I hesitate, imagining one of his teammates lounging inside.

"Charlotte?" Jack glances over his shoulder and then shakes his head. "It's just my laptop. I'm alone."

"Oh." I try not to let the relief show in my face. "Can I come in?"

The skin between Jack's eyes creases. Girls aren't allowed in the boys' dorms under any circumstances. Being found means automatic expulsion for both parties. Even Ariel only came as far as the window.

But the concern leaves Jack's face, and he leans out his window, reaching for my arm. "Here," he says.

I grab hold of his shoulder, and Jack wraps his arm around my waist, hoisting me up with a grunt. I wedge my free hand against the sill and pull myself inside.

I've never been in his room before. I take a moment to notice all the small things that make up his space. The plaid comforter, and the balled-up socks on the floor, and the framed photographs of his family and friends sitting on his dresser. I don't know a single other boy our age who has actual photographs printed out and framed, but it seems oddly fitting for Jack. A sweet kind of rebellious.

A photograph near the back of the dresser catches my eye. It's a picture of Ariel and me from freshman year, grinning at the camera like fools. Our heads are pressed together, our cheeks side by side. We've never looked anything alike, but in this picture, we could be sisters. We could be two halves of the same person.

I turn my back on the photograph. "Look," I say, "I wanted to ask you about—"

Jack's lips are on mine before I finish my sentence. His mouth is warm and tastes like sweat. His hands wrap around my waist.

I lean away from him. "Jack—"

"I've been thinking about this all day," he murmurs, kissing me again. He pulls me closer, but I press my hands against his chest.

"I need to talk to you," I say, stopping him.

He frowns. "It can't wait?"

I shake my head. Jack drops his hands, but he doesn't seem to want to move away. He leans over me, his broad chest rising and falling beneath a thin white T-shirt. He's still pink-cheeked from track, and his hair is wet and slicked back from his face. All Weston dorms are small, but his seems too small to hold us both at the same time. The walls have shifted closer. The ceiling is only inches from our heads.

There are only two places to sit—the bed and the chair at his desk. I choose the chair. Jack remains standing.

"This might sound kind of weird." I feel Ariel staring out of her photograph behind me and I have the sudden urge to turn her around so she's facing the wall. I knot my hands together in my lap to keep them still. "Did you . . . take something this year?"

Jack's frown deepens. He never frowns, and the expression looks strange on his face. "You think I'm on steroids?"

"*No.* It's not like that at all. This was kind of like a serum, and it came in a small bottle. Mr. Byron would have given it to you at the beginning of the year."

I don't say: *You'd know if you'd taken it—it gives you superpowers and makes you feel dead inside.*

"I don't know what you're talking about," Jack says. He shifts his eyes to a spot on my chin. I don't think he knows that I can tell he's no longer looking at me.

Ariel's voice whispers in my ear: *Liar, liar, pants on fire.*

"You can tell me," I say.

"I really don't know what you're talking about," Jack says. He's using his father's voice, the one that persuades donors to add another zero to their checks. "But you're not supposed to be here, so maybe you should head back—"

"Look, I won't judge you or anything. It's just that it's—"

"Judge me?" Jack's eyes snap back to mine. "It's funny, hearing that from you."

He's angry with me. I see it in the set of his shoulders, the tilt of his chin. I twist my hands together so tightly that the tips of my fingers go numb. "Funny?"

"After everything you and Ariel did. But *you* won't judge *me.*"

"Jack—"

"The sneaking out and the drinking. *Lying.*" He doesn't say *cheating*, but he doesn't have to. I hear it anyway.

"I didn't do those things to you," I point out. Jack laughs. It's just a single *ha* that doesn't contain any humor.

"No. You just cut me out of your life right when—" He stops talking, jerks a hand back through his hair. "And now you think I'm on drugs."

I don't know what to say. Finally, I come up with, "That's not fair."

It's both the truth and a lie.

Jack swallows. I watch his Adam's apple bob up and down in his throat. "Who said I was playing fair?"

It's the same thing I said to him just a couple of weeks ago, but hearing it now, here, feels like a slap. Anger flares through me, so hot and so sudden that it almost knocks me over.

"Fine," I say. I'm halfway to the window when Jack grabs my arm.

"Wait. I'm sorry."

I turn back around, my heart a rapid thud. For a moment, my anger was stronger than my need to solve the mystery. It felt . . . *wonderful*. I want to cradle it close to my chest, like a pet, but it's already gone, like someone flipped a switch. I look at Jack, and I can't remember why it bothered me that he pointed out how Ariel and I used to sneak out and drink and lie. We did all those things and worse.

Jack sits at the edge of his bed. I watch the muscles in his shoulders tense beneath his T-shirt, his back rise and fall as he inhales. If he can make me feel anger, maybe he can make me feel other things, too. Maybe I'm not totally numb inside yet.

I cross the room and lean against Jack's knees, stretching my arms around his shoulders and interlocking my fingers behind his neck. He looks up at me, hopeful.

"Are we good?" he asks, smiling with the left side of his mouth. There's so much feeling in his face—the optimistic curve of his lips, the fear in his eyes, the anxious set of his jaw. I study him. His emotions are raw as fresh wounds. They're so much more vivid than anything I've felt in days. He couldn't have taken the serum.

I press my mouth to his and feel another flare—*anger and heat and want*—but it's gone in an instant. Jack wraps his hands around my waist and pulls me onto his lap. I kiss him harder, wondering if I can suck the emotion out of his body like breath.

Would I do it, if it were possible? Take everything that he feels for myself and leave him a shell? Steal his emotions for myself?

Jack pulls away, leaving me gasping.

"I love you," he says.

I stare at him, dumbfounded. It's the first time he's said that since Ariel died. If I'd heard those words months ago, I'd have felt wonderful and guilty and terrible all at the same time. I'd have felt like flying. Like falling.

Jack lifts a hand to my face, brushing a strand of hair behind my ear. I let my mind travel through every inch of my body. I don't feel like flying. I feel hollow. I feel nothing.

"My parents are going to that gala at the Med Center tomorrow night," he says. "I'm supposed to go with them. Be my date?"

Outside, it starts to rain. Drops hit Jack's window and, for some reason, I shiver. They sound hollow and empty. Like I feel.

"Sure," I say, and Jack kisses me. I keep my eyes open, staring at the rain-streaked glass behind his head.

I wonder if I'll still be here tomorrow night. I wonder if I'll still be anywhere.

I wake up hours later, Jack's bedspread tangled around my legs. The sky outside is dark, rain tapping against the window. I groan and find my cell phone: *11:12*. We must've fallen asleep.

I lean over to shake Jack awake and tell him I'm leaving, but he isn't there.

". . . see why that matters . . . ," someone is saying.

I sit up in bed, suddenly wide awake. The voice came from the other side of Jack's door, but it sounded like it was right next to me. I push the blankets off my legs, standing.

"I hate this," Jack is saying. I cross the room and press my ear to the door. "Can't I—"

"Do you have any idea how hard we worked to get you in?" The new voice sounds like Jack's father, but why would his father be at Weston in the middle of the night?

Jack moves, and the wood creaks beneath my ear. I

picture him leaning against the other side of the door, his knees pulled up to his chest, but, hard as I try, I can't picture his father standing out there with him.

"I know," Jack says. "I'm sorry."

"Don't be sorry. Be *smart*." Jack's father's voice sounds the tiniest bit mechanical. My eyes widen as I realize what's going on. It's a phone call. I can hear both sides of a phone call Jack is having with his father out in the hall as clearly as if they were both standing right in front of me. This is deeply disturbing.

"I know," Jack says. "You're right. It's just that we were talking earlier, and she already seemed to know what was going on. I had to lie right to her face."

My chest clenches. He's talking about me.

Jack's father sighs. "If Dr. Gruen chooses to share the details of the program with her daughter, that's her business . . ."

Dr. Gruen. For a second, the entire world gets put on Mute. I hear only the sound of my own breath hitting my teeth. The flap of my eyelids blinking open and closed.

If Ariel were here, she'd laugh at my surprise. She'd say this was obvious.

I have to remind myself to start listening again. ". . . I will not have my son violating the terms of the program," Jack's father is saying. "Not after everything else that's gone wrong this year. Do you understand?"

A pause, then "Yes, sir."

"Good. Now, when is your next dose?"

"End of the week."

I back away from the door. That's enough. As quietly as I can, I grab my bag and slip my feet into the leather ballet flats lying next to Jack's bed. His window is cool to the touch, the glass slick with rain. I push it open and climb outside. Shadows stretch their long fingers across the dirt, leaving the trees around me dark and mysterious. Wind makes my skirt flutter, but I don't shiver.

I pull my cell phone out of my pocket and dial Mother's number. It just rings and rings. Her voice mail picks up after a minute, and a recorded message tells me her mailbox is full.

I stare at her photograph on my screen for a long moment, trying to place the emotion bubbling beneath the surface of my skin. It's like anger and betrayal and fear and hatred, all tangled together, their ends tied in knots. But though I can place it, I can't quite feel it. It's like it's behind a layer of glass.

I hear Jack's father's voice echo through my head: *If Dr. Gruen chooses to share the details of the program with her daughter . . .*

I squeeze my phone so tightly that a long crack snakes across the screen, splitting her face in half. It occurs to me that this is odd. I shouldn't be able to break a phone with my bare hands, but that hardly seems to matter. All this time Mother knew what had happened to Ariel and Devon. What's happening to me. And she said nothing.

That ends now.

Zoe still isn't in our dorm when I get back. It's probably better that way. I drop my bag onto the floor and dig an old math textbook out of my closet and flip it open, revealing a carved-out space in the middle of the pages. Mother's keys to the Underhill Med Center sit inside. I stole them during last Christmas break, when Dev and Ariel thought it would be fun to sneak inside after dark and look for painkillers. Mother had too much bourbon after dinner and fell asleep on the couch, some CNN special blaring from the television across the room. I slipped the keys out of her purse and into the pocket of my robe. The next morning I took them to the hardware shop around the corner and had copies made. Mother never even knew they were missing.

I take the keys out of the book and slide them into my pocket. If Mother won't answer my calls, I'll have to find the truth my own way.

The Underhill Medical Center runs on a skeleton crew after midnight, but the lobby and first floor appear to be deserted. I study Mother's keys. The largest is for the main doors, but there are two others on the ring: a smaller office key, and an even smaller key that looks like it opens a file cabinet or briefcase. I pick out the middle key. No one's allowed inside my mother's office unless invited. She'd disown me if she knew I was thinking of breaking in.

"She's out of town," I remind myself, digging the pad of my thumb into the key's metal teeth. I should be scared. I should feel nerves crawling along my skin, dread pooling in my stomach. But all I feel is impatient.

Mother's office is on the second floor, around the corner from long-term care and outpatient facilities. I take the stairs so I don't risk running into anyone in the elevators. There are patients up here and nurses wandering the halls. I slip my shoes off to keep from making any sound. I stop at the end of the hallway, listening at the wall for footsteps or the soft shuffle of scrubs. I don't hear anything, so I creep around the corner.

A nurse steps out of the last room on the left. I freeze. She's staring at her clipboard, so I don't think she's seen me yet. I duck into the nearest room and pull the door almost closed. I watch the hall through the crack, holding my breath to keep from giving away my location.

She walks past my door and disappears down the hall, her shoes padding quietly against the tile. I wait until I'm sure she's gone, and then I push the door open. Mother's office is around the corner and to the right. I move like a shadow, my bare feet pressing into the floor without a sound. I slip her key into the lock and turn, pushing the door open.

The light is on, which is strange—Mother never forgets to turn off her light. The closet door hangs open, and a pair of shoes lies in the middle of her floor. I spot bloodred soles and realize they're the Louboutin heels—her favorites.

I step farther into the office. Everything feels a little off, a little wrong. Her samurai sword is still crooked on its shelf. Mother used to shout at me when I'd touch it, warning me about how valuable it was. I reach out and straighten it now, careful not to let it fall from its stand. It's heavier than I expected it to be, the leather handle sleek and cool to the touch.

A half-full coffee cup sits on her desk, her lipstick smudged around the rim. There's a stack of newspapers beside it, and Mother has circled one of the articles: "Wildfire Rages Through Franklin County," the headline reads. She didn't write anything beside the article to indicate why she thought it was important, just circled it with a thick black pen. She pressed down too hard, ripping the paper.

I search her desk first, shuffling through outdated invoices and phone messages, and a few more newspapers. There's nothing about mysterious volunteer programs or vitamin supplements that make you feel numb. Nothing about Ariel or Devon or Zoe. I slam a drawer closed, frustrated, and the crash of wood against wood echoes through the room. I cringe, waiting for someone to storm in and check on the noise. No one comes.

The file cabinet is next. I drop to my knees and pull open one of the drawers. There are a few folders with scribbled names of corporations I vaguely remember her mentioning, and several more files with dates scrawled across the labels. I open a folder and find pages and pages of Med Center tax documents.

I close that drawer and tug open the one above it. It's empty except for a stack of glossy brochures. I take a second to stare down at the smiling, happy girls on the front. They're all wearing lab coats and huddling around a table covered in microscopes and test tubes. I reach for one—then pause. I smell something.

I sniff at the air. It's gas station cologne, heavy and sweet.

I hear something, too. The muffled sound of footsteps on tile. Someone's coming.

Ignoring, for the moment, the extremely disturbing fact that I could smell someone from down the hall, I nudge the drawer closed, glancing over my shoulder at Mother's office door. Still closed. And there's only one drawer left to search. A silver lock winks from beneath its handle.

The footsteps come closer. I pull Mother's key ring out of my pocket and slip the tiniest key into the lock. I turn—

The office door slams open, and the keys slip from my fingers. I swear and kneel to grab them when a hand clamps down on my shoulder. Someone spins me around.

A security guard glowers at me, one hand resting on the nightstick dangling from his belt, the other holding tightly to my arm.

"You're in a lot of trouble, miss," he says, his mouth settling into a hard line.

Chapter Twenty-Eight

The security guard's fingers dig into my arm. His beady eyes scan my face. Any second he's going to recognize my mother's straight nose and sharp cheekbones and realize that he's getting his grubby hands all over the boss's daughter.

I shift my face down so he'll stop looking at me. I'm not sure how much trouble I'm in, but getting my mother involved can only make things worse. His grip tightens and, for a second, I consider yanking my arm away. My muscles feel firm beneath the surface of my skin, my blood hot. I'm stronger now. I could hit him and make it out the door before he had a chance to recover.

I let the guard lead me out of the office without a fight. A teenage girl with super strength isn't someone you just forget. It's better not to chance it.

"I'm going to need to see some ID," he says.

"I don't have any," I lie. This guy might not recognize my face, but he'll definitely recognize my last name.

"Young lady, if you can't show me any ID, I'll have no choice but to call the police." He pronounces the word "*poe-lease*," his voice barely a whisper. He casts a wary glance back at the office door, and I realize something—he doesn't want my mother to know someone was snooping around her office any more than I do. "Do you want to spend the night in jail?"

I squirm under his grip, trying to think. Jail. Or Mother. The choice is surprisingly easy.

"Cuff me," I say, holding out my hands.

It seems to take the police forever to get to the Med Center, but it's probably not even an hour. I spend the time slumped in a folding chair in a tiny gray office, staring at a wall calendar from 2014. Someone wrote *Debbie's birthday* on the twenty-second and circled the date in red. Finally, the door opens and some guy who looks like he graduated from high school last week walks in, wearing a loose-fitting brown uniform and cap. He looks more like the UPS guy than an officer of the law. He slaps a pair of metal cuffs around my wrists and leads me out of the hospital, loading me into the back of his car so carefully that you'd think he was taking me to prom.

"Thanks," I say before he closes the car door. He actually blushes. I bet he'd rob a bank right now, if I asked him to.

The junior cop leads me to a small concrete cell. I slump

on the wooden bench, letting my head fall back against the wall. Cold air uncurls from the concrete and wraps itself around my arms. I glance down, watching goose bumps ripple over my skin.

I don't shiver. I barely even feel the cold.

"You get a phone call."

I open my eyes, flinching at the sudden brightness in my cell. It's morning. Sunlight trickles through the barred window above me.

I stretch, cringing at the stiffness in my back. "What?"

"Your phone call?" The junior officer dangles my phone between the bars of my cell. "The Med Center isn't going to press charges, but you need to call someone to pick you up."

I take the phone, murmuring "thank you" before the cop ambles away. I pull up my contacts list and stare down at the screen. There are only three people who might accept a phone call from me, from jail, first thing in the morning. Jack, Zoe, and Mother.

"Decisions, decisions," I mutter, staring down at the short list. I let my finger hover over Jack's name, thinking.

I press my finger to the screen, and the phone begins to ring.

Zoe has a Dora the Explorer Band-Aid wrapped around her middle finger.

"Cute," I say, and she uses the finger to flip me off. I climb into her car, and she slides into the driver's seat next to me. She doesn't smile as she starts the engine.

"You going to tell me why you broke into the Med Center?" she asks, pushing her glossy black hair behind one ear.

"You going to tell me why you ran out of the library yesterday?" I counter.

Zoe pulls her car out of the police station parking lot, studying me through narrowed eyes. Her eyeliner comes to razor-thin points. It looks deadly. "You found something, didn't you?"

I give her my best robot face. She groans, slapping the steering wheel with one hand. "*Fine*. Your info for my info, okay? My cell is in the bag by your feet. Get it. I want to show you something."

I pull her bag onto my lap and dig out her phone. Zoe takes it from my hand and keys in her password with her thumb, eyes never leaving the road. "Voilà," she says, dropping the phone into my hands.

A doc fills the screen, displaying three columns of names and numbers. I zoom in, narrowing my eyes to read the tiny type.

Darla Miller, 122

Kevin MacAvoy, 118

Steven Franklin, 131

They go on like that for pages.

"Are these IQs?" I ask.

Zoe nods. "Remember how we had to submit a test as part of our application?"

"Lots of other crap, too," I add, remembering. "Physical, grades, teacher recommendations."

The light turns red, and Zoe pulls her car to a stop. "These are the IQ scores this year's freshman class submitted before they started at Weston," she says. "Now scroll down."

I scroll to the next page, and find the same group of names.

Darla Miller, 135

Kevin MacAvoy, 129

Steven Franklin, 147

"They're higher," I say.

"Yeah. Those are from three months ago. Weird, right? A year at Weston and your IQ goes up ten points? And it's not just that. I found physicals reporting lower weight and improved agility and strength. And there are reports from teachers that detail behavioral improvements in class." She nods at the phone. "It's all in there."

I slide my finger over the screen to scroll through the doc. There are pages and pages of information. It would take hours to read all of it. "Where did you get this?"

"Byron's computer. I went back later and found his password on a Post-it under his desk." The light changes. Zoe starts driving again.

I chew on the inside of my cheek, thinking of students bent over textbooks in the cafeteria, the daily announcements listing one impossible achievement after another. Shiny hair and clear skin and perfect teeth. I suppose I should have found it strange that they were all so beautiful. But

I always felt like I was the strange one. I was doing something wrong. "So you think every student at Weston was given the serum?"

"No. I think every student at Weston was given *something*. A diluted form of whatever we got, maybe."

"Why didn't you tell me all this at the library?"

Zoe presses her lips together. I can practically see the gears grinding away inside her head.

"Before, when we were about to break into Byron's office, you asked me if I felt anything anymore," she says after a moment. "The truth is, I haven't felt anything in weeks. I kept hoping it would come back, but . . ." She glances down at her bandaged finger resting against the steering wheel. "I thought if I tried cutting myself that something would—"

"You *cut* yourself? On purpose?"

Zoe curls her fingers around the steering wheel, so I can't see the bandage anymore. "Just a knick. There was hardly any blood."

I think of the tiny pink pocketknife in her underwear drawer and feel sick to my stomach. "Well?"

She works at her lower lip, never moving her eyes away from the road in front of her. It takes a long time for her to shake her head. "Do you really think Devon and Ariel killed themselves because of something in the serum? That it was inevitable?"

My throat feels suddenly dry. "Why else would they have killed themselves?"

Zoe jerks her shoulder up and down. The shrug is trying

too hard to be casual, and all at once I realize how badly she wants there to be something else. Something we've missed.

But I saw Ariel floating below the water. I found the idiotic clues she left behind for me, like a trail of bread crumbs leading to God knows what. "Ariel didn't have any other reason to kill herself," I say. "Devon, either."

A muscle in Zoe's jaw twitches. "Whatever. Now it's your turn to share."

For a fraction of a second, I consider lying. Ariel left that video for me. I don't want to let Zoe in on the secret.

But we'd agreed—her info for mine.

"There was a video," I admit, swallowing. "Ariel left it for me on this burner phone she hid in the woods, but it's water damaged. Won't turn on."

Zoe's fingers tighten around the steering wheel. "Did you check the SIM card?"

"The what?"

She groans, shifting the car into second gear. Fields and phone lines fly past my window. "The SIM card. As long as it hasn't been damaged, you can pop the card out of one phone and into another and all the data will be intact." Zoe cocks an eyebrow. "Is that all?"

I tell her about the conversation I overheard between Jack and his father. "That's why I went to the Med Center. I searched my mother's office pretty thoroughly, but there was a locked file cabinet that I didn't get the chance to check."

Zoe glances at me. I wait for her to say something snarky

about my mother's involvement, but she keeps her mouth shut.

Weston's slanted gray roof peers over the tops of the trees just ahead. Zoe pulls into the parking lot, jerks her car into a space, and hits the brakes. My body lurches forward, the seat belt digging into my chest to hold me back.

"So you want to sneak into the Med Center?" she says. "Again?"

"Tonight's the anniversary ball. You could sneak in with the rest of the party, and after I arrive with Jack we can slip away. No one would ask questions."

"Won't your mother catch us in her office?"

"I don't think so. She's the president of the hospital. She'll be in the ballroom with everyone else." *I hope*, I add silently. "Why? Do you have a better idea?"

"Train station," Zoe says without blinking.

"You want to run?" I frown. "Why do you need a train? You have a car."

"Cars can be found. A train is safer. We could be in a different zip code before the dean even reports us missing."

It takes me a moment to understand what she's saying. "You want to disappear?"

Zoe chews on her lower lip. "We assume Ariel and Devon died because of what was in the serum, but what if we're wrong? What if they knew too much, and somebody . . ." Zoe slashes her throat with one finger.

I stare through the windshield. I don't believe my mother

would kill two teenage girls just to protect her secrets. But I didn't want to believe she'd be involved in any of this. Zoe might be right. This could be our chance to escape before it's too late.

"If we leave, we'll be like this for the rest of our lives." I stare at Zoe's bandage, imagining her dragging a blade across the pad of her finger. "Do you really want that?"

"If it means I get to have the rest of my life, then yes."

I unlatch my seat belt and grab my bag. "I don't think that's good enough for me."

"So you're going back?"

I nod and push the car door open. "Are you coming?"

Zoe doesn't let go of the steering wheel. Her knuckles are white. "I think I'm going to drive for a while longer."

"Zoe . . ."

"I'm not running away now. I don't even have any of my things. I just need some time to think, okay?" She flashes me a tight smile. "I'll text you."

"Fine." I climb out of the car and into the frigid winter cold, slamming the door shut.

Zoe backs out of the parking space and drives off, leaking exhaust behind her.

You could be next, I think, and I close my eyes. The darkness behind my lids seems to pulse. I wonder how I'll do it. Pills maybe? Or I could slit my wrists? I picture the sword in

Mother's office and imagine sliding it into my gut, committing seppuku like the samurai.

I pull my cell out of my pocket, clicking on Mother's name. Her photograph fills the screen. She promised she'd be back for the ball tonight, but she still hasn't answered any of my phone calls. I let my thumb hover over the Call button, and then change my mind and stick the phone back into my pocket again.

I need to change before my first class, so I head through the double doors and into the courtyard, hurrying so I won't be late. I race up the stairs and push the door to my dorm open. I'm deep inside my own thoughts and it takes a long moment before I realize there's someone sitting on my bed.

Mother lifts her blond head and fixes me with those cold blue eyes. "Hello, Charlotte."

Chapter Twenty-Nine

"Mother." The word feels lodged in my throat, like food I can't swallow. I glance over my shoulder to make sure there's no one in the hall behind me, and then I ease the door closed.

Mother straightens the front of her skirt, even though there isn't a single wrinkle in the fabric. She's never been in my dorm room before. Not even on the day I moved in. Darren helped me bring my stuff up while she waited in the car, memorizing case notes for a presentation she had that evening.

I feel something, but the emotion fades the second I notice it. It was like anger, but more complex. Bitterness, maybe.

Mother tucks a lock of hair behind one ear, considering me in silence. "You called," she says finally.

I usually have such a strong response to her presence. Light-headed, sweaty palms. It's like she takes up too much space in the room, leaving less oxygen behind for everyone else.

But I don't feel that now. She's just a person, like any other person. Strange.

I sit on the edge of my bed. "You could have just called me."

"I just got back into town so I thought I'd stop by."

"Did you find what you were looking for?"

"The missing asset? Yes, as a matter of fact. It's been recovered." Mother glances at my desk, wrinkling her nose at something she finds distasteful. A tense moment of silence passes.

"Something weird is going on," I say finally. "Zoe—"

"Is that why you broke into my office?"

Anxiety stabs at me with sharp, dirty fingernails. I should be grateful to feel anything—even this—but I fight it, hating that she can reduce me to a nervous wreck with just a few words.

"Who told you I broke in?" I ask.

Mother lifts an eyebrow, her way of telling me that no one had to *tell* her. She knows everything, always. "A few of your teachers have let me know you're skipping classes again. And Amelia says you missed your last shift at the Med Center."

I stand, my bedsprings creaking as they release my weight. "That's because—"

Mother lifts a hand, stopping me. My mouth snaps shut without consulting me first. The anxiety is still there, simmering below the surface of my skin.

"You had until the day of the anniversary ball to prove to

me that you were serious about staying at Weston. That was our deal."

"You're making me leave?" I manage to choke out.

"You were *arrested*, Charlotte. Honestly, what did you expect?"

I *was* arrested, and I have been skipping classes and shifts at the Med Center. I just didn't think she was paying attention.

"Grab whatever you need for the week. I'll send Darren for the rest tomorrow." Mother uncrosses her legs and stands. I catch a glimpse of bloodred on the soles of her shoes. She's wearing Louboutin heels, the exact ones I saw in her office. "I've arranged for several tutors to meet with you once you're back in the city. All you have to do is pick your favorite and send me an e-mail so I know who to make the check out to."

The order is like an itch that needs to be scratched. It feels weird to ignore it, to stay put when she's told me it's time to go. I imagine weeds growing out of my feet and digging into the floor beneath me, rooting me into place.

Mother lifts her head, noticing that I've made no move to follow her to the door. "Charlotte," she snaps. "Darren is waiting."

"When did you get back?" I ask, staring at her shoes.

"I don't see why that's—"

"Did you stop at the Med Center first?"

Mother frowns. "No, I came straight here."

But she couldn't have come straight here, because she's wearing the shoes she left in her office. It's such a dumb lie.

I can't imagine why she'd tell it. Unless she needed to cover up other, bigger lies.

"Don't you want to know why I broke in?" I'm surprised by how calm I sound. My anxiety has gone still as untouched water. Not a single bubble breaks the surface.

"I assumed you were looking for painkillers again," Mother murmurs, staring down at her phone. She's trying to pretend this conversation doesn't bother her, but a wrinkle creases the skin between her eyebrows, and her shoulders have gone tense.

I reach down deep, trying to find that numb place where snuffing an emotion is as easy as blowing out a match. I expect to search for it, but it's waiting just below my skin. It's like a current running through me. Like a river. I step inside, and it sweeps me away.

"Ariel left something for me before she died," I say. "A bottle."

To anyone else, Mother's expression would've seemed to remain the same. But I see fear reflected in her eyes, in the set of her lips. "Is that so?"

"Zoe told me she got the same thing from our school nurse. They said it was a vitamin supplement. But you know what it really is, don't you?"

Mother lifts an eyebrow, but otherwise her expression doesn't change. "Do I?"

"You know because you created it. You or some other scientist at the Med Center. You created it and you gave it to Devon and Ariel. You know what it did to them."

"That's a delightful little story you've concocted, but I'm afraid it's fiction. Now, come along. I want you on the road before the morning traffic into Manhattan."

She says this so easily that I almost don't notice the twitch at the corner of her mouth. I've known my mother's tells since I was nine years old. I know when she's lying to me.

"I drank it, too," I say, crossing my arms over my chest. "Am I going to commit suicide? Or do you still think this is a story I'm making up?"

My desk lamp illuminates the lines of Mother's face. For a moment, she doesn't look like a person at all. She looks like she's made of marble, all sharp angles and hard stone.

"Fine," she says through clenched teeth. "You win. I'll get you the antidote once we're back in the city. Happy?"

"There's an antidote?"

"Of course there's an antidote," Mother says, flippant.

For a moment I feel nothing, and then—*anger fear relief sadness loss hate*—it all slams into me at full force. I press a hand to my chest. I can't catch my breath. It's like being hit when you've never been hit before.

I think of Ariel, her lips blue beneath the surface of the water and partly opened, like she wanted to tell me something. I think of Devon lying on a bed of leaves, her fingers curled toward her palm.

"You let them die?" I ask. "How could you do that if there was a way to save them—"

The muscles in Mother's jaw grow taut beneath her pale skin. "The project you're referring to is highly classified," she says in a cold, deadly voice. "I'm not at liberty to discuss the details with my *daughter*. Now, for the last time, get your things."

"What about all the other Weston students? They're being drugged, too, aren't they? Are you allowed to talk about them?"

Mother passes a hand through her hair, leaving a few locks standing on end. She looks mussed, and she never looks mussed. She never looks out of control.

"The Med Center's relationship with Weston goes back decades," she answers finally. "The students here are intended to succeed. That's all you need to know."

"So you're drugging us?" I say. "How do you do it? Do you put something in our flu shots? The water?"

Mother presses her lips together, considering me. Her cold stare is a challenge. I don't look away.

"It's in the food, actually," she says after a moment. "In order for the supplements to work, you need to eat at least seventy-five percent of what you're served. I brought you here to be a part of the program, but you never eat enough for the supplements to take effect. Ironic, isn't it?"

I think of the dozens of half-full plates, of organic quinoa and locally grown broccoli going cold in front of me. I always saw the uneaten food as an act of rebellion. My way of proving that Mother couldn't control every aspect of my life.

Mother holds the door open. "Get your bag," she says, tapping her foot. The bloodred heel clacks against the hard wood.

I want to say no. I want to grab her by the shoulders and shake her until she tells me everything she knows about the serum and Weston and the Med Center.

But Mother has never told me the truth when she didn't want to. I could stand here glaring for as long as I want. Nothing will make her say anything she doesn't want to say. Even her revelation about the food felt like a slap. Her way of telling me that I can't even succeed when I'm being pro-grammed to.

My body realizes I'm giving up before my brain does. My shoulders slump. I lean over and wrap my fingers around the leather strap of my backpack.

"That's better," Mother says as I follow her into the hallway.

Chapter Thirty

Darren stands at the curb beside Mother's sleek black car. I follow her through Weston's double doors, pausing at the top of the concrete staircase so she can pull on her leather gloves. Darren nods when he sees us and crosses to the back passenger seat to open my door.

I stare at the car's tinted windows. That's it, then. My next five minutes are planned out, just like the next year and five years and fifty years of my life. Just as my mother knows that I will walk down the steps and wait while Darren opens my car door, she knows that I will go to whichever tutor she picks for me, whichever therapist she deems acceptable, whichever college she chooses. She knows I'll take the antidote she didn't offer to Devon or Ariel, and never speak about any of this ever again.

My phone beeps. Mother's head snaps up at the sound, and I half expect her to demand that I hand it over. But she just turns and starts down the steps without me.

I dig the phone out of my pocket and check my message. Zoe.

Screw it. I'm in. The last train leaves at ten. I'm on it if we don't find anything. Meet me at the Med Center at seven?

"Charlotte," Mother calls from the bottom of the steps. "Let's go."

I put the phone back into my pocket, and I glance over my shoulder at Weston. It looks like a cold concrete mountain in the middle of the trees. Row after row of empty windows stare down at me. I half expect to see Zoe appear, frowning, as she watches me leave her alone to deal with what's happening to her.

But there's no one. The windows stay empty.

I walk down the stairs. Darren opens the door, and Mother puts a hand on my shoulder to guide me into the car. It's like she knows I want to run. I squeeze the strap of my backpack, listening to the squeak of my skin against the expensive leather. Somewhere far away, a crow caws.

"Charlotte," Mother snaps. My feet obey even as my brain rebels. I slide into the car. The buttery leather seats are warm to the touch. I cross my legs, preparing for the long drive back to Manhattan. Mother slams my door. Darren starts up the engine, and the car roars to life.

"Wait," I say. Darren glances at the rearview mirror, but he doesn't move the car. I roll down my window. Cool air curls around me, chilling the leather beneath my legs. I recognize the cold but don't feel it.

Mother already has her phone out of her pocket, and she's staring down at it, studying something that makes her frown.

"You aren't coming with me?" I call back at her. She lifts her head suddenly, like I've shocked her.

"I have work," she explains, slipping the phone back into her pocket. "And the ball is tonight. Did you forget?"

I clear my throat, keeping my face cool. "When will you be back in the city?"

Mother gives me a curious look. I wonder if she's touched by the question. If she expects that I'm asking it because I'll miss her, because I want her home with me. Mother doesn't do emotion, not ever, and it doesn't show in her face now. But I can't help wondering if, somewhere below the steel, she cares about me at all.

She straightens her head. "Not before the end of the week," she says, her voice clipped. "I'll send someone to the apartment with the antidote but, otherwise, you'll have the place entirely to yourself. How lucky. No parties."

Her voice is so carefree when she says this that you'd think she hadn't realized that all my friends are dead. Almost all of them.

I clear my throat. "You'll get Zoe and Jack the antidote, too?"

"Of course," Mother says, too quickly. Her mouth twitches. *Liar.* She raises her hand in half a wave and turns back to the phone she's still holding. Darren pulls away from the curb.

I stare through the window at my mother until she becomes a tiny black dot against the gray sky. Darren turns onto the main road, and she disappears.

I need to break out of this car.

I come to this conclusion after we've been driving for roughly ten minutes. Pine trees and telephone lines and the odd red farmhouse fly past my window. I clasp my hands in my lap, thinking. Darren has the radio on, tuned to a classical music station that I'm sure my mother insists on listening to whenever he drives her around. Bach or Chopin or some other boring dead-guy music drifts through the speakers.

There has to be a way out of here. Darren pulls up to a stoplight. I move one hand off my lap and over to the door handle. Keeping my gaze focused on the woods outside my window, I place my hand on the door handle, and lift . . .

Locked.

I drive my teeth into my lower lip, trying to keep my expression neutral. Something must give me away, though, because Darren glances at the rearview mirror.

"Your mother insisted on the child locks, Miss Gruen," he explains, flashing me a sad smile. He says this like it's normal for a woman to lock her teenage daughter inside a freaking car. I suppose Mother pays him not to ask questions.

I press my lips together and go back to staring out the window. *Dammit.* With the child locks on, there are only two ways out of this car: I can either crawl out the window, or climb into the front seat and go through the passenger door.

I tap my fingers against my knee. Getting through the door would be easier, but I'd have to get into the front seat first, and that presents a challenge. Darren would have to stop for gas or something, and he'd need to be distracted enough that he wouldn't notice what I was doing. I glance at Darren. The slim muscles in his arms are visible, even through his work shirt, and his legs are so long that he looks cramped and uncomfortable in the front seat. He's probably fast. He'll catch me, even if I make it out.

That leaves the window, which is impossible. I examine the frame. I'm sure I could wiggle my way through, but stopping at a light doesn't give me enough time. Maybe if we were in an accident—

I sit up straighter. *An accident.* Even a little fender bender would mean that Darren would have to stop the car and talk to the other driver. He'd need to exchange insurance information and wait for the police to make a report. He'd be distracted, probably distracted enough that he wouldn't notice me climbing out the window, or crawling into the front seat. An accident would give me plenty of time to get away, and then I can hitch a ride back to Weston.

I run my tongue over my teeth. I'll need to distract Darren for a moment, get him to swerve or stop quickly. There are plenty of cars on the road. He's bound to hit something.

Ariel's voice whispers in my head. *Is this something normal girls do?*

Something painful twists inside me and, for a moment, I hesitate. Someone could get hurt. *Really* hurt.

But if I don't get out of here, people will die.

I reach for that cold place inside me and let it sweep my concerns away. I scoot down in my seat, keeping my eyes on the window so Darren will think I'm sulking.

I peek at the rearview mirror to make sure my reflection isn't obvious. I bend my legs, my feet aimed at the back of Darren's seat. He slows to a stop behind a line of traffic. For a long moment we're still. I take a breath and hold it in my lungs, counting the seconds ticking past.

One Mississippi. Two Mississippi . . .

The light changes, and the car inches forward. Darren hits the gas, making the engine purr beneath my feet. We start to pick up speed.

Three Mississippi. Now.

I slam my legs into the back of Darren's seat. I kick too hard, misjudging my newfound strength. Darren's body flails forward, like a rag doll, but he doesn't let go of the steering wheel and it jerks to the left. The car doesn't slam into the station wagon in front of us, like I'd expected. It veers out of our lane, into oncoming traffic.

Things happen very quickly after that. Horns blare, and headlights flash. I look out my window and see a truck speeding toward us. I imagine it slamming into the side of my mother's car, metal crumpling like paper around it.

Then Darren hits the gas and we zoom forward. The truck clips our back fender, making us spin. Tires screech against the asphalt. We crash through the barricade at the side of the road and tumble over the shoulder. There's a crunch of metal, and the entire vehicle shudders as we slam into a tree.

Darren lurches forward again, and I hear a sickening thud as his head slams into the steering wheel. I wait for him to groan and sit back up. But he doesn't.

He doesn't move at all.

Chapter Thirty-One

"Darren?" I whisper. His body is slouched over the steering wheel, his seat belt straining to hold him upright. The air bags didn't inflate. A trickle of blood weaves down from a crack above his eyebrow.

I unbuckle my seat belt and crawl forward, placing two fingers on his neck, just below his jaw. His skin feels cold to the touch. For a long moment, I don't feel anything.

And then—

A vibration against my fingertips, a *bomp bomp bomp* just below the skin on Darren's neck. He groans, and shifts against his seat belt. I yank my hand back. He's alive, then. Okay.

A few cars have pulled to a stop by the side of the road. People stand beside them, shading their eyes to peer down at the wreckage of the crash, but no one has approached us yet. I check out my two exit options. The passenger-side door faces the street, so that's out. I try the window, praying the button still works. I push down, and there's a dull buzz as the glass slides from the frame.

"Charlotte?" Darren moans.

I don't answer. The window is completely open now, so I prop my hands against the sides of the car and wiggle through. My hips clear the sides easily. The car's tilted to the left, and my window is only a few feet away from the ground. I lean forward until I can catch my weight with my hands, and then I pull my legs outside, tumbling onto the icy dirt.

"Charlotte?" Darren says again. His eyes are open but unfocused. It takes him a long moment to find me. I hesitate. He's awake, but that doesn't mean he's okay. I should call an ambulance. I should wait until the EMTs get here. I've known Darren practically my entire life. He and his wife just bought a puppy. I think they're trying to get pregnant.

Something flickers in my chest, and I recognize the emotion as guilt in the second before it vanishes. I'm the reason Darren's hurt. I caused the accident. I've spent most of my life feeling guilty about something, whether it was failing to live up to my mother's impossible expectations or lusting after Ariel's boyfriend. But now, when I've finally done something truly unforgivable, I feel nothing.

Sirens sound in the distance. An ambulance will be here soon.

I cast one last glance at Darren. His eyes are closed again, but he's still alive. His breath fogs the glass in his window.

I send Zoe a text—*I'll be there*. As soon as I press Send, another text pops onto my screen, this one from Jack.

What time should I pick you up tonight?

I stare at the words for a beat. I forgot I'd told him I'd be his date. I start to write back and cancel—then hesitate. I'm going to need a ride. And being on Jack's arm will make it easier to get through the door.

Seven, I write back. *I'll meet you in front of the school.*

I press Send and then pocket my phone, starting the long walk back to school.

At five minutes to seven, I'm standing just inside the school doors, the hood of my winter coat pulled over my head to hide my face. Mother's probably called the dean by now. Maybe even the police. I glance over my shoulder, anxious, but nobody seems to have spotted me.

Jack's car pulls up to the curb. I push the doors open and hurry down the stairs without glancing up. I open the door and slide into the passenger seat.

"Hey," Jack says. "What's the—" He stops talking when I push back my hood. "Oh. Wow."

"How do I look?" I ask. Jack stares, stunned, but my voice seems to jar him out of his stupor. He clears his throat and turns back to the steering wheel.

"Different," he says. He puts the car into drive and pulls away from the curb.

"Good. That's what I was going for."

I snuck into the locker room to take a shower. It was the one place I could think of where I could scrub the blood and dirt away without being seen. I keep some makeup and beauty products in my locker, and I used them to slick my short hair away from my forehead and behind my ears. It looks chic and French, nothing like my normal messy bob. I smudged eyeliner around my eyes and drew on deep ruby-red lips.

It's not a perfect disguise, and anyone who knows me will be able to see through the layers of makeup and recognize my face. But I'm hoping that, from across the room, in dim light, I might fool enough people to get through the Med Center doors.

I glance at Jack's tux as I shrug my coat off. Black tie, stiff shirt, slim jacket. "Nice duds."

"They were my dad's." Jack steers the car out of the school parking lot and onto the main road. I stare at the silhouette of his face as his drives.

Jack casts another look my way, and his gaze falls on my beaded cocktail dress. "And that was Ariel's, right?"

I shift uncomfortably in my seat. I had to risk sneaking back to my dorm to get Ariel's beaded cocktail dress out of our closet, but I didn't have another choice. I couldn't go to the gala wearing my ruined school uniform. "How did you know?"

Jack is quiet for a moment. "It smells like her."

The serum must be increasing his sense of smell and hearing, like it did to me. For a moment, I consider asking him about the phone call I overheard. But he already lied to me once. And I can't risk him mentioning something to his dad. Breaking into my mom's office is going to be hard enough without Senator Calhoun watching me all night.

Jack turns back to the road. "You look like her," he says. It doesn't sound like a compliment.

Silver lights twinkle from the trees as we pull into the Med Center parking lot. Two giant vases of white flowers stand to either side of the main entrance.

I climb out of the car and push the door shut behind me. Ariel's dress falls around my thighs, the lacy black fabric hugging my waist and skimming the skin just above my knees. The dress fits snug around my chest and dips low in the back to show off my pale skin. Rows of tiny golden beads glitter from the skirt. I feel like I stepped out of a silent film.

Jack offers me his elbow. "Shall we?"

"Thanks," I say, looping my arm through his.

The gala seems to be in full swing. I see the flash of the chandelier through the floor-to-ceiling windows, and a crowd of glittering, dancing people.

"Excuse me?" A small woman in a short black dress steps in front of us, blocking our way inside. She has one finger poised over an iPad. "Are you on the list?"

"Jack Calhoun," Jack says. He glances at me. "And date."

"Oh. Of course." The woman shuffles out of our way. "By all means."

Music envelops us as soon as we step through the doors, first a haunting snatch of cello, followed by the sharp blare of a trumpet. Talking, laughing voices fill the room, and I catch a whiff of food: skewered meats and something fried. My stomach rumbles. I can't remember the last time I ate a full meal. But then I think of what Mother said about putting supplements in the food, and my appetite vanishes. I wonder if the Med Center drugs the appetizers, too.

I glance at the elaborate grandfather clock in the far corner of the room. It's twenty minutes after seven. Zoe may have shown up, seen that I wasn't here, and hightailed it to the train station already. I pull my phone out of my clutch, my other arm still linked through Jack's.

Where are you? I type with one hand.

"Looking for someone?" Jack asks.

"My mother," I say, putting the phone back into my clutch. "I told her I'd say hi when I got here. You don't mind, do you?"

Jack looks disappointed, but he releases my arm. "Find me when you're done?"

"I'll see you soon." The lie comes easily, and it's then that I understand why Ariel lied so well and so often. When the truth is crazy, lies can feel almost real.

I duck into the crowd before Jack says another word. Women in gowns sweep through the room, followed by men in expensively tailored tuxedoes. The oversize chandelier glimmers from the ceiling, and the golden light catches on champagne glasses and serving trays, on diamond-studded bracelets and rings. I almost have to shield my eyes. The

Underhill memorial fountain twinkles from the corner, a string quartet playing in front of it.

I hurry across the room, grateful for the low lights and crowd. My mother will never spot me in this. I sweep a glass of champagne off a serving tray, for camouflage, and scan the room for Zoe's black hair and pointed face.

One minute stretches into two, and then five. I don't see her. I tap my fingers against the side of my champagne glass.

"Come on, Zoe," I whisper. "Be here. *Please* be here."

"Miss?"

The voice shocks me so much that I jerk and whirl around, the champagne glass slipping from my fingers. A waiter in a black tuxedo grabs the glass before I drop it.

"My apologies, miss," he says. "I didn't mean to startle you. I wanted to know whether you'd like more champagne."

I blink, and my eyes land on my empty champagne glass, now sitting on the waiter's tray. I don't even remember drinking it.

I flash him a tight smile. "I'm okay."

A familiar tinkling laugh rises above the other voices, sending a chill down my spine. I swear under my breath and turn my head, studying the people behind me from the corner of my eye. Mother stands at the center of the crowd. She's telling a story I can't quite hear, and a circle of eager party guests has formed around her to listen. She has her head turned away from me, so I turn all the way around.

Her gown is new. It's black satin, sleeveless, the sweetheart neckline coming to two sharp points just below her collarbone. She looks sleek and vicious. Like a predator.

A man makes his way over to her and taps her on the shoulder. She moves her head toward him, and he whispers something in her ear. She takes a sip of champagne as he talks, her expression never wavering. But I see the stone set of her eyes, the way her jaw tightens, almost imperceptibly. He's given her bad news. She says something back to him, and he scurries off.

A hand circles my wrist, yanking me away from the crowd.

"What the hell are you doing?" Zoe whispers. She's hiding in the dark alcove below the stairs, where it's unlikely that anyone from the party will notice her. I duck into the shadows next to her.

"Looking for you," I explain. "I got here late. I thought you already left."

"I should have," Zoe says, frowning. She's wearing her homecoming dress from last year. It's bright red, with spaghetti straps and a chiffon skirt.

"I'm glad you didn't," I say. I cast one last glance at my mother. She's still standing in the middle of her group of admirers, telling some story that makes them all throw their heads back and laugh. At least she's occupied. Her office will be empty.

"Come on," I say, taking Zoe by the arm. I don't want to risk climbing the main stairs—it'll draw too much attention—so I lead her down a back hallway, hoping it'll connect with another staircase farther on. I don't know this part of the hospital well, and twice I lose my way and have to retrace my steps to take a different turn. Zoe follows silently, like a shadow.

"Where did you get that?" she asks after a few moments.

She's looking at a jagged cut twisting from my elbow to my wrist. I noticed it in the shower after the car accident, but I can't remember when I got it. It was barely visible under the dim lights of the party, but the hall lights are brighter. Out here, it looks garish.

"Accident," I explain.

Zoe lifts an eyebrow. "Can you feel it?" she asks. I shake my head. "What about hot or cold? Can you tell the difference?"

"Not really," I say. "Sometimes I notice a breeze, but I can't feel temperature anymore."

Zoe whistles through her teeth. "You're almost as bad as me."

I dig my teeth into my lower lip. I focus on the sharp edges driving into my flesh, and I imagine nerve endings going off, sending warnings to my brain. *Pain! This is what pain feels like! Stop doing that!* When that doesn't work, I bite down harder. But I taste blood on my tongue before I feel even the briefest glimmer of hurt.

"I *just* took the serum," I say, licking the blood from my lips. "This is happening too fast."

Zoe shrugs. It's one of her slow, lazy shrugs that seem to involve her entire body. "Devon, Ariel, and I all took the serum at the same time. Ariel and Devon only lasted a few months, but for some reason, I'm still here. It doesn't seem to follow a schedule."

This seems violently unfair to me, but there's nothing Zoe can do about it. I nod at the staircase at the end of the hall.

"My mother's office is just up there," I say. "Come on."

Chapter Thirty-Two

Moonlight drifts in through the window, lazily illuminating Mother's desk and bookshelves. A car drives past, its headlights arcing across the room before it disappears into the woods. I find the switch on the wall beside the door and flick it on.

"Come on," I say. "Someone might see you."

Zoe steps into the office, pushing the door closed behind her. I drop my clutch on Mother's desk and head for the file cabinet. I fit the smallest key into the lock and turn, but it doesn't catch.

Zoe hovers behind me. "That's the wrong key."

I wrench the key to the left, like I can make the drawer open through sheer force of will. No luck. "I figured that out myself, thanks."

Zoe opens her purse, and removes the pink pocketknife I saw hidden in her drawer weeks ago. She opens the blade and gently threads the pointed, metal edge into the lock.

"That's not going to—" I start, but I'm interrupted by the sound of a click. Zoe pulls the drawer open.

"It's not going to what?" she asks, snapping the knife closed.

"Never mind." We crowd around the cabinet, Zoe standing on tiptoes to see inside. Dozens and dozens of files fill the drawer, each meticulously labeled in Mother's small, tight handwriting.

"Look." Zoe grabs a file and holds it out so I can read the label: "Ariel Frank." She points to the date scribbled beside her name. "That's when they gave us the serum," she says, flipping the file open.

A photograph of Ariel lying on a metal table stares up at us. Her eyes are open, and her hair billows around her head in lazy, tangled curls. Both the green of her eyes and the red of her hair look duller than I remember them. Like death has made her ordinary.

Emotion bubbles up inside me. I release a low sigh and lift my hand to my mouth, but the feelings vanish as suddenly as they appeared. I lower my hand back down to the file, lightly touching the photograph with two fingers.

"They did an autopsy," I say, reading the paragraph below her photo. I point to a line near the bottom of the page. "What do you think that means?"

"'Fail-safe kicked in,'" Zoe reads out loud. She shakes her head. "I don't know."

She reaches past me and grabs the next file, marked "Devon Savage." Her expression doesn't change as she reads, but, after a moment, her eyes flick up to meet mine. "Are you sure you want to see this?" she asks.

I pull the file toward me. There's another photograph, only now it's Devon lying on the slab with dull skin and vacant eyes. I wait for another kick of emotion, but it doesn't come. I look from the photograph to the block of text below it.

"There it is again," I say, pointing. "'Fail-safe kicked in.'"

Zoe flips through the rest of the files, frowning.

"More names. Hey, isn't this your boyfriend?"

Zoe pulls a folder out of the cabinet and hands it to me. *Jack Calhoun.*

I let the folder fall open in my hands. There's a photograph clipped to the inside cover. It's like looking at a funhouse-mirror version of Jack. His eyes are slightly too far apart, and his hair is styled strangely—too long on the back and sides. His smile is too wide, too perfect.

"This is Jack's dad," I say, pointing to the date at the corner of the page. "See? 1989."

"Whoa," Zoe says, leaning over my shoulder. "They look exactly alike."

I scan the text below Jack Sr.'s photograph, frowning. "This doesn't say anything about a fail-safe. And look"—I point to a row of additional dates—"he got more than one dose of the serum. Whatever he got must've been different from what they gave you."

I close the folder and slide it back in place. "They've been doing this for years," I say, examining the dates on the rest of the files. "Some of these files go all the way back to the sixties."

"They only chose a handful of kids," Zoe points out. "See? *1989, 1989, 1989*, and then it goes straight to *1994*."

"Weird," I say, quickly scanning the rest of the files. All names. "Do you see anything about an antidote?"

Zoe shakes her head. "These are all just patient files. Your—Dr. Gruen must keep the top secret stuff somewhere else." She swears in French, sliding the drawer shut. "This was a waste of time."

"Wait. There's still this." I grab my clutch from Mother's desk and pull out Ariel's mystery phone, which I grabbed while I was in the dorm changing into my dress. I hand it to Zoe. "You said you could switch the SIM cards, remember?"

Zoe lifts her eyebrows. "I'm going to miss my train."

"Don't you want to know what Ariel had to say before you disappear forever?"

Zoe hesitates, glancing at the door. "Fine," she says. She takes a paper clip from Mother's desk and uses it to pop open a tray in the side of Ariel's phone, removing a card the size of her pinkie nail. I hand her my phone and she does the same, then slides the card into my phone.

"That's it?" I ask.

Zoe jabs the power button with her thumb. "That's it. Is this the file?"

She shows me the screen. Ariel looks out at me through a fan of her eyelashes.

"Yeah," I say. "That's the file."

Zoe hits Play.

Chapter Thirty-Three

Ariel peers out from the tiny phone screen. Red curls rustle around her pale, heart-shaped face. Her lips curl into something that could be a smile or could be a smirk, and you could only know for sure which one it was by asking her.

"Hi, Charlotte," she says. "If you're watching this, that means I'm already dead. I know, such a cliché. But don't worry. This video isn't my suicide note, if that's what you're thinking. It's way better than that—one last game. You're holding the first of three clues right now, so listen closely."

She clears her throat, and when she speaks again, it's in her storyteller voice.

"Once upon a time," she says, "there were three beautiful princesses. Their families decided they didn't want them anymore, so the princesses ran away and hid inside an old castle in the middle of the woods. They told each other secrets and they drank stolen wine, and they explored the castle and the woods around it. Before long, the princesses became witty and brave as well as beautiful. They decided they would never leave the castle. It would be their home, forever and ever."

Ariel's smile curls into something darker, bordering on cruel. "But, of course, the castle was cursed. Castles are always cursed, you see. For while the princesses danced away inside, happy and safe, the world on the other side of the castle's walls was changing. Strange fires destroyed the woods they once loved. Children were being captured and transformed into terrible monsters. And an evil witch plotted against them. The princesses didn't know about any of this, of course. Not until it was too late."

Ariel holds the tiny bottle of serum up for the camera. "One day, while walking through the woods, two of the princesses met the evil witch. She appealed to their vanity and their egos, and persuaded them to take a magical potion. The potion changed the two princesses. It made them cruel and cold. They no longer cared about dancing or secrets or family. They no longer cared about anything at all. They became monsters themselves.

"And so it was left to the smartest, bravest, and most beautiful princess to save them." She winks at the camera. "That's *you*, idiot. There are two more clues following this video. I'm sure you'll find the second clue, but the last one is the hardest, so I'm going to give you a hint. All you have to do is go through the wardrobe. Like in the story, remember? Go through the wardrobe and you'll find the doorway to a new world. I know you'll figure it out. You're a lot smarter than you give yourself credit for. That's why I always loved you best."

Ariel pauses, and a tear slides down her cheek. She swipes it away with one finger, then stares down at her hand like she's not quite sure where it came from.

"I guess this is good-bye," she says in a small voice. "It's kind of strange that I can still cry. I can't feel anything. It's like I'm numb. "

Her eyes flick back up to the camera. They're wide and scared, but empty. Like she's hollow. The video stops.

"Are you okay?" Zoe asks.

I swallow. I don't know what I am. I'm dimly aware of emotions rumbling around inside of me, but they don't affect me like they're supposed to. It's like sitting in a warm room while a storm rages outside. I hear the wind howl, and I remember what it's like to be cold, but I don't feel it.

"'Through the wardrobe,'" I repeat.

"Like in the story," Zoe adds. "She's talking about *The Lion, the Witch and the Wardrobe*, right?"

"She liked that one," I say, nodding. I never read the book—Mother wasn't a fan of fiction—but Ariel made me watch the movie our freshman year.

"Do you think she meant our dorm?"

"I searched our closet pretty carefully. I think I would

have noticed if she left something for me there." I look up, my eyes landing on the closet on the other side of Mother's office.

Zoe follows my gaze. "You don't think—"

"She knew where I kept the keys. She could have gotten in here as easily as we did."

I cross the office and pull the door open. Three white lab coats and two dark blazers hang inside. A pair of black loafers sits on the floor. Otherwise, it's empty.

"Nothing here," I say. I start to push the door closed, when my fingers brush against a thread wrapped around the base of the doorknob. I roll the thread, frowning. It's bright yellow, like the bricks Ariel left in the woods.

My heart beats faster. Zoe says something, but I don't hear it. I try to dig the thread away from the doorknob, but it's attached to a tiny card wedged between the metal base and the wood of the door. The edge juts out, but I doubt anyone would notice if they weren't looking for it. I dig at the card with my thumbnail, but the paper's old, and it starts to tear. *Shit.* I try again, this time pinching the corner between two fingers. It gently pulls free and falls into my palm. Tiny letters dance across the creased surface.

Go through the wardrobe, they read. And at the bottom of the card: *3/3.*

I pull the door open again and, this time, I push past my mother's lab coats and blazers, to the very back of the closet. Zoe steps inside behind me.

"Charlotte—"

"In the movie, she goes to the very back of the wardrobe, remember?" I say. "The little girl pushes through the coats, and the back of the closet opens into another world."

I rise to my tiptoes, and then drop to my knees, running my hands over every inch of the back wall. I find nothing, no secret door or note or clue. It looks like my mother barely even uses this closet.

"I need a little help here, Ariel," I whisper.

I stare into the darkness, but the closet is just a closet, the wall is just a wall. Zoe drops to the floor next to me, my mother's coats rustling around her. She sighs. Music plays somewhere deep in the hospital, and the sound travels up through the floor, making the floor vibrate beneath my knees. I press my lips together, waiting.

Come on, I think. What is it? What did she want me to see?

Ariel loved fairy tales, and she could never figure out why I didn't love them in the same fierce, all-consuming way. Ariel wanted to crawl inside them and live her life there. It was the real world she hated.

I never got the point. They seemed simplistic to me. Boring.

"There's nothing really there," I told her once, and she looked at me like I was a damn fool.

"You're trying too hard," she explained. "Let it be what it is."

Let it be what it is, I think now as I crouch in my mother's closet. *Stop trying.*

I stare at the back wall, letting my eyes go unfocused. The distant sound of music fades away. I focus on my own heartbeat. My own breath.

Something flashes from the upper corner of the wall. I jerk my head up, and there—I see it.

A tiny silver keyhole.

Chapter Thirty-Four

My hands tremble so badly that Mother's tiny key slips from my fingers twice before I manage to hold it steady. I stand on my tiptoes and slide the key into the lock. Turn.

The wall stays still. Zoe stiffens next to me. *I guessed wrong*, I think. There's another key, a key I haven't found yet. Maybe I'll never find it, and this will stay a mystery forever.

Then a grinding sound rumbles from somewhere below me. The wall moves inward.

"Holy hell," Zoe whispers, and the breath I'd been holding releases in a huff of air.

There's a secret room at the back of Mother's closet. I remember the command to get my legs to move and step forward, hurrying down the short flight of stairs. It's probably good that I can't access my emotions right now, because I'm not sure what I'm supposed to think about this. My mother has been lying to me.

Fluorescent lights buzz to life the second my shoe hits the floor, illuminating a large room with high ceilings. Everything is white. White tile floors, white walls, white metal cots covered in crisp white sheets. The sleeping faces peering over the tops of those sheets are the only spots of color. Tubes trail away from their noses and wrists, connecting them to strange, beeping machines. I try to count them and quickly lose track. There are rows and rows of cots. Hundreds of unconscious people.

"Charlotte," Zoe says, stepping into the room behind me. "What is this?"

"They're patients," I say, but that can't be true. Patients wouldn't be hidden behind a secret wall in the closet. Patients wouldn't look like this.

I walk down the aisle between the cots, listening to the slow beep of the machines. There's a boy submerged in blue liquid, tubes trailing away from his body. And a girl with skin so dry it almost looks like scales. One of the cots is inside a metal cage, the bars warped. Whoever's inside must've been fighting to get out.

I glance at the girl lying in the cot nearest to me. She has short black hair and dark skin. Burns crawl up the side of her face and over her lips, leaving her skin black and shiny. A thin hospital sheet covers her body. I move it aside. Thick leather restraints bind the girl's wrists to her cot. The skin beneath them is raw and red, bleeding.

Zoe pulls a chart off the wall next to the girl's cot and squints down at it, reading. "She was doing some sort of experiment on her," she says after a moment. "It says here that she's *pyretic*, whatever that means."

Bits of old conversation flip through my head. I remember a lecture from a unit on Greek myth: *pyro*, from the Greek *pyr*, meaning "fire."

I think of the forest fires in the papers and on the news. The man brought into the Med Center in a coma, his face covered in burns.

The world on the other side of the castle's walls was changing, I hear Ariel whisper. *Strange fires destroyed the woods they once loved.*

Zoe makes a face and turns the page. "Gross. There are pictures."

The cot next to the girl holds a boy with a metal halo circling his skull. Thin metal rods stretch from the halo to his shaved head. There's dried blood crusted to his skin. Another cot holds a girl who's so thin she looks like she might break in half.

Children were being captured and transformed into terrible monsters.

I ball my hands into fists. Sweat coats my palms. I'm feeling *horror*, I realize. Full-on horror, like I haven't felt since I was a little kid hiding from the monsters under my bed.

"I'm going to be sick." I make a beeline for the trash can in the corner of the room and double over. My chest constricts and the acid burn of vomit climbs my throat, but I haven't eaten enough to throw up. I heave and spit something sour into the trash. My stomach roils.

I've never asked my mother about her work. I always told myself it was because we didn't have that kind of relationship—we weren't the type of mother and daughter who'd make cocoa and cookies and gossip about our days.

But there were other reasons. Even as a child, I knew there were rooms in my mother's life that I never wanted to enter. And now I'm standing in her most secret room, staring at the things she's kept hidden from the rest of the world.

"Charlotte?" Zoe touches my shoulder, and I flinch. I didn't hear her come up behind me. She frowns. "Are you okay?"

I straighten, wiping my mouth with the back of my hand. I look around the room, at all these people strapped into narrow cots, sleeping while my mother does God knows what to them. Zoe's plan to run away doesn't seem foolish anymore. We don't want to be found here. "We should go."

"But we haven't found anything yet." Zoe is still holding the chart she pulled off the wall next to the girl's cot. "Don't you want to know who all these people are?"

I shake my head. I've never known fear like this before. It squeezes my throat and pounds in my ears. I glance at the lab coats dangling in front of Mother's secret door and wish I'd never found this place. Some boxes should never be opened. There are some secrets you can never unlearn.

"Zoe," I say.

"Give me a minute." She studies the chart, her lips moving as she reads. "It says here that this girl came from a juvenile detention center called—" I rip the chart from Zoe's hands. "Hey! I wasn't done with that."

I slide the chart back onto its hook, not bothering to glance at what it says.

"*Look around*," I say. "These people were hidden. They're strapped down and locked away in cages. Something seriously sick is going on here. *Let's go*."

"I don't get it." Zoe crosses her arms over her chest. It occurs to me that she isn't even a little bit afraid. "You can't pretend this doesn't have anything to do with you. Your own mother is playing Dr. Frankenstein on a bunch of kids she found in juvenile detention centers. Meanwhile, you and your rich friends get handed a miracle serum that turns them into superheroes. Don't you think those two things are connected?"

My mouth suddenly feels dry. I swallow, tasting vomit at the back of my throat. "You think she did this for us?"

Zoe nods. "Ariel must've found this place when she figured out that the serum came from the Med Center. I'm guessing she wanted you to see it for yourself."

I glance at the boy lying in the cot beside me. His eyelids flicker. His chest rises and falls beneath the thin hospital sheet covering his body. I wonder how long he's been sleeping.

My fear is fading, bit by bit. Any second now I'll forget that feeling of bone-deep horror. I'll no longer hear the animal voice deep in my subconscious, warning me to run.

I turn, and stumble toward the door. *I have to get out of this room*, I think. I take the stairs two at a time. I don't turn around when Zoe calls my name. Things will make sense once I'm out of here.

I step into the closet, and—

Mother pushes through the lab coats, her eyes widening at the sight of me.

"What are you doing in here?" she demands.

Chapter Thirty-Five

Mother's black gown looks wrong in the white room, like a bug floating in a bowl of milk. The blue-tinted light gathers in the wrinkles around her eyes and mouth, making her face look old.

"How did you get in here?" she asks, but she sweeps across the room without waiting for an answer, her heels snapping at the tile. The sound vibrates off the walls, making the metal cots tremble. She stops beside a phone hanging from the wall and lifts the receiver to her mouth without dialing.

"I need security in room three-A." She pauses, and anger flashes across her mouth. It disappears a fraction of a second later. "Yes, that's correct," she says in a voice like honey. "Please hurry."

I press my lips together, not bothering to explain myself. Mother hates excuses. She says they're signs of weakness.

Zoe gives me an *Are you just going to stand there?* look. I shift my eyes away from her.

Mother places the phone back on the receiver and steps away from the wall. I grit my teeth, warning myself to stay quiet. But I must be weak, after all, because I can't do it.

"Mother," I start, "I—"

Mother lifts a single finger, stopping me. Her nails are bloodred, like the soles of her shoes. "Not a word until they get here," she warns.

I turn to Zoe for help, but she stares straight ahead, refusing to look at me. I shift my eyes to the rows of cots, the sleeping kids, and feel a quick jolt of rage. I want to scream and stomp. I want to throw things.

The empty feeling rises like the tide, washing my anger away. For a moment, I consider letting it drag me down into its depths. I'm so tired of being afraid, and horrified, and curious. Maybe Mother was right all along. Emotion is weakness.

If I let the numbness take over, I lose my humanity forever. I picture my anger like a flame inside my chest, flickering but not quite going out.

Hold on, I think.

A man in a dark uniform enters the room. I recognize him—it's the guard who caught me sneaking into Mother's office the last time I broke into the Med Center, the one who called the cops and had me thrown into a cell when I wouldn't show him identification. His eyes widen when he sees me.

"You again." He moves toward me, pulling a set of handcuffs out from his belt. The metal links clank together.

"You're going to have me cuffed?" I glance at my mother. "Really?"

She clenches her eyes shut, and a vein leaps to life in her forehead. "They're just girls, Phillip," she says to the guard. "Bring them back to your office. I'll be there to deal with them in a moment."

Phillip clips the handcuffs back onto his belt. "Yes, ma'am," he says. He takes my elbow in one meaty hand and grabs Zoe with the other. Zoe yanks her arm away.

"I'll carry you if I have to," he says, reaching for her again. Zoe dances backward, reminding me how easily she dodges her opponents in fencing.

"What's going to happen to us?" she demands, looking at the unconscious patients lying in the cots around the room. "Are we going to end up like them?"

Mother presses her lips together. "We'll discuss the ramifications of this incident in a moment," she says.

That wasn't a no. I glance at the cot nearest to the door, the one holding the girl with the burned skin and the leather restraints around her wrists.

The guard finally manages to catch hold of Zoe's arm. A muscle in her shoulder tenses, and I think she's going to pull away again. It'd be so easy. We're both strong. The guard is large, but he's more fat than muscle. He'll be slow. Clumsy. We could get away.

I catch Zoe's eye and shake my head, glancing at my mother. *Not in front of her.* She'll just call more guards—bigger ones. Better to wait. Zoe nods, and her shoulders go slack.

The guard leads us to the stairs. I pause before stepping into the closet, and glance back at the strange white room. Row after row of sleeping kids lie, motionless, in their cots. I look at their faces, wondering what they were like before they ended up here. If they were happy. Whether they had families.

The guard tugs on my arm, and I start moving again.

We let the guard lead us down the hall, around the corner, and toward the stairs. There's no one up here, not a single nurse or doctor. Everyone's at the gala.

I catch Zoe's eye and nod. *Now.*

We move together, and it's almost like a dance. Zoe twists out of the guard's grip, and kicks him in the back of the leg. He goes down, hard. I pull my arm away, and his grip breaks so easily. It's like he's not even trying. I start to run, but I stop at the end of the hall. Zoe's not beside me.

I turn and look back. The guard is standing again, and he has both arms wrapped around her chest. She throws her head, catching him in the jaw, and his face reels backward.

"Go!" she shouts. "I'm right behind you."

I don't stop or think. I just go.

Chapter Thirty-Six

Wind brushes against my arms as I push through the back entrance. It doesn't feel cold. It doesn't feel like anything. I turn around, gasping.

"Come on, Zoe," I whisper. The doors stay closed.

It starts to rain. I smell snow in the air, but the rain feels warm against my skin. A light flashes at the corner of my eye, and I turn, spotting Jack's car at the other end of the parking lot. What's he doing out here? I cast one last glance at the Med Center doors and then hurry toward him.

He leans across the passenger seat and pushes the car door open. "She returns."

"I'm sorry."

Jack shakes his head. "Get in. You look cold."

"I can't." I glance at the door again. Still closed. "I'm waiting for somebody."

"You're going to wait in the rain?"

The rain is coming down harder now. It pricks the bare skin on my back and plasters Ariel's dress to my legs. I climb into the car and pull the door shut. Rain splatters against the windows.

"Who are you waiting for?" Jack asks, not smiling.

I suck a breath in through my teeth. I should come up with a story. But there are so many lies between us already.

"I know about the serum," I say finally. "I know you didn't tell me the truth."

Jack's face falls. "Charlotte—"

I lift a hand, stopping him. "It's fine. Really."

Wind pushes against the windows of the car, making the glass creak. The heater spits and hums.

"It's that school, you know?" Jack places both hands on the steering wheel, staring through the rain-soaked windshield. "It changes you. I used to do things because I liked doing them, and if my dad or whoever was disappointed, well, that was their problem. But since coming here . . . it's like it doesn't count if I'm not the best. Taking the serum made everything easy—"

"Didn't you ever wonder where it came from?"

Jack looks politely bewildered. "Does it matter?"

His words buzz around my head like flies. I look at him, and it's like I'm seeing him for the first time. Only I'm no longer blinded by want, so I see him like he really is. The way he makes jokes so he doesn't have to talk about anything serious. The way he drifts from hobby to hobby because he's terrified he won't ever excel at anything. How he pretends he doesn't care what other people think, but he needs them to like him all the same.

Every line of his face tells the story of the privileged boy who will one day go off to live his perfect, charmed life.

I glance at the Med Center doors. Zoe still hasn't come out. Something must be wrong. "Look," I say, pushing the car door open. "I have to go right now. I'll be back in a few minutes."

I climb out, my mind already in the Med Center with Zoe, when another car door opens and slams shut.

"Wait." Jack grabs me by the elbow and spins me around. Rain clings to his nose and his cheeks. "What's going on? Where are you going?"

I try to pull away, but Jack doesn't let go. "It's a long story—"

"Is this still about the serum?" he asks, tightening his grip. He'd be hurting me now, if I could still feel. "I don't know what you're getting so bent out of shape for. It's perfectly safe."

"Who told you it was safe?" I ask.

"My dad," Jack says, looking puzzled. "He took it himself when he was back at school. He and my mom are on the board, so they know all about the program Dr. Gruen set up."

"Do they know about my mother's secret lab?" I snap. "Do they know she's keeping people's kids locked up in there? That she's doing experiments on them?"

I expect Jack's face to twist in horror. I expect him to

deny it, to say his parents could never be involved in something so heartless.

But he just blinks. "Those kids all volunteered."

"Have you seen them?" My voice sounds different now.
Too high. One more crack and it could break. Jack shrugs
with one shoulder. I'm not sure if it means yes or no, but I
realize I don't actually care. It doesn't matter if he saw them.
He knew. He knew and he did nothing. "Let go of me."

"I want to talk."

"I don't." I look down at the fingers pressing into my
skin, and violent thoughts flash through my head. I could
break those fingers, one by one. I could make Jack fall to his
knees.

Is that something normal girls do? I think. It's not—it's
something Ariel or Devon would have done. Something a
girl with no humanity would do.

His fingernails dig into my skin. "Please."

"Let me go."

He squeezes tighter. I feel the pressure in my wrist even
though pain is an alien concept. Bones crunch. Skin burns.
Jack's knuckles have gone white, and there's a vein pressing
against the skin in his neck. I don't know if he realizes what
he's doing.

"Charlotte," he pleads. He tugs my arm and I stumble on
my heels, knees knocking together like a baby deer.

Something inside me switches off. Like a light going dark.
I don't give myself time to think about what a normal girl

might do in this situation. I'm not normal. In a single, fluid movement, I grab Jack's arm with my free hand and twist the other. Something cracks, and Jack's fingers pop open.

It's easy. Like snapping a twig.

Jack stumbles, his foot slipping out from under him. He hits the ground, his head smacking against wet concrete. His eyes flicker, and I think he's going to pass out. He looks pale all of a sudden. The blood drains from his face.

It takes a moment for my mind to catch up with my body. I blink and it's like I'm seeing what I did for the first time. Jack's hand flops to the side at a strange, ugly angle. A bit of bone pokes at his skin, not quite breaking it. All it took was a second of losing control, and look what I did.

First Darren, and now Jack. I should be disgusted with myself. But I'm just glad he let go of my arm.

Jack forces his eyes back open. He cradles his hand to his chest. "Charlotte?" he groans.

"I'm sorry." I keep backing toward the Med Center. There needs to be distance between us. Miles and miles of space to keep me from hurting him again. "Go home, Jack," I say. "Just please go home."

"Zoe?" I call once inside the Med Center. I make my way through the labyrinth of hallways. The sounds of music and laughter fade. Something's wrong. Really wrong. I call Zoe's name again, but nobody answers. I make my way up the stairs, back toward Mother's office.

Something glimmers from the floor. A tiny red spot against the tile.

I press my hand to my chest, to the exact spot where I'd feel horror if I could still feel. It's blood. There's blood on the floor.

I keep walking, scanning the tile as I go. There's another splotch of blood near the wall, and one at the corner, where another hallway connects. I follow the trail like someone compelled, like the drops of blood are bread crumbs leading me out of an enchanted forest. A smear of red below a water fountain. A smudged handprint. A single, bloody boot.

I kneel and pick up the boot, turning it over in my hand. Men's size 11. It must be Phillip's. I turn down one last hallway.

The security guard lies on the floor, a pool of blood gathered below his head. I stop beside him and stare down at his broken body.

His throat has been slashed. The skin gapes open, spilling blood so dark it looks black under the garish light. His eyes are open, the whites nearly yellow, the pupils too large and unmoving. There's blood on his teeth and his hands, and on his remaining boot.

He doesn't seem real. I could be looking at a photograph. There are bruises along his arms. They must've fought hard. He's a big guy, not as easy to take down as we thought he'd be.

I place the boot next to the security guard's body and stand.

"Zoe?" I call. She couldn't have gotten far. I turn the corner, and there she is.

She lies on her back on the floor, her arms stretched to either side of her like she was crucified. I can't see the blood against the red fabric of her dress, but it's everywhere else—splattered across the floor and the walls. In her hair. On her cheeks. There's a bit of it crusted in her eyelashes. Her pink pocketknife lies on the floor beside one of her slashed wrists.

I drop to my knees and Zoe's blood seeps into my dress, staining the lacy, beaded fabric. I check for a pulse, even though I know she's dead. Blood clings to my fingers and my wrist.

It's still warm.

Chapter Thirty-Seven

I stumble away from Zoe's body, my feet slow and heavy, my dress soaked with blood. There's a disconnect between these physical sensations and what's happening inside my head. The pain buzzes against the surface of my skin, like a dragonfly skimming over a pool of water but never landing. I don't feel sorrow or horror or shock. I don't feel anything.

I walk through Mother's office and into her closet. Her samurai sword winks in the darkness. I push her coats aside, revealing the secret door to her secret lab.

Mother stands in the middle of the white room, surrounded on all sides by the monsters she's created. She has her back to me, her shoulders stiff beneath the soft silk of her gown. I start down the stairs, and she jerks around, fear and fury carved in every line of her face.

Her shoulders droop when she sees that it's just me. "What are you doing back here?"

"Zoe's dead." My voice doesn't crack. "She killed that security guard, and then she slit her wrists."

I hold out my hands so she can see the blood staining my palms. Mother stares for a moment, and then she sinks into a metal folding chair beside the nearest cot. It's like all the energy has drained from her body. Like she can't hold herself up any longer.

"You were never supposed to be a part of this," she says in a voice that belongs to a different, softer person. "That's why it took so long for me to bring you to Weston."

I kneel on the floor in front of her, the lace of Ariel's dress pulling against my thighs. "Why are they killing themselves?"

Mother stares down at the clenched hands in her lap. "Every year, we choose six students, three boys and three girls, and we give them a concentrated dose of the same drugs every other student gets in the food." Mother's eyes go hazy, like she's remembering a fond memory. "The serum is the most important thing I've ever done. It makes people smarter, stronger. Whoever takes it excels at everything he or she attempts. In the past, students who were given this serum went on to do extraordinary things. They became world leaders. Politicians. Writers and artists. The results have been so impressive that the Med Center's board of trustees encouraged me to tweak the formula. To see if I could stretch the limits of human ability even further.

"Unfortunately, this brought about unsettling side effects. Loss of fear translated into a loss of all emotion. The early subjects we tested became dangerous. I warned the board that the serum wasn't ready, but they insisted on moving forward with our next stage of trials."

Mother pauses. She presses her lips together so tightly that they seem to disappear into her face.

"I was scared, Charlotte," she says. "You have to understand that. I was worried that I was unleashing monsters into the world. So I built a fail-safe into the early doses of the serum—the ones given to Ariel and Devon and Zoe. It was designed to kick in the moment the subject did something inhumane." Her eyes flick to mine, guilty. "If she burned down an animal shelter, or broke another student's arm, or killed a security guard, she would—"

"Commit suicide," I finish.

"It was supposed to be a precaution," Mother says weakly. She closes her eyes. "I never thought . . . all of them."

I rub my hands against my thighs. It wasn't all of them. I took the serum, too, and I'm still here.

I see the same thought flicker across Mother's eyes. "The girls were dosed first. Once we saw the side effects, we discontinued their treatment, tweaked the formula. I don't know which dose you took," she explains. "The doses given to the male subjects were fine. Maybe—"

"You said there was an antidote."

"There is," Mother says. "But it hasn't been tested yet."

I look over the rows of cots holding sleeping kids. Tubes twisting away from noses. Strange machines beeping. The boy with the metal halo around his head twitches in his sleep. The girl with the burns up the side of her face moans softly.

"Human trials are imperative," Mother continues. "The students at Weston are the sons and daughters of the most powerful people in the world. We couldn't use them, so we found . . . others. People who no one would miss. They all volunteered," she says as though that could possibly make this better.

"So they're guinea pigs?"

"I know it seems monstrous to you, but we aren't hurting them. We've given them gifts. How many of these kids, in their old lives, would have a chance to be part of something extraordinary?"

I look out over the cots, trying to see what my mother sees when she looks at them. *Gifts. Extraordinary.*

"One of our patients got loose several weeks ago," Mother explains.

"Patient?" I repeat. "Your *missing asset* was a kid?"

Mother nods. "That's why I was gone—I spent the last few days trying to locate her. She—well, many of them can be dangerous."

The girl with the burned face lies a few feet away, her chest rising and falling beneath a thin blanket. I stand, examining her under the harsh fluorescent light. Her eyelids flicker while she sleeps. Beneath the puckered, blackened skin, she doesn't look any older than me.

"How was she dangerous?" I ask.

"That's classified."

I stop beside another cot and stare down at another girl. Blankets cover her frail body. Her cheeks are hollow, her arms all skin and bone. She doesn't look dangerous. She looks like she's dying.

Mother said the antidote hasn't been tested yet. What she means is that it hasn't been tested on *her*. They haven't studied its effects on this girl's broken body. They haven't sacrificed her to make sure I'll be safe. Yet.

I focus on the last struggling flicker of humanity left inside me. I picture it like a flame growing higher and higher. I may be doomed, but this girl—these *people*—don't have to be.

A medicine bag hangs from the metal stand beside her cot, and a thin tube trails away from it, attaching to her arm through a needle taped to her skin. Clear liquid drips through the tube. It must be what's keeping her asleep.

I yank the needle out of the girl's arm, and a new machine starts beeping. The sound is frantic—an alarm.

"Charlotte?" Mother snaps. "What are you doing?"

"You're wrong." I turn to the machines behind the girl's bed and flip switches until the beeping stops. "*This* is wrong."

Mother's heels pound against the tile. I flip one more switch before her hand circles my wrist and yanks me away.

"Let me go." I pull out of Mother's grip and lunge for the machine.

Mother wraps her arms around my chest, restraining me. "*Decades* of research have gone into this project."

I shake my head. *No.* These people aren't a project. They aren't assets or experiments. Mother is strong, but I'm strong now, too. So much stronger than her.

I wrestle an arm free of her grip and shove her. She stumbles and trips over her feet, slamming into the floor in a heap of black silk. I don't stop for long enough to check on her. I fumble with the straps binding the girl's wrists to her side. Leather snaps between my fingers. I undo the buckle, letting the straps fall to the floor. Then I move to the next cot.

Mother pushes herself up to one elbow. "Charlotte, *stop*," she begs. "You don't know what you're doing."

But I know exactly what I'm doing. Mother is wrong, and I'm right, and I've only ever known that for sure once before in my life, when I was nine years old and tossed some wooden blocks out the window of a hotel room. When I saved the tiny princess, at last.

I move from cot to cot, unlatching leather and unhooking needles. My fingers work quickly, frantically. Moans echo through the room behind me. Blankets rustle.

They're waking up.

I pause, and glance over my shoulder to watch Mother's prisoners climb down from their cots. I expect them to move like zombies. Dazed and slow, and confused about where they are. I expect them to need my help.

They don't. The frail girl stands, immediately alert, and hurries to another cot. She pulls the leather restraints apart with her bare hands. A boy with a shaved head and a bandage covering the back of his skull yanks the needles out of his neighbor's arm. He hits two buttons in tandem, stopping the blaring alarm before it even begins.

It's like they'd been expecting this. Planning for it.

I make my way to the cot holding the girl with the burned face. Despite the burns, she doesn't look as frail as the others. Her arms are muscular and her cheeks don't have that caved-in, hollow look yet. Tape peels, easily, away from her arm. I slide the needle out of her skin, ignoring the blaring siren as I fumble with her restraints. The buckle is stiff and awkward in my hands, so I grab the leather and pull. It snaps apart between my fingers, like tissue.

She wakes quickly, like the others, and turns to me with bleary, bloodshot eyes.

"You," she murmurs, and I wonder if she recognizes me from the Med Center. Her eyes shift to my hands, still holding the strips of leather that bound her to her cot. She sits, rubbing her wrists. "What are you doing?"

"You have to get out of here," I choke out. I nod at the rest of the patients. "Take them and go far, far away."

Gratitude flashes across the girl's face. She climbs out of her cot, heading straight for the cage in the back of the room. She tries to yank the padlock open, and, when that doesn't work, she curls her hand around the metal and closes her eyes. The padlock glows red beneath her fingers. Molten metal drips to the floor.

The cage door swings open, and a large boy with thickly muscled arms climbs out.

Mother pushes herself to her feet, wobbling on her heels. A rip tears across the side of her gown, and torn silk flaps around her legs. "Angela," she shouts. *"Don't!"*

The girl with the burned face—*Angela*—flashes a predatory

smile, her gnarled lips pulling tight across her teeth. "What's the matter, Dr. Gruen?" she asks. "Afraid to face your monsters?"

The boy from the cage slams his fist into a cot—it crumples like paper, the sound of grinding metal echoing off the walls.

Mother backs toward the door, eyes moving over the faces of her patients. Her prisoners. They circle her, anger etched on their pale, tired faces. The fluorescent light above her flares—red and orange sparks rain down on us.

Mother lifts her head, finding me at the back of the room. Animal terror fills her eyes. Maybe I've already lost my humanity. Maybe this is the last choice I'll make before taking my own life. But as I stand at the back of the lab, watching the monsters she made descend upon her, I don't feel a shred of guilt or sorrow.

She should face what she's created. It's only fair.

"Charlotte," she calls to me. "*Please.* I'm your mother. Your family."

I think of Ariel laughing as we sat beside the river, braiding hair and tossing stones into the water. Devon signing my mother's name in perfect, loopy handwriting. The three of us making cookies on a Friday night because none of us had—or wanted—dates.

"No," I say. "You killed my family."

Angela stops beside me. Her breathing comes faster. She blinks, and when she opens her eyes again, they're an oily, perfect black. The air becomes a staticky crackle. Like all of the moisture has been leached from the room.

She's dangerous, Mother said. *Pyretic*, it read in her notes.

I catch a whiff of smoke, and before I can process what's about to happen, fire blazes to life around me, coming from nowhere and everywhere at once. It erupts from the tile. It manifests out of thin air, cracking and flaring, exploding from nothing. It rolls between the cots like waves. It curls around my mother's feet, a circle of flame holding her in place.

Smoke stings my eyes. I drop to my knees.

The boy from the cage lifts a beeping machine above his head and hurls it at my mother. It crashes into the far wall, exploding into shards of plastic and white-hot sparks of electricity. My mother cowers, and it misses her face by inches. Her prisoners crowd closer around her, blocking any chance of escape.

I should run. The heat is too much. My head pounds and the ground seems to lurch. For a moment, all I see is black. I blink again and again, until the room comes back into focus. Until Angela and my mother and the flames feel real.

Is this what it feels like? I wonder absently. I did something inhumane, just like Mother said I would. I stood aside and let her monsters destroy her. This must be the fail-safe kicking in, preventing me from saving myself. Letting me die.

I open my mouth, but ashes coat my throat and tongue.

There's too much smoke, too much fire. I don't try to stand up again.

"Want to see a trick?" Angela says. Before my mother can answer, Angela curls her hands into two tight fists, drawing the fire close to her. The flames waver and then disappear. It's like they've soaked down into the floors and walls. Like Angela's absorbed them.

Mother's body begins to glow. It's subtle at first, almost like light bouncing off her pale skin. But it gets brighter. There are flames beneath her skin. She is heat and fire. I can't look directly at her. I shield my eyes and turn away.

I understand what's happening a moment before it does. Fire erupts from Mother's mouth. It flares in her eyes and curls from her nostrils. Her skin begins to boil and peel. Her gown turns to ash as her body succumbs to flames.

I close my eyes, trying to feel the horror of what I just saw. I replay the image again and again, but everything seems so far away. Like I'm seeing it through a veil.

The fire closes in. I imagine it destroying my face. Skin peeling away from my nose. Lips bubbling and turning black. Is it suicide if you let yourself die? If you do nothing to try to stop it?

I blink, and then I'm no longer in the lab surrounded by flames. I'm in the woods, in our secret cove. Tree branches form a canopy of leaves over my head, sunlight painting their bark gold. A soft breeze rustles the new grass. Somewhere in the distance, a bird chirps.

Ariel and Devon wait on the path ahead of me, their

familiar laughter echoing through the woods. Shivers race over my arms. I found them. *Finally,* I found them.

They turn, beckoning to me. There are other paths through the woods to explore. Paths that lead to places we've never seen.

I take their hands, and darkness falls, like a light switching off.

Epilogue

I wake to a world of ash and blood. Ariel and Devon are gone, but they were never really here, were they? I close my eyes, remembering the feel of their hands in mine, the sound of their laughter in the trees. I should have died. Why didn't I die?

I count to three, and then I open my eyes again.

Angela is gone. Everyone in the small tile room is gone. The cots lie empty, blankets tangled on the floor beside them. Machines beep angrily. Lights flash.

I sit up and look around. I'm not where I'm supposed to be. I collapsed at the back of the room, near the cage, but now I'm sitting at the foot of the stairs. Footsteps trail through the ash-coated tile and, beside them, a swath of clear floor. Like someone dragged me.

All at once, I realize: the kids my mother tortured and

experimented on and imprisoned moved me to where the flames couldn't touch me. They saved my life.

I blink, and letters float before my eyes. Someone wrote me a message in the ash.

Come find us, it reads.

Acknowledgments

A big, wet, sloppy thank you to Mandy Hubbard, as always, for everything you do to help my books become more than funny little images in my head. We're talking email therapy sessions, near-constant cheerleading, and an uncanny ability to answer the exact same question numerous times without calling me out on it. You're a rock star. I'm so glad we fell in love.

Thank you to Mary Kate Castellani for loving these characters as much as I do, and for helping to lead them out of the woods. To Claire Stetzer, thanks for everything (including endless patience as I actually write this). To Cristin Stickles, thanks for holding my hand during events and fielding crazy email requests. HUGE thanks to the rest of the Bloomsbury team for working so hard to get this book out into the world. I particularly want to call out Vicky Leech in the UK for everything you've done for my books overseas.

I also have to spend a second thanking all the usual suspects. Mom and Dad, thanks bunches for reading this one, and all the others, and for screaming like children every time I hand you a new book. Thank you, Ron, for loving this one (and, let's be honest, every new one I write) the MOST. Thanks Leah and Anna, for workshopping this bad girl to within an inch of her life. She's a better book for it.

I dedicated this book to nice girls and monsters. Throughout both *Breaking* and *Burning*, I played with concepts of image and femininity; namely, how to walk that increasingly narrow line between what's considered good and bad when you also happen to be a girl. I hope I did an okay job, but these things are always works in progress. If you have any questions, or want to discuss it more, you can find me almost anywhere @vegarollins.